BEAUTY

Also by Faith Baldwin
in Thorndike Large Print

Give Love The Air
No Private Heaven
He Married A Doctor
And New Stars Burn
Enchanted Oasis

FAITH BALDWIN

BEAUTY

Thorndike Press • Thorndike, Maine

Library of Congress Cataloging in Publication Data:

Baldwin, Faith, 1893-
   Beauty / Faith Baldwin.
   p. cm.
   ISBN 0-89621-952-6 (alk. paper : lg. print)
   1. Large type books. I. Title.
[PS3505.U97B4   1990]   89-48535
813'.54--dc20   CIP

Thorndike Press Large Print edition published in 1990 by
arrangement with Henry Holt and Company.

Large Print edition available in the British Commonwealth
by arrangement with Harold Ober Associates.

Cover design by James B. Murray.

This book is printed on acid-free, high opacity paper. ∞

For Mother

Chapter 1

There is a section of Brooklyn, New York, to which summer comes with more of tenderness and less of cruelty than is her habit in a city. Perhaps it is because she has not forgotten how recently Bay Ridge was country.

There are struggling lawns, and thousands of roses. There are little trees, and tall trees, sycamore, maple, oak; there are bushes in flower and beds of bright geraniums, and everywhere window boxes and ornamental grass and the perky, velvet faces of pansies.

But few people pick their cherished flowers; and they are left to die upon the stem or bush. And they die dustily in a whirl of city débris, their petals stirred by the wind from the Narrows.

This is a section of houses once called mansions; of encroaching apartment houses, some proudly advertising elevator service, all advertising mechanical refrigeration; and one or two offering swimming pools and tennis courts to people too used to progress to be astonished, and too accustomed to depression to be elated. Here, there are towns within towns and villages within a city, complete with business section and playground and park, complete with sea wall and drive and the occasional establishments the grounds of which nearly approximate small estates.

Here, too, are the one-family houses of brick and frame, the "apartment to let" signs in the windows of hitherto private homes, the two-family houses with their cemented walks in small back yards, their handkerchiefs of rather browbeaten, dog-ridden, child-infested lawns.

In one such two-family house, two long downhill blocks to the Narrows, and two shorter level blocks to the subway, Letty Lawson had lived with her father.

Now, she lived there alone. For the past three weeks, quite alone, for despite the kindness and familiar affection of the family who owned the house, death leaves its intimate survivor more alone than anything in the world.

The Merricks were her landlords. For seventeen of her twenty years she had known the Merricks. And today, a warm Sunday afternoon, she sat on their small enclosed sun porch, the replica of her own, with their daughter Carol, and tried, under the running fire of Carol's conversation, to think what she meant to do.

John Lawson, having brought his only child up in comparative comfort, had died, quite suddenly, leaving her in comparative poverty. He had been a silent, lovable sort of a man, for many years head chemist in an old and famous drug firm. He had been impractical and charming, a man with an inquiring turn of mind. But he inquired into things which did not touch the actual mechanics of living. He and Letty had been very close. She barely remembered her mother but her father was so indestructibly woven into the very fabric of her life, that life without him seemed an immense confusion.

Shortly after her mother's death John Lawson had encountered Daniel Merrick, a genial man with a good contracting business, and the acquaintance leading to friendship of a sort, had moved from Manhattan to Brooklyn and taken half of the Merrick's new two-family house. "The baby will have good air, and green grass," said Merrick, "and she and Carol and Tom are all about an age. And we couldn't wish for better tenants."

Thus easily, it had been settled. Merrick had built his home before that particular section had been closely populated and for all of Letty's childhood they had run almost as wild as if they were in the country, she and Carol, one very fair and one very dark, perfectly normal small children, laughing and mischievous and quarrelsome, gay with the miraculous unrelated gaiety of youth and melancholy with youth's inarticulate brief sorrows.

Tom was older, a gawky boy, with propensities a little beyond mere mischief, an inclination to set fire alarms and explore empty houses and run with gangs. And with of course, a vast scorn for Carol and also for Letty, until the close of the unexplained discomfort of his adolescence.

The Lawsons' part of the house was run by a succession of housekeepers, some good and some bad. The first of these acted as nurse as well, but Letty soon outgrew nurses and, besides, Mrs. Merrick was always somewhere near-by, ready to scold or comfort, advise or command, as the case might require.

Mr. Lawson took two weeks' vacation in the summer. During these breaks in the routine, the current housekeeper went away also, and the big, thin man and the little girl took their holiday together, somewhere in the mountains, perhaps, at a quiet hotel, or at some fairly near-by beach.

These vacations were really a concession to Letty's youth and need of change. For himself, John Lawson would have much preferred to have stayed in town, working in the laboratory which he had built and equipped in the cellar of his house and in which he conducted all sorts of curious and, to him, amusing experiments, some of which smelled to high heaven and penetrated into the Merricks' part of the house; others of which Mrs. Merrick said, resigned, were likely to blow them all to Kingdom Come; but which never did.

Letty liked poking carefully about the laboratory, when permitted. She enjoyed regarding things in test tubes, things boiling in a frenzy of action, or freezing. She liked the odd odors and the excitement when something came out right. As often as not things came out wrong, but that was part of the game her father played, a game in which as time went on she took more than a desultory interest. It was this interest which caused her father to decide to send her away to college after she, together with Carol, had been graduated from a local high school. And Letty, torn between the necessity of leaving the person closest to her in all the world, and the desire to get away from her narrow circle and see something of another city and another life, finally went. But only as far as Syracuse, where she spent two happy and informative years, and to which she had planned to return in the autumn.

But autumn was not far away, and now she knew she would never return. John Lawson had died during their summer holiday together, succumbing to an obscure ailment which Letty did not know possessed him. The Merricks had come at once, to the shocked and addled Long Island hotel; the Merricks had made all the necessary, somehow brutal arrangements; and Mr. Merrick had seen that his own lawyer attended to the financial details.

Now it was over, the dreadful lonely moments in the hotel bedroom with the strange doctor looking down at the strange quiet figure on the strange bed; now it was over, the Merricks' coming and the trip back to Brooklyn; the funeral was over, and realization had begun.

Dying, John Lawson had left his daughter without relatives, with unattained ambitions, with an immeasurable, unbelieving sort of grief, and with very little money.

He had expected to live a long time. His salary had been sufficient to enable him to live well, if simply. He had not saved very much, he spent a good deal on his laboratory, and more on Letty. Letty must have the best. She was entitled to it. He was inordinately proud of her, of her very genuine beauty, of her quick mind, inquiring like his own, and of her basic character.

He had carried a large amount of life insurance, enough for his young wife's and Letty's protection. At his wife's death he had dropped one policy and much more recently he had permitted others to lapse because, as the majority of his savings had been invested in securities promising large returns and appreciation, in prosperous times, he had been badly caught in times less prosperous. This had worried him, but not for long. He was a fixture in the chemical concern. He had worked out formulas of his own which he fancied would be valuable some day. He could start saving again. He was still a young man, in his early fifties.

But now he had died, astonishment and rebellion written plain upon his thin fine-featured face, and Letty was alone. And Letty had found that her material assets consisted of some very bad stock, a thousand dollars in a savings bank and five thousand more in life insurance, which had been added to the account.

She was just past twenty. All debts and expenses had been paid. A second-hand dealer had made an offer for the laboratory equipment. The head of her father's firm had written her a letter of condolence and the firm had sent flowers to the funeral. Letty, at twenty, must close her mind to college and must go to work. She had some six thousand dollars back of her, which she assured Carol she mustn't touch . . . that is, as soon as she got a job she wouldn't touch it.

They were together on the sun porch. Carol was lying full length in the swing, very scantily, very becomingly clad. She was a small girl, dark, with a bright, hard vivacity. She wore her lipstick like a banner of defiance, and her eyeshadow on the heavy lids of pretty, greedy brown eyes like a promise of softening.

Carol, on graduating from high school, had gone into what she termed the beauty racket. She had been employed for almost two years at a beauty salon in Manhattan. She liked her work. That she came home from it once or twice a week was a concession to her mother. The rest of the time she came home, mornings, with just margin enough to bathe and change and subway over to work again. Sometimes she didn't come home at all. She "stayed at a girl friend's."

Carol was very fond of Letty; and Letty of Carol. It was an affection based on long duration and habit more than one resulting from any mutual tastes. But it had strength.

"I've no assets," Letty was saying.

She leaned back in the wicker wing chair. Carol cocked a brown eye at her.

"Did you ever look in your mirror?" she inquired.

"Yes, often," Letty answered, smiling faintly. Of course she looked in her mirror, frequently. She was a perfectly normal person. And what she saw reflected there was not at all discouraging.

She was tall, but not too tall, with a figure almost perfect, according to present-day standards. She was fair, her short, thick hair was of that curious, lovely shade, too warm for the prevalent platinum and too pale for glowing gold. She had no especial beauty of features, her nose was insignificant and pert, and her mouth sweet and stubborn and her chin too firm for yielding roundness. But she possessed an absolutely flawless skin, very fair; and the amazing complement of eyes so dark that they were as nearly black as it is possible for the human eye to be. Her brows and lashes were a pale, dusty brown, quite charming when they were left to themselves, but when deftly touched by pencil and mascara, grace notes of beauty in her oval face.

"You've looks," said Carol dispassionately, "and how. You should cash in on them. There's the stage, and the screen; there's modeling; commercial photography and the rest."

They had been all over these grounds before, as far back as high school days and of

15

course more recently. Letty shook her head.

"Not for me," she said decidedly.

"I know. You're a fool," said Carol affectionately.

Letty was not drawn toward stage or screen or posing. She had absolutely no gift. She possessed a pleasant speaking voice, but was tone deaf when it came to music. She had had no business training. And the day had gone by when elderly ladies engaged personable young women, of good education and "pleasing personality," as companions.

It had been out of the question for Letty to maintain her share of the house. Besides, with building conditions slowing up to a point where they had become almost invisible to the naked eye, she knew that the Merricks depended upon the rental for almost their sole source of income. Carol brought nothing home, except now and then an expensive gadget or a dress for her mother, or a chicken for dinner. Tom, whose father had bought him a share in a small, moderately thriving garage, contributed now and then to the family income but not much.

The Merricks, however, had been unwilling to let Letty drift, and had proposed that she move in with them and share Carol's room. They were genuinely glad to have her, and she knew it; she knew she was welcome to stay as long as it suited her. Her father's arrangement with Merrick had always been from a month to month basis. The month had ended and there were prospects of new tenants. There was nothing for Letty to do but move into the Merrick half of the house. She had insisted upon paying, although Mrs. Merrick had been rather wounded by the idea, at first; "why, when you're like one of our own?" she'd said.

So Letty had moved. Some of the furniture had been sold to neighbors, the rest was stored in the Merrick's cellar. And Letty spoke to Carol, out of a deep trouble.

"I don't feel right, living here, Carol — on your people. The little I draw out to pay my board, it doesn't cover it, by half. And I make things so cramped for all of you, you must admit that."

"I never admit anything," Carol said cheerfully, her rusty black hair ruffled but her disposition surface-smooth. "Don't be an Airedale. Letty, come over here and look at my chin, do you see anything?" asked Carol anxiously.

Letty hitched her chair closer, leaned over and peered obligingly. Carol's skin, over which she spent hours, was olive in tone, and clear. "I discover no blemish," said Letty, laughing, "except a speck of coal dust."

"It itched," explained Carol, "and I thought — This beauty business has its drawbacks. You can't even enjoy a pimple — excuse me, acne — in comfort, it's as much as your job is worth. 'Why, of course, madame, I always use Sonia's preparations,' " said Carol in a high, mincing voice, " 'I had a wretched skin when I came here.' Anybody," said Carol more naturally, "would know that for a damned lie. Anybody, that is, who isn't coughing up eight bucks for an hour and a quarter of Sonia's boloney."

Letty laughed. Presently she sobered. She said, going back to the previous conversation:

"I can't live here indefinitely, Carol, and not pay my way."

"Oh, shut up," said Carol, "it's too hot to fight. You know we're tickled pink to have you. You belong to us. A Merrick in all but name. And if that bothers you, Tom would be happy to attend to it," she said with a hint of mischief.

Letty flushed slightly. She replied, after a moment during which Carol reached for a cigarette, pulled an ornate standing ashtray close to her, and, looking out through the shimmering screens, murmured indifferently, "God, it's hot":

"I know, you're all dear, but —— "

"Nix on the buts. They belong in the gutter."

"No, seriously, Carol. I must find something to do. I can't be a burden to your people, honey. Especially now, with the building business the way it is and your father taking punishment and saying nothing ―― "

"You could get a job tomorrow," Carol told her, "but why bring that up? We've been over it before. But there's always Ziegfeld. Modeling, wholesale houses or shops, that isn't so hot, now, of course. And posing ― well, there's a girl at Sonia's who used to get two hundred and fifty to sit on a table and swing her legs. They'd make Dietrich's look like an English bull's. Boy, she's gorgeous. But business was lousy and so she took some money out of the triple sheer sock and grabbed herself a beauty course and now she's wandering about Sonia's saying, 'I recommend the muscle-strapping treatment, moddom, it takes off ten years.' Lord," said Carol, suddenly sitting up, "what a prize ass I am! Why didn't I think of that before!"

"Of what? Muscle strapping?"

"No. Taking a course. You. They're down in price. Risk that much, it's a good gamble. I think I can get you a job at Sonia's. It's only a question of time before two of the girls will be leaving. One of 'em, Mae Allyn, you remember her, don't you, she was over one day last year? has had a row with her meal ticket. She

19

told me yesterday that the conditions under which they'll kiss and be friends include a trip to Europe and a house at Great Neck. She wants to retire. By the time you've finished the operator's course," Carol went on, "there's sure to be a place for you. It won't be much money, at first. But you'll get tips and sales commissions and all that. Sonia's pretty regular. Holy cow, what a chump I've been! You were made to order for the business. With a skin like yours you can sell a truck-load of Sonia's stuff — not a blotch in a carload," said Carol, laughing.

She swung back and forward in the glider. Letty regarded her doubtfully.

"Do you really think — " she began, her eyes bright with excitement.

"Only when I have to — and then I think damned fast," Carol interrupted. "Look here, Letty, can't you see it's a swell idea? You aren't a steno or a typist. Of course you could learn, but could you get a job and work at it? You wouldn't be so good behind a counter, even if there was a counter with a vacancy. You give me the horse laugh when I talk about studio tests or stage tryouts. Come on into the beauty game, Letty, and watch your own smoke. You'll be able to eat, and you'll get a lot of laughs. If you want to pass on some of the stuff you hear to Winchell or Sullivan or Sobol or the rest, you'll see yourself in print. Boy, it's a riot, what I mean! And I'll give Sonia a line, see, meantime, and get her interested and then when you're ready you can come in, refined and a little high-hat, college girl interested in the science of the skin, or something. Look here, wasn't your father sort of keen on that stuff anyway?" asked Carol, remembering.

Letty nodded, her eyes somber.

"Yes, during the last few years or so," she answered. "He used to say that most of the preparations used were either pure fake, bad medicine or simply harmless. So now and then he amused himself fussing around in the lab. He got up a sulphur lotion and a couple of heavy creams — expensive, because he used good almond oil in 'em — and then there's a thing that has cucumber and strawberries in it. He made up some for me, I gave you a little once, remember?"

"Of course," said Carol, excited. "I'd forgotten though. He didn't sell them to the drug firm, did he? Oh, of course not, I'd have heard."

"No. He offered them two of them, I believe. They weren't interested at the time. There was nothing in his contract to prevent him from selling the formulas elsewhere, I suppose, but he just didn't bother. I remember he said once that if he sold outright, he'd get very little. And that even if someone bought them on a royalty basis the returns would not be so great. He said that when he got around to it he might get them made up for himself in larger quantities than he could make and try selling them himself; that if someone else took them over he was sure that, eventually, inferior ingredients would go in. 'What you need is a clever advertising campaign,' he told me, 'and to start small, and work up slowly.' He used to laugh and say that I wasn't much help; my skin didn't need improving," Letty stated without vanity, "and so he couldn't tell, on me, whether the things would do any good or not."

"What happened to the what-you-may-call-'ems?" asked Carol, excited.

"The formulas? Oh, I have them, and a lot of others. There in the tin box in my trunk, with," said Letty, "the securities." She spoke without bitterness, smiling, but there was a catch in her voice.

"Hang on to them," advised Carol, "they may be worth jack some day. But if you come in with us, don't tell Sonia. She's all right, but she's a good business woman and that means she'd do you in the eye as soon as look at you, provided she could do it gracefully, and then sell you something to paint on the shiner. But

22

don't chuck them away, they might come in handy."

"I've thought of that," admitted Letty, "but at present they're not much of an asset."

"There's Dorothy Gray," Carol reminded her; "didn't she start by selling her father's preparations to drug stores? He was a doctor, I think —— Well ——

"Oh, Lord, here comes Tom! Why that gawk exerts himself in hot weather God only knows. He can't shake a leg when it comes to building a furnace fire in the winter," said Carol, viewing the advancing form of her brother with resigned annoyance.

Tom yelled, "Hi!" and came loping up the steps. He was a big young man, very tanned. He spent all the time he could spare at the beaches, in season, and left his older, more sober-minded partner to run the garage. He was excessively good-looking in a large, unextraordinary way, in a bathing suit or a pair of overalls. Even in the hot blue serge he now wore he was attractive, light brown hair curling damply, tanned face shining, white teeth showing in a lopsided grin. He came up the steps, opened the door, fell into a chair and tore off his collar and tie, all, it seemed, in a single gesture.

"Howdy, women," said Tom, "how about a movie tonight?"

"Oh, it's so hot," Letty began.

Tom looked at her with that curious mixture of anger and adoration which had been growing on him for three years now. Carol said briskly:

"Well, the theater's refrigerated. Swell place for pneumonia. I might allow myself a soda afterwards," she said thirstily, "I haven't had any this week. I have to lay off 'em. I haven't your figure, Letty, or your skin —— "

"If you'd lay off the gin you'd be better off," Tom told her.

He disapproved of Carol. They regarded each other with a sort of sulky affection, tinder to the spark of anger. They were close in years and that was all. Tom complained bitterly of Carol to their parents. Her "nights out," the imported cars that sometimes called for her, the life she led, away from home, away even from business, about which she said no more than was necessary.

"Sez you!" said Carol indifferently.

Letty intervened hastily. She'd go to the movies, she said, and be glad of it. How hot was it anyway? Hadn't it cooled off a bit? She was about to ask Carol if she didn't want to walk down to the shore.

Mrs. Merrick poked her head around the archway leading into the living room. She viewed the little arena of the sun porch with a

24

complacence as yet unshaken by fear. The sun porch was stable. It stood for something. Canary cage, radio, wicker and reed, Tom lolling in a chair, Letty cool in green, Carol showing more leg than was necessary but not more than was attractive, supine in the glider.

Mrs. Merrick had gray hair and a round unlined face. She wore an apron over her chiffon dress. Her small feet, plump and tired, were in house slippers. Her hands were older than her face, and the left hand wore a broad uncompromising gold band. She said:

"Tom . . . ? run down to the corner, will you, and see if you can find your father. He may have stopped in at the Clanceys'. Mike has a new short wave set. Supper's about ready," she added.

"Come along, Letty," said Tom. He nodded at his mother, rising as he spoke. "O.K., Ma," he said.

Letty came to her feet. The thin cotton dress worn over a slip, a net brassière, and a very light, supple girdle showed every line of her slim figure, long thighs and rounded waist and small bust, low and firm. They ambled down the steps together, Letty looking back; "Coming, Carol?" she asked, with the merest hint of appeal. Carol cursed silently, rose and followed. Tom's look at her was black. Carol grinned, glad she had come.

The wind came singing down the street, stirring the dusty leaves of the city trees. A robin was singing, singing his heart out, his brave red breast vibrant. Letty's curling short hair was a halo about her face.

"I've persuaded Letty to go into the flattery business," Carol told Tom, trying to suit her shorter heel-stilted pace to Tom's long stride and Letty's freer step.

"What's that?" asked Tom, instantly suspicious.

Carol explained, enjoying her brother's obvious ill humor as her story grew, exaggerated, absurd. Letty laughed, without interrupting.

"Does she mean it? Do you mean it, Letty?" he demanded.

Letty nodded. "Of course. . . . There's Uncle Dan across the street," she said, waving, and hastened ahead a little to meet him. Tom dropped back a pace and took Carol's arm in a fraternal grip which lacked all affection.

"What the hell are you putting her up to?" he demanded.

Carol wrenched her arm away.

"Hey, have a heart! I bruise easily and when I do I get paid for it!" she said angrily.

Tom dropped her arm with a mutter of annoyance. Carol said, rubbing her injury with the tenderness she always expended upon her own body:

"Letty's going to take an operator's course. I'll try and get her into Sonia's."

"That's hooey," Tom interrupted. "Why ——" Words appeared to fail him. He swallowed and went on, "It's all very well for you, Carol, but not for Letty."

Carol glared, not any too well pleased. Letty was coming back toward them with Dan Merrick. Walking home Tom managed to detach Letty and keep her beside him while Carol and her father went on ahead. He said sourly:

"I thought Carol would make some fool suggestion, Letty, why do you want to work? You know you needn't. I've saved a little money, we could take the other half of the house, pay the old folks just what — what they've been getting," he said clumsily, "and ——"

"Please, Tom," she said quietly, "don't let's discuss it. That's impossible. I'm sorry, but it is. I've told you so, a dozen times ——"

"A hundred," he amended, sullen, "but that don't make it any easier to hear. Anyway, if you won't have me, don't listen to Carol. She's running with a crazy crowd, I don't trust her, for a minute. But they won't listen to me, they think she's gold ——"

27

"So she is," Letty told him hotly. A moment later as they turned toward the house where Mr. Merrick was admiring the strong green shoots of the new rambler and announcing that next year they'd have flowers, she added, "I do think Carol's idea is a good one, Tom. I don't understand why we didn't think of it before."

A little later they went on in to supper, in the cool, dark dining room, and sat together about the round, scarred table. There were stuffed birds and plated silver on the sideboard and two staring fish anchored to varnished boards testified that, once, Mr. Merrick had taken a holiday in Florida. Everyone talked at once, there was laughter and gossip, cold meat and potato salad and iced tea and fruit and Letty slipped from her seat now and then to help Mrs. Merrick carry plates in and out. It was all friendly and homelike, all something to which she had been accustomed, for years. Many a night she and her father had come down to Sunday supper with the Merricks . . .

She mustn't think of her father.

She looked up and saw Tom glowering at her across the table, hurt and appeal and something more terrifying in his blue eyes. She didn't want to think of Tom either.

But she would have to. Tom was one reason, the strongest probably, for her dislike of living in the Merrick house, now. Tom couldn't be ignored, he wouldn't let himself be.

She did not love him. She had never loved him; she never would love him. She had never loved any man, in that way.

At Syracuse there had been men. . . . A senior or two. The brother of a girl with whom she had spent weekends in the town. Nice boys. Something exciting about them, something which both warned and warmed her. But she hadn't been in love.

She mustn't think of Syracuse.

Chapter 2

Letty had definitely decided to take her operator's training at the academy in Brooklyn where Carol had taken hers. She elected for the three months' course although Carol said, "You won't need it. You won't be asked to do anything but facials at Sonia's and you'll have to learn her method, anyway."

But Letty shook her lovely head. She wanted, she said, to learn all she could, she would take the six months' instruction if she felt she could afford the time and money. As it was, the course cost her about two hundred dollars, plus the extras, which included certain books and her small black bag containing irons, scissors, combs, polish, files and the rest.

She found the work both interesting and entertaining, to her silent amazement. Manicuring came first and Letty would arrive home to display, ruefully, raw and bleeding fingers, bestowed upon her by her "partner" for the day. Every student had to have a partner and one's arrival at the school was heralded by wild cries of "Will you be my partner today?" as if it were some strange and childish game.

In the morning from nine to twelve Letty would permit herself to be practiced upon. Then, she had an hour for lunch. From one to two there would be a lecture; and from two to the close of the day's session Letty would have her revenge upon her day's partner.

The beginners were nervous and awkward. Letty felt despairingly that she was all long arms and large, unwieldy hands. But she learned rapidly. And she made some friends. All sorts of girls buzzed busily about the big rooms. Tall girls, short girls, pretty girls and plain girls. Pretty ones predominated. It seemed to be a provision of nature that good looks drifted into the business of good looks.

Letty had considerable advantage over most of her school companions. She had not only the quick mind and the adaptability which many of them lacked, but she had Carol at home to give her a good deal of sound advice. Carol laughed long and loud when Letty bore home the books. "The same old stuff," said Carol. "I suppose you thought if you bought 'em you'd have a short cut to the operators' heaven. I have 'em, myself, forgot all about 'em or I'd have saved you the money. They didn't do me any good. And look here, nothing is going to do *you* any good but experience. Marcelling, for instance. You can learn the motions, all right, but before you can do it properly it will have taken you years of practice. You won't have to, anyway. Sonia has a couple of very good men. Saps, both of them, but swell with the irons. You needn't have bothered with that course, I told you so."

But Letty was stubborn. She might as well get all she could in the time at her disposal, she argued. And she wanted to go to one of the permanent wave equipment places and learn permanent waving, later, as she hadn't signed for it at the school.

Carol snorted. "You can learn it in a couple of days," she said, "as far as operating the machine is concerned. It takes about ten years to really know your onions though, except now and then when you have a lucky break. Why you want to clutter yourself up with all this dope is beyond me. Learn as little as you can to get by, that's my motto," said Carol.

Manicuring was the most uninteresting of the courses, thought Letty, shuddering as she painted her partner's nails the bright, prevailing red. Her own were painted in a like manner, but she removed the evidence as soon as her partner had brushed it on to her own satisfaction. The partner, a plump little blonde, held Letty's hand a moment and looked at it with a wistful envy.

"You have the prettiest hands I ever saw," she said, sighing.

Letty's wrists were round and fragile looking but they were strong. Her hands were strong too, slender, long-fingered, soft and firm. She had, although she did not then realize it, a fortune in her hands.

The three months passed quickly, and the season slid from summer, late, hot, lingering summer, into the crisp clear autumn. Letty was generally too tired by the time she reached home to do much more than go to bed. Sometimes Tom persuaded her to go with him to the beaches, evenings or Sundays. But not often. Carol was away a great deal of the time. She was sent to one of Sonia's summer branches for a couple of weeks to finish up the season there. Her own vacation had been taken earlier in the summer, with some people she vaguely designated as friends, in a Catskill resort from which she sent home scrawled postcards.

Letty progressed evenly and steadily. She was very well liked. She could, the other girls found, always be counted on to help when they ran into difficulties. She went out to lunch with one or the other of them, consuming a sandwich and a glass of milk somewhere and perhaps walking afterwards and window-shopping along the crowded stretches of Fulton Street filled with stores and people, dust and blowing papers.

Dora, the plump blonde, was often Letty's partner; and there were other girls she liked. One, a young widow, using her husband's meager insurance to see her through the course in order to support a little son; another, a Brooklyn girl who had been a beauty contest winner and who had drifted, after a brief, disastrous trip to Hollywood, back home and had finally decided to take a course and earn her living, as she put it, with some bitterness, "as honestly as most."

The marcel waving was amusing, working at the long tables before the round wooden heads of the models, equipped with switches, while the instructor walked by and commented. "Must you make your client look as if she had slept with her head on a washboard?" was one of the usual remarks.

The facial room had long chairs and mirrors and there you practiced on your partner or she on you; and later perhaps you listened to a lecture on the nerves and muscles of the face and the texture of the skin. Or if hair was the order of the day, upon the nerves and condition of the scalp and hair. Letty liked the lectures. Many of the girls yawned their way through them, preferring practice to theory;

but Letty listened and took notes. She had been fortunate, thanks to Carol, in the selection of her school. The instructors were well trained and the lecturers who came to them from all over the city and country were the best of their kind — if one wished to take advantage of them.

Finger waving came easily to her, her long fingers soon learning to press the deep wide waves close to the shingled heads upon which she experimented. But the facial treatments she liked best of all; she liked dipping ice-cold satin-smooth fingers in the clinging cream and smoothing and tapping it into the quiet face which to her had always such an other-world look, with the white towel bound close about the hair line. She told Carol, however, that the one thing she must get over if she was to be a success was her instinctive dislike of some faces. Carol laughed. "You've said a mouthful," she announced, "you'll have some laid out before you over at Sonia's that you'll want to slap. And not with any gentle slapping to bring up circulation either!"

But what Letty couldn't quite explain was that she had to school herself to what she mentally termed indiscriminate handling. She herself disliked to be touched; and disliked, as heartily, to touch strangers, people for whom she had no liking, no affection. Something of this crept into her fingers, tempered by her knowledge that to be fastidious in her fingers as well as in her soul was not going to help her to success. But the result was that her touch upon the face and throat and back of her "partner" was impersonal yet not indifferent. A feather-soft, firm touch which was learning to feel out the little nerves and muscles, learning to bring the bright blood singing to the surface, learning . . . learning. But most of all learning to consider that this unique combination of flesh and blood, skin and bone, muscles and nerves, under her sagacious fingertips was merely something that she was modeling toward beauty and so learning to detach it from the person who possessed it, so to speak. And this would stand her in good stead when at Sonia's, instead of the eager, familiar fellow students whom she was growing to know, she would have querulous, short-tempered women, women whose faces were marred by the stamp of too many cocktails and too little sleep, by hatred and greed and fear, by frustration and desire, by luxury and selfishness. For there would be women coming to Letty at Sonia's who, unless she considered them as so much clay to press into fleeting shapes of beauty, would turn her sick with a mental and physical nausea, not because their outward surfaces would

36

be repulsive, these well-dressed, prettyish women, but because unless she trained her fingers to that quality of impersonality which is not cold and not indifferent but which is detached, she would feel, somehow, the ugly, the almost terrifying emanations.

Something of this she tried to put into words to Carol. Carol stared at her.

"You're nuts," said Carol with finality.

Letty laughed and gave it up. Perhaps she was.

And so the course ended. Her beautiful hair was burned sometimes and her delicate skin reddened from the attacks upon them. She was almost always tired, but she was always interested. She would tell Carol what she had found that seemed good and sensible, and what she had found which was merely harmless or actually harmful as the case might be. Carol would yawn. "Why take it to heart like that? It's only a racket, and a good one," she'd inform Letty. But Letty was obstinate. It needn't be, she'd say.

Toward the end of her course she had found herself practicing upon genuine customers. There were the women who came in, quite aware that the operators were merely students but willing to take a chance for the sake of saving money. Letty's first experience, a facial and finger wave, confused and frightened her. She had become accustomed to her classmates, who accepted what she gave in the spirit in which she accepted their student blunderings. But a "real" person was different and she found herself shaking with excitement and fear of failure. But she acquitted herself well enough and later stood staring at a ten-cent tip, not knowing whether to laugh or cry.

She'd forgotten about tips. And that the anxious, aging little woman to whom she had given the treatment, and who had confided in her that she had been tramping the streets for jobs and simply had to look her best in order to land one, if at all, should have added the dime to the painful quarters squeezed out for the facial and finger wave seemed to Letty infinitely pathetic.

The Merricks, all save Tom, had approved of her decision. Carol would find her a good job, they said comfortably. They added that working would take her mind off things. Mrs. Merrick was still volubly objecting to Letty's paying board from her little principal. "You might let it wait until you're earning," she said.

But Tom had grown sulky and demanding.

"I suppose once you get over there in that swell dump," he told her, "you'll get the same big ideas Carol has. Do you think for a minute

I believed all that hooey about a young married woman, sister of a girl she works with — that vacation story? Not on your life. But ma's as blind as a mole where Carol's concerned."

He intimated that he would keep a sharp eye on Carol and that if ever he caught Letty going out with her — or ——

It wasn't very pleasant.

Carol knew. Carol had been present on several occasions. "Tom's past all endurance," she told Letty irritably one night. "I wish he'd go jump off the sea wall or something. I think I ought to get Dad to speak to him," she said. But she said it doubtfully. Neither she nor Letty really wished to bring the uncomfortable situation to the older Merricks' attention. It would only make things worse, Carol agreed finally.

"Besides," said Letty reasonably, "it's natural that they'd take his part and think I'm ungrateful or crazy or something. I think they do already. . . . I know they're fond of me, bless them," she added, "but after all Tom's their son."

"Well, he's my brother," Carol retorted, "and I couldn't see you wasting yourself on that great gawk." She regarded Letty from her kitten-like posture on the old-fashioned bed they shared. Letty was standing before the mirror in a wisp of a nightgown, brushing her hair, burnishing it, letting the strands spring back to their deep natural waves, pressing the waves in with her fingers. "If I had your looks — " said Carol. She stopped. Then added, "Well, they're yours. And if you play your cards properly —— "

She halted again. Letty was no prig, nor was she ignorant. But there were some things Carol hesitated to say to her. Letty stopped brushing.

"Go on," she said quietly.

"Heck," replied Carol, unusually embarrassed, "you belong on Park Avenue, what I mean. And you know it. With a couple of goofy butlers in rompers and a penthouse all decked out in Christmas trees and *Mrs.* on your calling card."

Letty's eye twinkled. She put down the hair brush. She said, looking at Carol in the mirror:

"The Park Avenue bit might be easier than the Mrs."

Carol was mildly astonished. Recovering she nodded vigorously. She then remarked, a little wistfully, "Virtue doesn't pay dividends. That's one stock that's sunk. People," said Carol, giggling, "have been selling short."

"It may not pay," said Letty after a moment, thinking of some of the things she'd heard lately, at the school, "but it's safer."

"You've only one life," retorted Carol after a moment, "who wants to be safe? Most of the nice respectable people I know end up in the gutter. Some of them slave all their lives away and what do they get for it? Mortgages and worry about the grocer's bill. Look at ma," said Carol gloomily.

Letty was silent.

This brief conversation took place shortly before Letty entered Sonia's. There was no difficulty about placing her there as Carol had spent three solid months throwing out mysterious hints. They had been one girl short at Sonia's, as Carol had predicted, her volatile co-worker having become reconciled to her aging boy friend in a manner satisfactory enough to the lady. In summer it had not mattered; but it was autumn now and people were back from the country, those who had gone at all, and many of them were not going South this year.

Therefore, one morning in early November Letty presented herself at the Sonia Salon, for an interview.

The salon was housed in a building on Fifth Avenue. The elevator rose eight floors and stopped. The doors opened and Letty stepped into the reception room, a large square room, which ran to touches of rose and mauve, which had eccentric rosy lights housed in

41

glass and metal along the walls, overhead and at the sides. There was a desk, occupied by a pert and pretty little person. On the desk were several telephones. "Appointment desk," explained Carol, her guide and mentor.

All around the wall were glass cases where Sonia's preparations were shown to their best advantage, housed in crystal and sealed in mauve and silver, bottles, jars, compacts, lipsticks, the latter aids to titivation in black and mauve and silver. The atmosphere was curiously hushed, the room wore the aspect of some strange cathedral erected to the modern manifestation of a very ancient goddess, a goddess who had it in her power to bestow inestimable favors but who could be cruel and capricious, and who, at all times, demanded a ceaseless vigil, a prayerful service and golden propitiation.

Presently Letty found herself alone in Sonia's private office. Carol had ushered her in, spoken briefly and briskly and then vanished. Sonia sat at her desk and regarded Letty.

The office was small. It was paneled in dark, expensive woods and there was no sign of unguents about it, no preparations were on display. There were flowers instead, roses in a silver bowl, roses in a tall modern vase worked in some bronze, metallic material.

Sonia behind her severe desk, a fine piece of furniture, Sonia leaning back in her tall chair, as her own advertisement.

In another corner a typewriter, unobtrusive. Sonia's secretary and bookkeeper came in and went out again, a good looking woman, not young.

Sonia herself was perhaps fifty; or over. With her back to the light she looked no more than thirty. She was handsome. She had preserved a slender tall figure, broad shouldered, deep chested, and a smooth, heavy skin, by God knew what deprivations. Her eyes were unlined. But they were tired and a little shrewd, their brilliant blue had blurred. They betrayed her. Her mouth was firm, her teeth very lovely, her blond hair brilliantined and closely waved. She had big, square-fingered hands, beautifully kept, large-knuckled hands. She spoke slowly, with a very faint Scandinavian accent. She looked at Letty with the measuring eye of the habitual dealer in human flesh as Letty answered the first commonplace questions.

Age, education, home —— "You live with Miss Carol's parents, do you not?"; experience, schooling in beauty technique . . . "that's a good place, a very good place, you were wise to take your course there."

Then, "Have you any outside income?"

Flushing, Letty explained the situation, the legacy, such as it was, which she hoped to keep intact from now on.

Sonia's lids drooped. She fidgeted with a pencil for a moment.

"I pay fair salaries, even to begin. At twenty, my girls begin. Later, it is thirty. I permit them to accept tips, and of course Miss Carol has explained to you that when you have doubled your salary you will have a commission on your work, commissions also on your sales. But you understand in this business the girls must always be at their best, rested, refreshed, well-groomed, the skin perfect, the eyes bright. If there is too much struggle to make ends meet, if there are large amounts to be paid in at home, this is not always possible. Some of my girls have families not dependent on them; some have — oh — other means of assistance. You understand?"

Only dimly, at the moment; later, perfectly. But Letty nodded. That evening Carol, at her questioning, would enlighten her. Sonia's girls, the majority of them, had friends. Oh, not *kept*, you understand. They would have resented that, they would have been outraged. They had jobs, they were technically self-supporting. But they lived in rather good apartments, in better sections than Sonia's salaries would have afforded. Many of them

44

sent money home. They wore good clothes, they had plenty of recreation. They were "seen" everywhere, they had an ample supply of silk stockings and were rarely called upon to pay for their dinners . . . or breakfasts . . . or lunches. . . .

There were eight girls, including Carol and the one girl who did manicuring. There would be eleven with Kitty, the bookkeeper-secretary and the appointment clerk.

Sonia was watching Letty. "Let me see your hands," she said abruptly.

Letty put them down flat on the desk. Sonia touched them with her blunt, strong fingers.

Enchanting hands. The girl herself, as lovely a girl as she had seen in years. A skin you could eat, thought Sonia, there were no words for it. In the rose-colored uniform with the organdy collar and cuffs she would be delectable. Yes, she would engage her. This was no ordinary girl, she thought. Clever, quiet, watching out of the amazing black eyes. . . . If she were a little cleverer she would go far. . . .

"I'll take you," Sonia said in her husky voice, "at twenty, to start. You must, of course, learn my methods. Miss Carol will teach you, and Madame Nelda, my secretary. You will at first be given the very simple facials, once you have learned the technique required. You will also learn to make the masks. . . . I have a girl who does only manicuring, you will not be required to do that. Perhaps in the beginning an occasional shampoo . . . ? The waving, the permanents are taken care of by Kean and Louis, two very good men."

She explained that when a new client arrived she herself came into the room for a consultation, examined and prescribed. Also, if an old customer came for, say, a five-dollar facial it would be the operator's task to suggest another, at eight or ten; or, better still, a "course" of the most expensive. The buying of preparations also was up to the operators, more or less. "Each of my girls has her own following," Sonia said.

It was a large establishment. It occupied an entire floor, and had been established for six years in its present situation. Times were bad but old customers were faithful, Sonia said.

Letty was dismissed. She would come to work on the following day. Madame Nelda came in to take her measurements for uniforms. The uniforms were supplied to the operators at cost. The cost was considerable, thought Letty, who had been dreaming of sales commissions and of more than doubling her salary. But she must wear the regulation uniform. Nelda showed her one, rosy and crisp and pretty. Later, leaving, she saw Carol similarly tricked out, spotless, looking quite lovely with her dark skin and hair.

"Sure, I knew you'd make it," said Carol. "See you in the morning. No, I won't be home to dinner. . . ."

Letty left, perfectly aware that those of the girls who were idle were watching her frankly or from behind doors. The appointment clerk smiled at her as she stood waiting for the elevator. "You're in the army now," said the appointment clerk.

News had traveled. The new operator, to take Mae's place? Well, time would tell.

Chapter 3

Letty puzzled considerably over what she called the "outside income clause." She spoke to Carol about it several times during her busy, rather nerve-racking month of probation.

"It's putting a premium on —— "

"If you say immorality I'll scream and pull the emergency cord," Carol interrupted her.

Letty laughed. They were traveling home together, swaying to the jerky progress of the crowded car, clinging to straps, brushing with knees and shoulders and torsos the bodies of complete strangers, in the brief, rather appalling intimacy of the subway.

"I wasn't going to say immorality," she said, "I was going to put it a little more delicately. How about primroses?"

Carol chuckled. Her hard little face was tired but her eyes were bright with the defiance of her species.

"Primroses are as good as lilies," she remarked; "when they're both dead they smell the same."

"You get hay fever or something from primroses," Letty reminded her.

Carol's original explanation of Sonia's question had both interested and repelled her. But now, after working for a while with Sonia's troupe of pretty girls, she was beginning to understand more clearly; and Carol assured her that the system was not at all unique. Sonia hadn't invented it.

The doors opened at Cortlandt Street, the crowd surged forward, people crowded out . . . and in. A small child dragged along by one arm whimpered; it was as if he struggled through a jungle consisting of trouser legs and shining silk stockings and trampling feet. There was no air and no light, merely a confusion and a terror.

Conversation was an impossibility. The doors started to shut again, and a man, dashing in at the last moment, held them braced open a moment with his shoulders until he could slide through to the sticky, breathless safety of the car. Carol let go her strap and made a dash for the center post, grimy and slippery with the clutch of many hands. She hooked an arm around it and opened her paper. "See you later," she called to Letty, grinning.

Letty held fast to her own strap, thinking, as they shot around curves, or halted in the echoing reaches of tunnels, and then moved on again.

She liked Sonia's. The work interested her. Already she was beginning to be in demand although she had been permitted to give only the very simplest facials. But several times when they were rushed and the girls were busy she had been pressed into service. And two of her customers had asked for her again . . . "the tall girl with the lovely hands," they had specified over the telephone and Gracie, at the appointment desk, had said brightly, "Oh, you mean Miss Letty? Very well, mod-dom."

She had not been content to learn her routine, that first month. "Snoopin' Sam" Carol called her. She would waylay the girls and question them, she would talk to Gracie, to Madame Nelda, who liked her and showed it, even to Sonia, when Sonia was in one of her benevolently, consciously gracious moods. She had asked if she might go through one of the downtown laboratories and Sonia had said yes, with an astonished lift of her eyebrow. And Letty had taken her lunch hour one day and gone; and talked to chemists and clerks and stockroom people, and peered into the mysteries of beauty in the making; and asked about bottles and jars and packaging and trademarking. Carol had laughed at her.

"What's the big idea?" she'd demanded.

"Nothing. Everything. What's the use of working at anything if you don't find out everything there is to know about it?" Letty had countered.

"Well, if that's your idea of a hot time," Carol had told her, shrugging, "you can have it. But don't get too interested; I mean so that Sonia's on to you. She likes her girls smart but dumb. Get me? That is, she's always been strong for the exclusive stuff, the touch of Garbo, as it were. Doesn't want anyone wise to all her tricks. Nelda is, I suppose, but then Nelda's been with Sonia since she was knee-high to a hoptoad."

Letty was remembering this now, as they reached their station and emerged into the cool, brisk air. The wind was sharp from the Narrows and the shops along Fourth Avenue were bright and garish with their reminders that Christmas was not far away. Letty turned her eyes from the tinsel and the red paper drapings and the little dusty Christmas trees. She and her father had made a good deal of Christmas . . . it would be hard this year. And all the years, she thought, with the blessed ignorance of the young.

She took Carol's arm as they walked and went on with their interrupted discussion.

"Look here," said Letty, "I can't get it,

quite. There's Gloria — and Francesca and some of the others. But then, there's you — and —— "

"Oh, we don't all get the breaks," Carol explained carelessly, "and there's the middle way, you know."

Letty was learning more about Carol's middle way; the dinners and theaters, the gifts carelessly given and as carelessly received; or so it seemed; an occasional frock, stockings, bits of jewelry . . .

She neither approved nor disapproved. It was Carol's business. In more ways than one, it was Carol's business.

Carol was urging her these days to go out more. "Come along with me, make a fourth, there's always an extra man. It's good business to be seen places, the right places."

But Letty wasn't interested. Even Tom, sullen these days, could see that.

The month passed. Christmas came and went. Christmas was what you made it, a love feast, a festival, or something meaningless, commercial. Christmas at the Merricks' was pleasant, with a tree to trim and an odor of turkey roasting and little gifts for everyone. Tom, flushed with the Christmas cocktails he had insisted upon making, caught Letty and kissed her under the rather bedraggled piece of mistletoe. She freed herself, laughing, not at all indignant, but a little sorry for him, while Mrs. Merrick watched them, her eyes shrewd and thoughtful in her amiable, round face.

Carol had certain gifts which she did not exhibit to the family. A bar pin, for instance, small square diamonds and sapphires. Very pretty and rather costly. Letty raised her eyes from the shining thing in the leather box to Carol's face. Carol laughed, a very little.

"It's only Snooks," said Carol.

"Snooks? Carol, for heaven's sake!"

"Oh, he's old," said Carol carelessly, "and he likes to be babied. He's pretty sweet, though."

She didn't add that she had given up most of the younger men for Snooks. She said merely: "I've known him ages. He has lots of what it takes, Letty. This pin — it isn't more to him than a couple of handkerchiefs to us. After all," said Carol, "I amuse him, don't I?"

During the holiday season Sonia's was busy. Letty found herself booked straight through the day. Sometimes the days passed in a blur. A blur of color and scent, of the soft darkness of sables, and the silver darkness of fox. A blur of women, coming and going, talking in their low or shrill or clipped accents, coming alone, coming in pairs, always in a hurry, unable wholly to relax on the yielding couches,

53

their little faces, thin or plump, smooth or haggard, masked in creams and lotions, their hair bound back with a strip of rosy linen, their hands restless, their tongues clattering . . .

Always in a hurry, thinking ahead to the next appointment, the shop, the luncheon engagement, tea, dinner, bridge, anything. . . . "Hurry, Miss Letty, I've only an hour. . . ." "Hurry, can't you . . . ? I have to be at the St. Regis at one . . ." "Have I time for a muscle strapping . . . ? hurry — hurry ——"

Beauty, on the wing . . .

Letty's hands were miracles. "You should have them insured," Carol told her for the hundredth time. They were firm and cool and soft. They had strength and they were gentle. They learned quickly, the soft tapping movements, the even pressure against the bones, the smoothing and soothing, the coaxing at the little drooping muscles, at the tired, jaded nerves. Faces bloomed under them gratefully. Women spoke to Sonia. . . . "That girl, Letty, her hands are marvelous, she takes years off you — and heaven knows I could spare a few years . . ."

Perhaps it wasn't beauty so much that they sought but youth which is beauty . . .

Sonia noticed and nodded, well satisfied. She was always in and out of the rosy rooms, observing, advising, consoling. Women turned their briefly nunlike heads to her and complained or confided, frightened sometimes, sometimes angry, sometimes hopeful of contradiction, never resigned.

"Oh, my God, Sonia, look at the hickey on my chin . . . and I have to go out tonight!"

"That's all right, Mrs. Messinger, Miss Letty will use a little of the pore-paste when she makes you up. No one will notice."

"Sonia, what'll I do? My skin's shot to hell. I haven't been in bed for a week . . . "

Sonia regarded the patient under a magnifying glass. Dry, hot skin, tight, taut, faintly lined, faintly blotched. There were skins you didn't love to touch. Sonia might have said . . . cut out the pastries and get eight hours' sleep a night for a couple of months — cut out the cocktails and the highballs — go on a diet — exercise — walk — breathe a little pure air for a change. Sonia might have said, change your mode of thinking. Sonia did not. She was a business woman. To be sure she spoke of rest and diet and exercise, but vaguely, in a routine, automatic way. And her client squirmed under Letty's hands.

"Have I the time? Of course I haven't!" She started to recite her program for the next three weeks. Letty was fatigued, listening. Sonia nodded and soothed.

"Acne lotion," she suggested, "yes, and the pore-cream. Meantime Miss Letty will give you the circulation treatment and the mask . . . and make you up for the evening. If you could spare the time for a course of circulation treatments . . . ?"

She had no time, but she would make it.

This was the life of the Sonia Salon; insistent, demanding, soft, hurried, terribly, even terrifyingly feminine, with its constant odors of perfumes, creams, tonics, distilled femininity. It amazed Letty, it frightened her a little. The procession of women amazed her even more, old and young, thin and fat, laughing and melancholy, anxious and complacent, married and unmarried, kept and lost; dowager, matron, débutante, actress, writer, business woman — there was no end to them. They came and they went, a sea of them, a surge, looking for beauty, looking for youth, crying for it, needing it. Why? To keep something, to hold something, to gain something . . . a man, a job, a lifelong vanity, a love — someone's love, sometimes their own, for themselves.

Processions of women . . .

They came without appointments, demanding instant attention. They came after too much drinking, they came a little drunk, a little drugged; they came worn and feverish and nervous; they came in bronzed and glowing from southern sun on shipboard; they came anticipating something, atiptoe with it, a raise, a proposal, a wedding. They came, all of them frantically, with the most amazing hope about them, a little tragic. They came deploring the time they must spend, and the money; but they threw themselves down, their nerves tight strung and waited for the miracle. And then they relaxed. And, looking into mirrors, they smiled. They left smiling — as a rule.

And almost always they came and went, talking, talking, talking . . . lying back under the deft, impersonal but, somehow, giving hands, scented soaking-pads over their restless eyes . . . talking. Yes, the hands were impersonal. They could talk to the hands.

"It's incredible," Letty told Carol one evening at home where, like the sailor rowing about the lake on leave, she was giving Carol a facial, not with the Sonia preparations, however, but with creams and tonics from the fat plain jars and the tall plain bottles she cherished.

"What is? Boy, can you charm away the wrinkles," Carol murmured.

"The things they tell me."

"Sure," said Carol, "why not? We all know enough, at Sonia's, to break up a hundred homes. What of it? Gosh, this is swell stuff, Letty. You're almost out of it, aren't you?"

"Yes, but I can get it made up again. Steaner, the old druggist, over on Sixth. He made it up for father, you know, before the lab was working. It won't cost anything, really."

"No, it never does," said Carol, laughing, "that's the joker. Those boobs come in and pay five-fifty for a jar you could put in your eye — and for what?"

"Of course," said Letty, "good almond oil's expensive."

"Sure, but how many use it in their racket? And if so, how much of it?"

She was silent. Then she chuckled.

"If all the advertised turtles who had sacrificed their dear little glands were laid end to end," she began, but Letty was not listening; she was still thinking of the women who talked . . . and talked.

"One client," she interrupted, "today — said —— Oh, it doesn't matter. But it was about her husband . . . and . . . her sister." She shivered a little and then asked inadequately, "Can you beat it?"

"Sure I can beat it. And how!"

"Why aren't they afraid of blackmail?" asked Letty.

"Oh, that's been done too. But it doesn't

58

pay, really. Not the out and out sort. But, remember that sometimes they remember the things they've said and they come back to you and keep on coming back and the tips are pretty good —— "

"Women are fools," said Letty, cleansing Carol's face with tissue.

"If they weren't," Carol responded briskly, "we wouldn't make our living off 'em."

It was beginning to be a living for Letty. The twenty a week did not go far, but her tips were increasing and her commissions. She banked her tips, gave Mrs. Merrick ten dollars a week and managed on the rest. From the middle of the first month she had been able to double her weekly salary in work; and she was developing a sales talk. "Sometimes," she told Carol, "I feel ashamed. Look at Mrs. Winzer! She has more stuff now than she can use in a hundred years but every time she comes, and she comes once a week, I sell her another truckload. It's absurd."

"You're nerts," Carol told her briefly. "What's it to you, except your commissions, if she wants to set up a warehouse? I've met her Big Moment, Old Man Winzer himself," Carol announced, *"and* . . . the girl friend. There's the answer."

Letty was silent a moment. Then:

"I see. I don't think I'll ever laugh at her

again." She thought of Ella Winzer, small and dark and horribly harried and so believing; believing you could buy things back again, in bottles and jars; youth and loveliness and love. . . .

"It seems," said Letty soberly, "dreadful."

"What? *He's* dreadful, if you like," said Carol, "fat and sticky and oily —— "

"I wasn't thinking of him," said Letty.

"Stop thinking of any of them," said Carol, "and look here, be a sport and come out with me some night. Letty, you're a fool. I run with a keen crowd, all you have to do is look beautiful and act dumb and be clever. It's the payoff."

Carol was, as usual, rarely home. She told her mother, now and then, that she had made outside appointments for extra work. It wasn't, of course, true. Sonia did not permit it. Letty held her peace. Toward spring, however, she spoke to the other girl.

"Look here, aren't you setting a pretty rapid pace?"

"Lord," said Carol without rancor, "you've got to be amused. And I get so damned sick of women. And you know, by now, Letty, that that Chanel copy wasn't four-ninety-five and it wasn't a copy."

Letty knew. She had known for some time. Her eyes on Carol were without censure but they were hurt.

"Is it worth it?" she said quietly.

"Why not? What do I give except my charming company for dinner, show, night club? A little knee-squeezing perhaps and some goings-on in the taxi. Not too much. I manage to ruin a frock now and then . . . they spill highballs easy. Once, you could drag down a hundred for that but now it's fifty or twenty — still, that's better than nothing."

Letty shrugged and said nothing. Her generous, lovely mouth was set, a very little.

"Hell," said Carol, "don't bawl me out. I'd go nuts around here. I haven't seen the man I'd marry yet — or if I have, he's married. They're all married and not working very hard at it, or they're keeping away from the handcuffs. Now and then I get hold of someone who has honorable intentions. No, thanks. I'm having a swell time and I've got my virtue," said Carol coolly, "but, if anyone ever met my price —— "

"Would you?"

"Why not? You live just once as far as I know. No one's ever come back to tell me different. I don't like the sort of things you do. I don't like books or music — unless it's a snappy serial or a hot jazz band — I couldn't be bored studying to get ahead — on my brains, if any. So don't get hot and bothered, Letty, I am as I am, I see no reason to change.

61

I'd have been out of this dump years ago if it hadn't been for ma. Women get a rotten deal anyway and any little thing you can get out of life, free, is that much to the good, see?"

Letty saw.

But Carol refused to let her friend alone. She would ask her half a dozen times a week if she wouldn't change "what she called her mind" and go out with her, on a blind date. Why, she herself hardly knew. She knew a number of girls who would be glad of the opportunity. Somehow she wanted to make Letty see a little of the other side of the picture. Or perhaps she would feel more at ease if Letty — not that Letty "acted superior" — only ——

For a while Letty was adamant. But things were not comfortable for her at the Merricks' when Carol was not at home. Tom was importunate, she could not refuse to go to a movie with him now and then, Mrs. Merrick was obviously hurt when she refused. In order to escape, occasionally, she had signed for a night course in chemistry at one of the schools. She had always liked chemistry, in high school and college. Now, as she took a more advanced course, which was open to her that winter, she grew intensely interested, and tried to work out certain experiments of her own, using her father's notes, his formulas, and those he had worked out only in note-books. But the extra work tired her and once or twice Sonia spoke to her sharply.

"You're not looking your best," she said; "what do you do with your free time?"

Letty said, vaguely, that she was studying. Sonia shrugged and did not inquire into the nature of the studies but said, merely, "You need more recreation. It's no advertisement to my business to have my operators looking worn and fagged out."

When summer came in the course ended. Business slackened a little at the salon and as usual the girls were sent out to open up the branch places, one in Newport, one in South-ampton, one at Bar Harbor. The girls were drafted in turn, it was like an extra vacation for them, Letty supposed that she would re-main in town with the skeleton force, being new; Carol would go to Southampton.

And before she went she persuaded Letty to go out on one party with her.

"Just one," she said, "and you needn't turn up your nose. These guys are regular."

Chapter 4

Parties, reflected Letty, didn't cease with summer. Not Carol's kind. Numerous men, it appeared, stayed in town during the middle of the week and paid their wives' expenses by long distance.

They dressed at home, perhaps Sonia knew, they were able to leave the salon early. Mrs. Merrick was vague and incurious. . . . "Going out with Carol, Letty? That's nice," she said, with her comfortable smile, "you should go out more." Tom slammed in and out again. The slamming in was friendly enough. . . . "Hey, Letty, how about a movie . . . or let's go down to the Island." Letty, Carol informed him, had another date. "Is zat so?" said Tom, ugly. The door rocked the house, shutting like that. Mrs. Merrick said, "Oh, dear —— " as his voice floated back to her . . . "won't be in for supper, mom," he shouted.

She'd planned something he liked. "Cub," commented Merrick, looking up from the home edition of his paper, "no more manners than an ape!"

64

Letty felt a little pang — what was it? She hated Tom in that possessive humor. What right had he? But she and Carol were dressing now, quickly, laughing, taking turns at the tub, with the lavish scent of bath salts steaming up from it.

What to wear, Letty wondered, looking at her frocks. Not many. The two dresses, one new, which she alternated in wearing to work. The linen suit, marked down, very good lines. The cool, inexpensive chiffon. She hadn't bought much since her father's death.

Carol, red organdy, perky as a flower petal, laid out on the bed, was walking around in stepins, smoking. She vanished into the clothes closet and came out with a gown of Letty's which had been carefully hung in a scented bag; a gown Letty had never expected to wear again, an extravagance committed before her father's death. He had made her buy it for their occasional cherished evenings at the opera, during her winter vacation from college.

It had been a year ahead of fashion then; or rather it was the sort of dress which never goes out of fashion, really. White heavy crêpe with supple lines, severe and classic. Carol said, "This is the ticket. Make-up, of course. Not that you need much."

She'd never used much; often, none at all.

But Sonia had taught her. Now, laughing a little at Carol's fussing — "When did you become a mother hen?" — she sat down at the dressing table obediently. Eye shadow, a little with a metallic glint; mascara, the merest brushing; a fine pencil touch along the brows, the rosy pearl powder which so exactly matched her fine, glowing skin, the very brilliant, frankly artificial lipstick, the glass stopper of Carol's loveliest perfume drawn back of her ears, touched to the deeply curling hair; sheer stockings, satin sandals, a plain velvet wrap in a dark brown, shirred high at the neck.

Herbert Gordon's car came for them, impassively chauffeured. A small, compact, luxurious car. Carol, her red skirts disposed about her, cuddled her chin into the unnecessary fur collar of her wrap; a fur which her mother believed to be "very good rabbit" and was not.

"This is the life," said Carol.

The car sped down Fourth Avenue, snaking in and out of traffic, halting reluctantly for lights, reaching Flatbush Extension and starting to cover the crowded blocks to the bridge.

"You might tell me something about — our host," Letty reminded her. She felt — exposed, overdressed, underdressed; something uncomfortable. Yet she had no feeling of inferiority. The last year's — oh, was it eighteen months ago? — frock was good, the wrap was good. She looked well. She knew it. But she felt a little ridiculous. Why had she come? She hadn't wanted to. But Carol had nagged and nagged; put it finally on a personal basis, "I know you don't approve . . . you don't want to be seen with me — you think ——— " "Oh, Carol, I don't, I don't — of course I'll come if it means so much to you. Just this once."

Letty now asked: "Whose car?"

Carol explained; Herbert Gordon's. She had read about Herbert Gordon, hadn't she? The banker? A good egg. The other man? She wasn't sure, said Carol vaguely, it might be Morty Fisher. If it was Morty Fisher, she, Letty, would have a marvelous time. You know, the promoter . . .

Over the bridge, a clear summer night, the sky still lighted with a faint saffron glow. The buildings were tall and dominant, their illuminated windows like small squares of gold. Light and shadow drifted across them. Below, the boats went by.

Letty knew Carol was talking. She wasn't listening. She was looking at the skyline. Lower New York, lower Manhattan, not sprawled, but close-knit, building on building, rising, rising, some like the blocks which children build, some like strange cathedrals, all like some monstrous flower garden, giant flowers twisted from steel and stone. And farther uptown, yet looking so deceptively near, the triumphant soaring of the Empire State, the silver needle of the Chrysler.

Her town. Beauty in it, brutality, strength, a strength that might crush but which could inspire.

"You haven't heard a word I've been saying!" said Carol, with reproach.

After a time they had left the cluttered, filthy pushcart atmosphere of Hester Street behind them, the children crying in the gutter, the women arguing . . . a little way off was the Bowery, there were men lying in the gutter, doors swinging to and fro, people passing, indifferent. . . .

Her town. Filth in it, sorrow, tragedy, laughter, survival, if not of the fittest, of the one with the will to live.

Now they had left New York's Fourth Avenue and were sliding uphill, turning, past the Commodore, into the covered causeway, looking ahead through the arch, seeing Park Avenue framed there, a conventional picture, lights winking out. Letty loved that particular view. She said so now. This was her city, too, seemingly so permanent, so solid, so arrogant. The yellow signs on the fenced-in, mid-street grass plots amused her and she laughed. "Dogs not allowed for any reason . . ." she said, and wondered if Manhattan dogs were literate.

She was, she told Carol, enjoying the ride. She said, "You don't see New York from subways. Or — do you?"

But the ride was an old story to Carol, and many of Letty's questions she considered purely rhetorical.

Presently, turning into Fifty-fifth Street, they drew up at the St. Regis.

The two men were waiting in the lobby. Letty saw them at the moment when Carol said: "There they are ——"

One was, Letty judged, almost sixty. That would be Herbert Gordon, the banker, a slender man, quite tall, with a tolerant blue eye and, of all things, a trimmed and tended Van Dyke, as white as his thick hair. He must be, Letty realized with a start at her own stupidity, the Snooks of the diamond and sapphire bar pin. That a man of his appearance and personality and reputation — for Letty read the newspapers — could permit himself to be called Snooks by Carol or anyone like her — or unlike her — was an interesting commentary on character.

The other man was, as Carol had hoped, Mortimer Fisher. Mortimer Fisher also figured frequently in the daily press. He promoted, heaven knew what. He engineered railroads in strange countries and backed businesses all over the world. He had been himself originally an engineer, Letty remembered, as they shot upwards, twenty floors, in the small lift. Now he engineered other engineers. "A big shot," Carol murmured once at an opportune moment.

He looked it. He was, Letty judged, about forty-five. She was at once repelled and attracted by his good-looking ugliness, or was it his ugly good looks? If Herbert Gordon reminded her of a greyhound, Fisher was the perfect bulldog; the undershot jaw with its outthrusting chin, the small brilliant eyes, the tremendous physique. Some day he might run to paunch and jowls. Not now; never, perhaps, if he was careful. There was an air of bodily well being, fitness about him; of grooming; the pepper and salt hair sleek, the evening clothes a miracle of cut.

The roof was lovely, blue and silver, the orchestra, Lopez speaking, quite perfect. Letty looked through windows to the green of the Park, looked at lights in the buildings. No whisper of traffic came to her; she was, literally, on top of the world, she thought.

Dinner was as it should be. Eugene, his square, sagacious face smiling at them, was mindful of their comfort. There were corsages at their places, frail green orchids, dream flowers, gardenias, creamy, thick-skinned, over-fragrant . . .

"I'm not used to an atmosphere of top hats," said Carol calmly, regarding an artichoke heart with tenderness, "but as long as Letty finally consented to a night out I thought I'd better not frighten her with my favorite haunts."

Carol was different, her dark, mobile face sparkling above the red dress. She was not as hard, not as slangy. She was sweet to Gordon, amiable to Fisher; not too sweet, not too amiable. Letty, slightly amazed, looked around her. Pretty women, lovely girls, men, music, laughter. Carol of Sonia's Salon was not out of place. She fitted perfectly, anywhere, she had a quick, chameleonlike quality.

"Don't be silly, Caro," said Gordon with paternal affection. But Carol twinkled an eyebrow at him.

"Oh, be sensible, Snooks, and admit I belong in darkened speakeasies, where the sidecars are as they should be. But Letty —— " She looked at her friend and laughed.

"I understand perfectly," said Fisher, quite gravely. He had been regarding Letty with astonishment, through the original introductions and the trivial, general table conversation. Carol, whom he had met before, was one of a thousand pretty, pert, rather clever, one of a thousand little shrewd drifters who nevertheless kept an anchor to windward. But this girl — Letty — Letty Lawson, wasn't it? — was one *in* a thousand.

He said something about Ziegfeld.

"There," cried Carol triumphantly, "didn't I tell you? That's what we all say. But she just isn't interested."

Gordon couldn't believe it; nor Fisher. Not interested in being glorified! Letty shook her lovely head. "I'm too lazy," she said frankly.

But she wasn't lazy, Carol contradicted, she was a fool for work. She was graphic about it, about Letty's interest in manifestations of Sonia's business which needn't concern her, about her studying — "nights, if you can tie that," said Carol tragically.

Letty was flushed, a little. She said, "Let's not talk about me. . . . " She asked Fisher something, anything, about the room, who had done it . . . was it Urban?

They were late, of course, at the theater. They came in during the second act. It didn't matter except to the people who moved aside for them, glaring, making audible comment. The show was summery, light, amusing, with good music and a hard-working comedian.

After the theater, the Central Park Casino.

Carol, as the evening drew on, became more and more absorbed in Gordon. Letty, watching under level brows, saw that she amused, relaxed him. Saw too that she liked him, that it wasn't all singing for her supper. And could understand why. There was that aura about him, not alone money or success or a species of fame or the background of a family which had had money for three generations. Not any of these things singly, but a combination of them all. It meant something to Carol, that a man whose quiet voice at a meeting of men like him could send the sensitive temperature of Wall Street up — or down, a man who conferred with kings and who lent money to monarchies, a man who walked in the security of his own position and pride, found her amusing and excellent company and showed it, unabashed.

Fisher was different. Not that he seemed less secure, but he lacked something Gordon had; or did Gordon lack something Fisher possessed? Letty tried to recall what she knew of Mortimer Fisher; nothing, really, except that he was a self-made, a "recent millionaire," if he was indeed a millionaire. She didn't know. Not that it mattered.

She was there, of course, to entertain Fisher. That was part of the unspoken bargain. She could not and did not resent it.

After all, this blind date differed only in quality from a thousand others being fulfilled all over the city.

That he talked down to her at the beginning of their encounter was obvious enough. She made no effort to guide him, but after a time he ceased to talk down.

They danced together. If Gordon danced beautifully but dutifully, Fisher danced as if he loved it, as if for the moment nothing existed for him but dancing. That was the way you should dance, Letty thought, surrendering happily to his strength, his sense of accurate rhythm.

He said, "You really care about dancing, don't you?"

"Very much —— "

"Then why don't you —— ?"

"Dance more?" Letty laughed, her astonishing eyes on his own. "There hasn't been much opportunity —— "

"You don't expect me to believe that," he answered conventionally but sincerely.

"Oh, yes, I do. I don't mean that I couldn't . . . that Carol hasn't been very generous, wanting me to share her evenings. But, I've not really missed it, recently, not since I left college."

She stopped abruptly. She wished she hadn't said it, how absurd it sounded; it sounded the way headlines read . . . "Follies Girls Passion-ate Readers of Einstein. . . . " or "Beauty Operator a Ph.D." . . . or something of the sort.

She thought bitterly that all chorus girls were either ministers' daughters or flowers of decayed Southern gentility — according to themselves and the press agents.

But Fisher was genuinely interested. What college? he wanted to know.

She told him. Later, when they were seated again at the table and watching Gordon and Carol dance, he questioned her further, care-lessly, naturally enough. He said that, yes, Carol had told him that she had recently suf-fered a loss.

Letty thought, so Carol has been talking about me. She reflected that that was per-fectly natural; natural too for Carol to offer as an excuse that Letty was not available because of mourning.

Some curious little barrier which she had unconsciously erected between herself and this man tottered and fell. She found herself talking to him quite eagerly and normally about the two years away from home which seemed ten years away now; about her father's sudden death; and a little about her training for her work with Carol. Things came back to her, amusing incidents. Fisher listened to her, chuckling. He had not, he thought, seen so beautiful a girl in many years; to find her intelligent; to suspect something strong and enduring about her, as well as a sense of humor, seemed too good to be true. But it was true.

"You won't," he prophesied, "be content to stay long where you are."

"No. And yet, why not? I've no other training," she said frankly, "and I've grown to like the work — that is, some aspects of it. I've no inclination toward, or talent for, the stage or screen; I'd dislike modeling or posing. So — what else am I to do, really?"

He said thoughtfully: "I know, but even without talent — although I doubt that limitation — you're quick, you could learn to get by —— "

She said quickly: "You mean, on looks? Oh, I knew perfectly well what doors were open to me, because of looks. But they didn't open on, to me, particularly interesting or attractive vistas."

He was astonished, mildly. And said so, turning the slender stem of his glass between strong fingers. Letty laughed, a low delighted sound faintly tinged with mischief.

"You find that unusual? Why? I look in my mirror as often as any other woman," she told him, amused, "and I deal with looks, good

76

looks, indifferent looks, the remnants of beauty, say, all day long. Why not be honest about it? Nature, accident, heredity, something, gave me a good skin and a good figure and a happy arrangement of feature and coloring. I had, really, no other assets. I was forced, therefore, to consider these when I had to make up my mind what I should do to earn a living. I did . . . and thanks to Carol I found a niche which, if it isn't exactly what I had planned, at least contents me for the moment."

Carol came back, flushed, her eyes bright, laughing over her shoulder at Gordon. She inserted herself into a chair, put her elbows on the table and laced her fingers under her chin. "It's a large night," said Carol amused. "Snooks saw some out-of-town big-wigs. They didn't know whether to cut him or to ask to be presented to his —— " She stopped and the flush deepened. Gordon said smoothly: "Daughter. Don't try and spare my ancient feelings, Caro. I only wish Lottie were half as pretty and a third as amusing and a tenth as sweet as you are, my dear."

He was quite unperturbed.

It was late when they left the Casino. The sky was dark and starry above the Park. Letty said, "How in the world can I ever get up in the morning?"

Fisher's car waited outside to take the two men home. Gordon's sleepy chauffeur would drive Gordon's car over the bridge to the Brooklyn wilderness. Carol said, "We could drop you," but Gordon shook his head. "No, Morty's man will take us. I know you youngsters. You'll want to relax and lean back and talk over the evening and perhaps add a little color to our already colorful reputations." He laughed, thanked them for a charming evening. "Just like Mr. Van Porter," said Carol, who was an Amos 'n' Andy addict.

Fisher held Letty's cool, offered hand a moment; briefly, warmly. He said, not too low, but low enough, "Of course, you know I must see you again?" She was aware of a quickened heartbeat and found herself replying automatically, "That would be very nice," or something equally banal.

Riding home, Carol yawned. She'd had a good time, but not a very exciting one. She asked, "Enjoy yourself?"

Letty had, she admitted honestly.

It had had, she reflected, its drawbacks. There had been moments early in the evening when she had seen Carol and herself as paid entertainers. But not later. Nothing had been said or done to offend her, ever so slightly. She had liked Herbert Gordon, his amused and weary air; she had liked Mortimer Fisher, his vitality, his enthusiasm. He had talked to her, between dances, of some of his new projects. He painted them with a slashing brush on a big canvas, in crashing colors.

"Snooks," said Carol, "is all right. He makes the younger men seem pretty average tame. I've known him a long time now. He's sort of spoiled me for most men. What did you think of him?"

"I liked him."

"And Morty Fisher?"

"I liked him, too," said Letty.

"Well, it was fun; if only to prove to you that I don't go out on — what's the word? — orgies. . . . Did you see the woman at the next table in the shell-pink lace? I think I'll scrap my lace dress," said Carol discontentedly, "I thought it was good when I bought it — but — most of 'em look like twenty-two-fifty, don't they? Lace has to be darned good to be right."

Letty wasn't listening. She was drowsy, leaning back, feeling the swift, smooth motion of the car. The streets were comparatively deserted. She wondered what they looked like at, say, four in the morning; they would be, she thought, dark and strange and empty, with the shadowy taxis suddenly appearing, sliding through the night, with milk trucks lumbering by, and in the wholesale produce district, the great trucks of produce from

Jersey and Long Island.

They reached home safely, said good-night to the resigned chauffeur, who was well paid for his night work, his discretion and impassivity, and let themselves in with Carol's key, tiptoeing to their room, inclined to stumble and giggle a little, as one is always inclined to do, reaching home late, keenly aware one must not arouse the sleepers.

While they were undressing Carol remarked, creaming her face:

"Fisher was crazy about you."

"Don't be silly," said Letty.

"I'm not. I've been out with him before, foursome. I never saw him like that."

"Like what?"

"Oh, I don't know," said Carol vaguely. "He's a grand guy to know, but he might be bad medicine."

"Why?" asked Letty. She looked at her mirrored reflection and laughed. "Why?" she asked again, stripping a stocking from her slender leg. "I think," she murmured, "that a run's started, that's the worst of these —— "

But Carol was explaining, running nourishing cream under her eyes, not, she would explain, that it mattered, but it's a habit one can't break.

"Oh," Carol answered, "he's married, of course, and —— "

Letty was conscious of a chilling, a vanishing glow. Naturally he was married. Weren't most men in young middle-age, successful men, married? She had rather taken it for granted that he would be — and yet ——

"How about Snooks?" she asked lightly; "isn't he?"

"Oh, yes, but it didn't take. Snooks is harmless," said Carol definitely. "All he wants is to be told that he's a man. He's probably not much of a one, that way," said Carol lucidly, "but he likes 'em young and pretty and he doesn't cause 'em any tears. He gives 'em tips on the market, when there are any tips, or any market for that matter. He pays for all he gets and he doesn't ask for much. But Morty — that's a dangerous guy. He's not to my taste though I like him well enough. But what I mean is, he — well, he'd be dangerous to fall in love with. A man isn't, really, until you do fall in love with him; and Morty's the kind that you might —— "

She was yawning; she was involved; very sleepy, her words were tangled.

Letty took off her dress and hung it back in the bag. She wrapped a silk robe about her and said, carelessly:

"Well, don't worry about me. I'm not susceptible and, besides, I'll probably never see him again."

"I wouldn't be too sure," said Carol, "I heard him say —— "

"That was routine," Letty told her, laughing. "I wonder if I'm very careful sneaking down the hall if I can make the bathroom without waking —— "

The door opened, quietly, suddenly. Letty turned, more in anxiety than amazement. Had they wakened Mrs. Merrick after all?

But it was Tom.

Chapter 5

Carol made a noise like a mouse and jumped for covering, of a sort. Letty was too astonished to speak.

Tom was still dressed. He had been drinking, a little; not enough to make him drunk, but enough to make him reckless, dangerous. He came into the room and shut the door softly behind him and leaned against it in the fashion of certain motion picture heroes. Absurdly, Letty thought of that. And Carol spoke first. She said, in a small harsh whisper, "You get the hell out of here, Tom Merrick!"

Tom shook his head. He spoke directly to Carol but he looked at Letty. His eyes were angry and hurt and a little frightened. He said to Carol, "So you've done it, have you?"

"Done what, you fool?" inquired Carol. She sat down on the bed, a wisp of silk about her, her bare legs dangling. She added, "Will you get out or must I yell for pop?"

"Made her into another little gold-digging bitch like yourself." Tom answered her first question. Letty, still standing, grave and troubled, made a small, disturbed sound. She shrank back against the sharp corner of the crowded vanity table, leaned on it with one hand. Scattered powder rose at her touch, in a little scented cloud. She did not speak, waiting, as Carol flushed and paled, and thrust herself from the bed and went up to Tom and looked at him and said, "You —— !"

But he paid her no attention. He was looking at Letty, he spoke to her with a curious courtesy, rather unpleasant to see and hear.

"I wasn't good enough for you to marry, Letty," he said, low but clearly, "but now you've gone in for the other thing, I've got a little money saved, I could pay my way for a while —— "

Carol was pushing at him with frantic hands. There were sounds next door, a drowsy murmur — her father. She stood on tiptoe, she put her hands on Tom's shoulders and shook him futilely. All the time she was saying, in a savage whisper — "Get out — *get out* — do you want to —— ?"

Letty had not spoken. Tom nodded in her direction. A jerky sort of bow, boyish, stiff. Suddenly, he'd gone; as suddenly as he'd come. The door shut, with exaggerated care. Both girls listened. They could hear nothing, not even a footstep. He walked lightly, lightly as a cat.

Letty stood where she was. She was quite silent. Her eyes were wide with some emotion, perhaps a deep astonishment. Her face was uncontorted but the tears ran down it quietly.

"God," said Carol sincerely, "I'm sorry — the — the damned fool!"

She went to Letty and put her arms around her. Letty bent to kiss her cheek. Then she drew away.

"It wasn't your fault," she acquitted her in a still voice, "but, you see, Carol," said Letty, "I can't stay here any longer. Not any more. I've got to go."

There was nothing for Carol to say. She said, after a minute, with a forced flippancy, "Well, you can't go now, in your shirt-tail. Let's get to bed, hop along and wash, I'll follow. I think they've gone back to sleep."

Letty asked, "You'll come with me, down the hall?"

Later, in bed, she thought she couldn't sleep. Pictures unrolled before her, on the uneasy screen of her mind. The evening; innocent enough; pleasant; Tom, the persecution of what he fancied was his love for her, the weeks of it, the months; Carol, getting along, by herself, knowing where she was going, hard as nails, seemingly.

And herself. Did she know where she was

going? She inquired, drawing away from Carol, sleeping soundly, healthily, an arm flung above her head, drawing away from her warm vitality, in the still heat of the night, "Where do we go from here?" she asked herself silently, half stupid with fatigue, trying to smile, in the lifting darkness.

She thought of her father; turned her mind away with a sick, heavy effort. Soon it would be dawn. A cool breeze had come up, was stirring the curtains. She lay on the edge of the bed, the sheet flung off, her lithe body quivering with the effort to lie still, not to arouse Carol.

Somewhere near-by, in the scrap of back yard, on the dusty branches of the lilac bush, a sleepy bird clamored.

Letty slept, falling fathoms deep with the abruptness of astonishment into the dark and dreamless depths. It seemed a year or a moment later that Carol shook her into consciousness.

Sunlight and heat, the city sweltering between the hot hands of summer.

In the days that followed there was confusion and hurt and a consciousness of sorrow. Carol had argued, had even pleaded; but even she knew to what useless end. Letty must go. There was no sanity in the present situation. So Carol stood by through all Mrs. Merrick's wounded expostulations. Mrs. Merrick "couldn't understand." What would Letty's father think, hadn't he left her to them as a sort of legacy, and Tom, poor boy, what would he do? Tom, "poor boy," looked uncomfortable and sullen, and escaped, as much as possible, his mother's appeals and protestations. Mr. Merrick was neutral. He was fond of Letty, was, perhaps, more genuinely hurt at what seemed her desertion, than his wife. But he washed his hands of this headstrong generation. Hadn't he, of Carol, long ago? Hadn't he said, after bitter quarrels during which his wife had sided with their daughter, "Very well, have it your way. I'll not interfere. You run things. Only don't come whining to me if they go wrong."

Tom managed to see Letty once, alone, after the night of Gordon's party. He had been abashed and remorseful, blaming things on his own "large" evening. "I drank too much, Letty." But she was adamant. And he turned plaintive. "It's your fault, you drive me screwy. I can't stand seeing you every day and —— "

Here she had interrupted, reasonably. "All the more reason why I should clear out, isn't it?" And that had irritated him. He couldn't understand Letty. She was, of course, lovelier than any girl he'd known, cooler, with those strange black eyes of hers looking a hole through you and the fair hair like a halo about her face. But she couldn't be cold, really, with eyes like hers, and a mouth like hers. He'd thought she liked him. They'd been like brother and sister for a bit. Later, he hadn't felt fraternal. But she hadn't changed, kidding him a lot, confiding in him — before she'd gone away to college, sharing her surface thoughts ——

Hell, there were other girls. Girls who fell a lot easier, girls who weren't cheap, really, who'd had a reputation of not falling. Women liked him, after all. His strength and vitality, his wisecracking, his awkward, youthful good looks. But Letty didn't. Why not? Wasn't he good enough for her? Of course not, no one was, he supposed. And yet ——

"Carol's fault, then," he said finally, turning ugly again. "She's no good. I've known it all along. *They* won't listen to me, they think she's gold."

The Merricks had had to accept Letty's explanation; that there were certain courses she wanted to take in Manhattan; and that the subway trips were too hard on her. They must, she cried, understand how grateful she was, how much she appreciated all they had done for her, how much she cared for them all. And she'd come to see them. It wasn't as if

88

she were moving far away.

But where would she go? Mrs. Merrick asked her practically.

By the end of the troubled week, she knew. She had been looking. To keep up even a one-room apartment was out of the question unless she wished to touch her little principal. To live in a furnished room seemed to be the only solution. She shrank from it but steeled herself to face it. She had always had a home; with her father, with the Merricks. The impersonal, if cluttered, coldness of a makeshift lodging somewhere filled her with horror. She went looking, after hours, and the best of them seemed miserable, wretched. But apparently there was no other way out. Perhaps it would be just for a time, perhaps when she had more salary, when she built up her own following so that she could rely more definitely on her tips and commission, she might be able to manage a room in one of the pleasant, inexpensive hotels run for women in her position. There were, of course, the cheaper clubs, the institutional sanctuaries. But even a furnished room was better, somehow, she thought.

It was Carol who showed her the way out, through a chance remark of Nelda's. Nelda, Sonia's bookkeeper and secretary, augmented her income by renting rooms in her large pleasant apartment on Riverside Drive. The rooms were for the most part occupied by nurses and school teachers. Now one of her teachers, who had a single room, was leaving and Nelda was looking for someone to take her place.

She was delighted to have Letty. The house was, she assured Letty, most respectable. Letty would have her key and come and go as she pleased. There was a common sitting room in which she might entertain by prearrangement.

Letty went up by bus one early evening to look at the apartment. It had a good exposure, plenty of light and sun and air and the room which would be hers, while not large, was pleasant, well furnished, had even a certain charm. There was a capable maid of all work and a tray breakfast was included in the room rent.

She moved there, to Nelda's delight. Mornings she came downtown on the bus with her landlady. Nelda, despite her hard, aging good looks and her grafted "English" accent, was "getting on" for the beauty business, she admitted to Letty. That was why Sonia had transferred her to secretarial work and bookkeeping after she'd taken the requisite courses. One day she would retire. She owned her apartment and made a good living, with the room rent and her salary at Sonia's. She had a bit saved, too.

She was Mrs. Garrison to her roomers. Whether or not there had ever been a Mr. Garrison, Letty didn't know, never knew. She liked Nelda. Nelda had a curious practical generosity, a streak of fibrous common sense. She said, one day, bus riding down the Drive, Letty beside her, her rather glassy, prominent blue eyes indifferently regarding a battleship riding at anchor: "Youth. Looks. In this business they're essential. Unless you own your own place. I take that back; even if you do, you have to keep up. Look at Sonia. I tell you, Letty, I'll bless the day when I can quit and go home and put on easy slippers and take off my corsets and let my hair go gray and not bother about what's left of my skin." She laughed shortly. "I would have done it a year or more ago but my investments washed up. I pulled out and stuck what was left in government bonds. Now I'll keep on working for a while. You, you've got everything. Looks, youth," she said again, with a hard shiny wistfulness, "and brains too. As much as Sonia had when she started; more in some ways. Not as much in others perhaps, not as much drive, the trampling, get-the-hell-out-of-the-way sort. Take my tip, feather your nest, save. You'll marry, perhaps. Rich, if you've any sense. If you don't — well, feather it anyway. Sometimes I wake up, sweating, wondering what would have happened to me if Sonia hadn't kept me on. Of course, if I'd started out with enough capital saved to go in for myself, but I didn't. Where do you land? Maid in some ladies' room, if you're lucky; or a theater job, wardrobe, dresser, what have you. Or hustling —— ?"

She was silent.

That day as they went into Sonia's together Letty was still thinking of what Nelda had said. In the salon a man was talking to Gracie at the reception desk. Letty noticed him. You didn't see men there often; and it was too early for the very occasional man who wandered in to meet some woman by appointment, to take her to lunch, or tea, or home.

This man was noticeable enough; excessively tall, almost exaggeratedly broad-shouldered. He was twenty-six or twenty-seven perhaps, with nondescript fair hair and big features. He was smiling, leaning on the round, high reception desk, half turned toward the elevators. He had an engaging smile. Gracie was smiling too; she lifted her hand with its crimson nails and patted her wave, unnecessarily, into place.

Then he'd gone, in the direction of Sonia's office.

Nelda's hand was on Letty's arm, hard, pinching. Letty looked at her, in inquiry.

"Who on earth . . . ? Surely, not a salesman?"

"No. That's Sonia's son, Burt Barker," Nelda said, "we don't see him around here often. Good-looking, or don't you think so?"

Letty didn't know. She said, puzzled:

"Son? I supposed she was married but I didn't dream . . . or. . . . Yes, I suppose I had heard, but it didn't register."

She remembered. Carol had said something once. About Sonia's boy — "the only thing she cares about." Letty hadn't listened, not really.

"He's not much in evidence," Nelda was explaining. "Too big. Too old. Sonia's taken for forty, sometimes for less. She's fifty, of course. Burt doesn't live in New York. She divorced his father, a good-for-nothing good-looking lad with a straight American background and a yen to be supported. That was ages ago. Barker remarried and then died, all in a couple of years. Sonia was having a struggle. So she finally let his people take the boy. They lived in Pennsylvania. Sonia has put him through school and college — Harvard, no less. He had a reputation there. Football and all that. Now he is an engineer and wanders all over the globe. She sees him, when he's in town, but they don't live together. Better all around. Oh, she doesn't conceal him and he doesn't conceal her — but —— "

Nelda shrugged. They had been standing some distance away from the desk talking. "What's the conference?" Gracie wanted to know. Her telephone rang. She picked it up and spoke over it to Letty. "You've an early appointment," she reminded her, "Mrs. Hallam."

Mrs. Hallam would be in town for the day. She'd want the works, all Letty could give her, and then Louis for her hair. Letty went on to the locker room in the back to put her things away and slip into the crisp rose-colored uniform. Later, as she stood at the desk, looking over the day-book to see if she had any special appointments after Mrs. Hallam, Barker came out of his mother's office. Sonia was famous among her guild because she arrived earlier at her place of business than her employees and stayed later. Barker had come directly to the salon from his train. Now, leaving, he smiled again at Gracie and hesitated, the barest moment. Letty, cool under his direct gaze, turned away and went into the room allotted to her to set up Mrs. Hallam's tray. She heard through the open door the sound of the elevator as it stopped at the floor, the metallic clash of its closing gate.

Burt Barker went down in the, literally, gilded cage thinking of the girl he had seen. He would have liked a glimpse of her eyes, a close-up. Blue, of course, a very dark blue. They had to be blue, with that skin and hair. He had spoken to his mother about her . . . "the tall girl, very fair. Isn't she new?" And his mother had responded briefly, "You must mean Miss Letty. Yes, she's new, since last fall," and had gone on to speak of other things. Did he want money? Times were rotten, business was impossible, but she could manage. But no, he had replied, smiling at her, no money. He didn't need it. He was off to South America, on a new job. He'd come to ask, would she dine with him and do a show?

She'd exclaimed, leaning forward, regarding him with that somber affection overlaid by the show of indifference which didn't, always, fool him. Wasn't it sudden? He'd said nothing in his letters. But then he wrote rarely. Yes, he told her, it was sudden enough, he'd heard only a day or so before, he'd had just time to run over to Lancaster and say good-by to the old people and pack a bag and hop a train. He'd sail tomorrow.

Sonia had looked at him with pride. What was beneath it he could not tell, nor could she, always. God alone knew.

After he had left she sat there thinking, her desk piled with correspondence, bills, bills of sale, reports from the laboratory. She did not notice Nelda, in and out; did not hear the click of the typewriter under Nelda's brisk fingers. She sat there, thinking.

Burt always made her think.

She'd slaved . . . how she had slaved; at a job that sometimes made her sick at the stomach; and to produce — what? A bank balance, a good name in the trade, the profession, a reputation . . . and the man who'd just gone out, whistling, gone window-shopping, he'd said, whistling his way down the Avenue, six foot three, bronzed, his own man, independent, adventurous.

Sonia thought; of the struggles, the deprivations, some of the makeshifts, none of them very happy. Of other things, too; of, especially, the lovers she might have had, the lover she had wanted and had denied herself, as practically as a woman shopping to feed her family on substantial things stops before a confectioner's window and then goes on. She hadn't wanted Burt to be ashamed of her; not ever. If she'd bought that cake — or was it cake-eater? she asked herself, laughing shortly in the loneliness of the office — he might have found out; hated her. No, not hated her, but been ashamed. He wasn't ashamed of her now. He laughed at her business, called it The Racket. All tenderly enough. "Hey, Sonia, how's The Racket?" He understood. He was grateful, he tried to make it up to her, in little ways.

She might have married again. She hadn't. She was afraid of splitting her emotions, afraid of any other claims but Burt's and The Business. They were, in reality, one.

But they weren't close, Sonia and her son. They were good friends, but they weren't close.

How could they be?

Much had been denied her; the little years, the rounded, tireless days of childhood; the delicious, scowling, dirty little boyhood, the awkward, trampling years, loud, sensitive, ridiculous, pathetic and lovely, the adolescent years. These had been denied her. They had been given to an elderly man and an elderly woman whom she disliked intensely and whom she respected deeply.

You couldn't have everything.

Well, she'd built up her business, it was a good one. Her books proved it, even in these days. She made her profit. Her investments had been safer than most. Not since the earlier days had she gambled. Now she couldn't afford it, it had been too hard won. She was decent to her girls. If she didn't inquire very closely into their private lives, that was better, wasn't it? Obliquely it brought her trade; it made for friendship of a sort; for smaller salaries. That was all to the good, wasn't it? Sometimes her girls left; married, a few of them; some didn't marry, but left all the same. They came back, as customers, most of them. They weren't the type to ignore the time they'd put in, smooth hands dipped in smoother creams . . .

There wasn't a soul to leave the money to but Burt. It had been made for him. She wanted him to marry; desperately she wanted that. She had urged him, cleverly, even carelessly, afraid to let herself go lest he learn how much it mattered. She'd kept her hands off him, paid his bills, left it to those old people to see that he had a proper rearing. No, she hadn't interfered.

With his charm and education he could marry anyone; a girl with money, a girl with social backing. He'd laughed at her. Just this morning he'd laughed when she'd asked him hesitantly: "Burt, isn't there a girl you're sorry to leave . . . back there in Johnstown . . . or in Lancaster?"

What had he answered, with his big laughter running through the words? No, thank God. That had been it, hadn't it? "No, thank God. What would I do with a girl?"

But this was her dream. Burt married, settled; good times again and then the sale of the business at a fair price, keeping a hold on it through the preparations; settling down, herself, seeing Burt and Burt's children, able to live in her grandchildren as she hadn't been able to live in Burt; at closer quarters; and going back now and then to Denmark, eating what she pleased, drinking what she pleased, sitting in the sun; no more damned women to cajole and flatter.

Sonia, for the rest of the day, was crotchety. She was crotchety now when Nelda came in to tell her, "Mrs. Hallam wants to see you. Miss Letty has her — she says —— "

"What do I care what she says?" growled Sonia. "I'll be in when I'm good and ready."

Burt always did that to her, Nelda reflected philosophically, ready to pinch-hit if necessary. "Madame Sonia is in consultation. She will be with you as soon as possible, Mrs. Hallam."

Sonia, growling, all day long. The egg masks weren't made to suit her. She went into a room, touched one, drying grotesquely on a woman's face, with the tip of her finger; she went out and spoke sharply to the girl who had prepared it. Not enough oil, too much this, too little that; where was her mind, if any? She would make the next one herself.

Nothing pleased her. Burt always upset her, that way.

It was a strange jealousy that would beset her then, a wounding pride, a sense of frustration.

Chapter 6

The weather was dreadful. Heat. The sort of heat that melted the asphalt, left you gasping if you so much as walked across the room. Even the occasional breeze which wandered across the Drive was sticky, a fretful affair. A cold shower left you warmer than ever. Nothing did any good. There was a hot, dry wind in the heart of town, idle papers swirling in the gutter. There were children bathing in the public fountains and from the wharfs, there were children, naked, on fire escapes in the crowded sections. The subways were filled with sweltering people going to sweltering beaches at which you couldn't possibly see the water for the bathers. And filled with children. Crying children, sick children, sunburned children, dragging at the hot, dirty hands of irascible, unhappy mothers. . . .

At the Sonia Salon there was much less to do; but even that little required more effort. The only women who came, presenting hot, dry, baked skin to the hands of the operators, were those who had to be in town. Work was

101

very slack, despite the summer price scale which Sonia, in an attempt to augment her business, had recently instituted.

Carol had gone to Southampton. She told Letty before she left, "Morty Fisher wants to see you again, Letty." Letty shook her head, the heat curling her soft hair into damp, small tendrils, very appealing. Carol, ignoring this, said: "Wish you were coming with me." She added that Snooks had a place in Southampton. She'd see him. "Not that I'll be among those present, when it comes to society columns; and if I'm careful I'll keep out of the other kind," she had explained, unabashed, "but — I'll see him. Why not? And, boy, if you could see my bathing suit! What there is of it!"

She remarked that Snooks, if he wished, could throw some business her way. A word to his women guests, and the Sonia Shop would be busy. She had then remarked casually, "I told Morty where you were living."

Letty said: "I wish you hadn't."

They were lunching together in the drug store of a skyscraper. Carol regarded the dregs of her iced tea with distaste. She replied, "Don't be dumb, darling. An occasional man with the price of a roof garden in his pocket is the only thing that can make the next few weeks bearable for you." She poked at a sand-

wich on her plate and said "Swill," in a resigned tone. Later she remarked, "I wish Tom
would jump in the lake. He's all wet already,
of course — but . . . Look here, Letty, has he
been bothering you?"

Letty answered "No," and looked away
from her friend, but Carol's dark eyes were
shrewd.

"You're lying," she said accusingly, "aren't
you? And not any too well."

"He's been up to Nelda's flat a couple of
times," Letty admitted; and then quickly,
"Why did you tell Mr. Fisher . . . ? I mean
. . . I don't want to see him, Carol, I really
don't. Why should I see him?"

"If you don't know, I won't tell you," Carol
informed her. "Do go over and see ma while
I'm away, won't you? She's still fretting about
you. Some Sunday? It isn't as hot there, that's
one thing, and she still makes the swellest iced
coffee and potato salad in town."

Letty promised.

But her mind wasn't on Mrs. Merrick. She
was occupied with Morty Fisher. Why had
Carol . . . ? Oh, Carol had no sense, but one
couldn't prove it to her! It would mean that
if he called up — not that he would — she
would simply have to find an excuse.

He called up. The first time she refused to
see him, arguing stoutly against his half-

laughing, half-serious protestations that she had no right to bury herself and snub all her friends. The second time she was very short with him. The third time she laughed, defeated, standing at the telephone in Nelda's little foyer, feeling her few garments cling to her body, feeling the sweat run in a thin, icy trickle between her breasts and down her back.

Heat. Dragging yourself around, sitting hatless on a bus, fighting for breath, experiencing the almost incredible relief of the cold motion picture houses and then coming out from them again to have the heat rise up from the pavement and strike you in the face, palpable as a physical blow.

She asked, tentatively, "If we could go somewhere where we needn't dress?"

That suited him perfectly. They went, in his fast car, himself at the wheel, to Arrowhead and dined out of doors. An oak tree grew up from the dancing floor itself, there were other trees, the lights were like small street lamps, the orchestra played from a stone shelter, the inn itself was of stone, somehow cool looking.

There were a good many people but their table was on the dancing floor. They did not dance. They sat and watched. "Too hot for frogs' legs?" he asked her, smiling. He had, she thought, an enchanting smile. No, not too hot. Frogs' legs and waffles, iced coffee. But she shook her head at the flask he produced. He put it back in his pocket. "I guess you're right," he agreed.

Boys and girls, two older women in deep black, alone at a table, elderly men, middle-aged men. One man was having a marvelous time. He had just had an experience in Kansas City . . . they could hear him telling the others at his table, laughing. Another couple, obviously professional dancers. Their night off perhaps and they had come to dance. "Busman's holiday," Fisher said, laughing, watching.

Intricate steps, fast and slow; mannerisms. The girl was tall and dark, pretty in a spectacular way, Hollywood eyes, lovely teeth, too much rouge. The man was short and small and agile. He had effortless grace. He was dark too, feline, Latin, not very young, or was he ageless? He closed his eyes, dancing . . .

Dinner was over. They danced just once before they left, Mortimer Fisher and Letty. She said to him on the floor, "We're crazy, I think . . . in all this heat — and frogs' legs!" He said, banally, but there was something in his eyes, eager, alive, "It's nice to be crazy . . . isn't it?"

Before they left for the drive home he knew all about her, had filled in the missing parts of

105

the pattern. He asked, standing with her at the sedate entrance to the apartment house: "Look here, why not? Business will keep me in town, quite a lot. I've an apartment, of sorts. I go — home" — here his mouth twisted a little — "weekends. But — I'm at a loose end, in town. And you? Surely working all day, dragging yourself back to a hot bedroom . . . ? That's not much fun. Let me see you. I'd like to. I'd be grateful. I like you, so much," he said gravely, even boyishly.

She said slowly, "Perhaps."

She liked him, too. He attracted her. Definite, the attraction. She said perhaps and she meant of course. She was lonely. New York can be deadly, if you're alone. Even if you're not.

That was the beginning. Almost every night that he was in town they saw each other. Always publicly, always in a tea garden, on top of some miraculous roof, somewhere in town, or a little way out. Claremont and Arrowhead, Nikko, Woodmansten, and sometimes quieter places. There was one place in the Village, an Italian place, a garden. It was quite cool, a fountain tinkled, the wine was good, the food superb.

She told herself savagely: "You're being a fool. You think you're falling in love. You're not. If you were you'd have to stop seeing him. It isn't love, isn't anything like it. You like him. You're lonely. Physically he disturbs you. You're not in love with him, you can't afford to be. He's married —— Or doesn't that matter? It doesn't to a lot of women."

It did to her.

Now, he was building up in her mind a picture of himself, painting in sometimes with broad, crude, slashing strokes of color, sometimes with small, careful, distinct lines, delicate and purely revealing as those of an etching. There had been the small Midwestern town. He made her see it, how narrow it was, how difficult, how somehow dear. And the girl he had married. He made her see her also, although Letty listened and shrank and once or twice raised her hand and said, "No, don't tell me any more, it isn't fair to her, is it?"

But it was fair to her, he insisted, or at least to him. He had married Eva at nineteen. He had brought his wife, he told Letty with a grimace at his own pitiful immaculate dreaming boyhood, an innocence — or was it ignorance? — as great as her own. Two youngsters, lost, in love, awkward, physically and spiritually . . .

Ambition and work, and struggle and dreams; and the hardening process through it all. The climb up.

"Hard, Letty, grueling. But, by God,

worth it. Or so I thought."

Five children, three of them living.

"But I don't know them, Letty. They won't let me. I pay the bills. I'm the 'Old Man.' I count, as a bank roll. But I can't get near them. Why not?"

"Have you tried?"

"Has there been time?"

The first fortune won; and lost. The second, won, precariously. Plenty of money now, to play with. Always the spirit of the gambler. He could lose again; and win it all back. But loss would be harder now, he had become accustomed to too much. *They* had become accustomed.

Eva had stayed small-town, narrow, frightened, lacking poise, lacking graciousness. Too small a woman to be stately, small mentally, small physically. Petulant she had grown, and distressed by money, terrified of responsibility, shrinking from the social obligations it all entailed. Worrying, always; about herself, about his, Morty's, health, about her children, whom she couldn't "manage." About everything. And for the last few years expending all her vitality on charity boards.

"I'm not a plaster saint," said Morty Fisher, regarding Letty over a dinner table, "I'm a man, and a pretty human specimen at that. I've played as straight with Eva as I knew how.

108

I've given her everything —— "

Letty raised her eyes to his. Black they were and earnest, in the startling fairness of her face. She repeated "Everything?"

Fisher flushed.

"Everything," he said, looking at her directly. "I swear I have. But — of recent years — Letty, when a man is freezing to death and the woman he married provides no fuel and no fire, he — he goes elsewhere."

"Elsewhere" hadn't been happy, she judged, more from the things he left unsaid. "Elsewhere" had been gay and venal and bitter. . . .

They talked, as intimately as that. Yet he said nothing to her, nothing she was able to think over afterwards, and find composed of adventure, rapture, terror. Nothing except, "You're very lovely, Letty." And that was all. But there were great boxes of flowers, and, until she asked him not to, books and perfumes and even delicate silks fashioned into a smoke screen of a stocking. All save the flowers and the books went back. But even the books were too much. She said so. "I'd rather not take — *things*," she said.

His eyes spoke to her sometimes, and his arm about her as they danced.

Clever man, Mortimer Fisher; not rushing his fences. This wasn't, he knew, Carol, sweet and disturbing and cheap; a dear and expensive little person. This was a girl with a brain; with ambition, with background. Nevertheless, a girl, alone; a lonely girl; a girl without ties.

Without ties. Letty was realizing that. She had gone to Brooklyn twice while Carol was away. The first time it had been all right, the elder Merricks had been glad to see her. But Tom walked with her to the subway, they had quarreled, standing there, at the station, the people, indifferent or amused, milling all about them, the heat welling up. Quarreled and parted, like the popular song. He had made various childish threats . . . "you'll be sorry — I'll clear out — you'll be sorry — " over and over again.

She had been annoyed; but she hadn't believed him.

The next time she went back she had to believe him. She found Mrs. Merrick at home alone. She had not telephoned she was coming, that Sunday afternoon, and Mrs. Merrick had wept, seeing her. Not, by any means, tears of joy; tears of reproach, of anger even.

"How could you do it Letty? How could you be so cruel to my boy? What has Tom ever done but love you? He would have carried you on his hands — worked for you —— "

It sounded like a third-rate play. But it was

real, *real*. People do talk that way, quite simple people, and even sophisticated people under the stress of emotion.

Merrick had come home, his face darkening when Letty rose to greet him. He was pretty short with her. It was he who told her what had happened, his wife obviously in a condition which did not even faintly border on coherence.

Tom had kept his word; cleared out. Tom was *spurlos versenkt*. He had signed over his share of the garage to his partner, taken the money, which wasn't of course much "in these hard times," and gone. Where, no one knew.

His mother was frantic; his father no less so. They had blamed Letty. She listened, distressed, a little sick, wanting to defend herself, unable to do so, unable to make herself heard.

He'd come back that other Sunday, sullen, unhappy, vowing he was through with women, fed up with everything, everyone. "You quarreled, didn't you?"

"Yes," said Letty, "we quarreled."

"About what?" asked Merrick, and before she answered he said sharply: "See here, Letty, you've been one of us, we've treated you like a daughter, but Tom's our son. We've a right to know."

111

She said finally that it was nothing, really. Merely a matter of dates . . . or of no dates.

"Well, why wouldn't you give him a date?" asked Merrick bluntly, while his wife wept.

Letty stammered. . . . She liked Tom, she regarded him as a brother; but not as anything different. She couldn't. He — he couldn't see things her way, and so — well, what was the use of seeing him? she asked frankly, it would only make matters worse, make him unhappy.

Merrick said, "Wasn't good enough for you, eh?"

She said quickly:

"Please — Uncle Dan. Of course. But — I don't love him."

There, she had said it. They couldn't understand. Why not? Wasn't he as good-looking, as clever as the other men she knew? Or wasn't he? Or was it money she was after?

Anyway, he had gone, without a word, before or since.

She left, after a supper she scarcely tasted, feeling as if she had been beaten. Exit, Tom. Exit, the Merricks. And Carol. What would Carol say?

Carol said plenty. Tom was a such and so, her mother and father were crazy, and the whole thing was too much for her to fathom. But it was obvious that Letty would not go again to the Merricks' for supper on Sunday or on any other day. "Good riddance," said Carol loyally to Letty. "I'm only afraid he'll come back." But she was alone in her opinion and it was one she kept to herself when she was at home. And the atmosphere would be, she agreed with Letty, far too strained to permit the old relationship again.

So Letty stayed away from Brooklyn and the two-family house with the roses and the handkerchief lawn and the view of the river.

Girl without ties . . .

In the late autumn Carol was absent from work. Her mother was ill. And in three days her mother was dead. Flu pneumonia. No, Tom hadn't come, they hadn't been able to send him word, they didn't know where to send it.

Letty had telephoned every day of the three brief, age-long, terrible days. Could she help? Could she come? She was sick to go, to do what she could. But it was of no use. Merrick had stormed, tiptoeing awkwardly in and out of the room in which his wife lay, refusing to fight for life, not caring much about it. There was a nurse there, a strange, kind, alien woman. And Carol, stricken, twisting a wet handkerchief, her brightness gone, everything gone.

After the funeral, which Letty attended, sitting well at the back of the crowded parlor,

113

looking — and looking away again — at the old man's stricken, bewildered face with its red-rimmed eyes, and leaving before he should see her, Carol came to Nelda's one night and told her all there was to be told.

"Uncle Dan's bitter, isn't he — about me?" asked Letty, shaken.

Carol nodded.

"He blames me, I suppose?"

Carol said swiftly, "He's half out of his mind, he doesn't mean it, he can't. It — oh, he has to blame someone, something."

Letty understood. She followed his simple reasoning. If it hadn't been for Letty, Tom wouldn't have left home. If he hadn't left home, his mother wouldn't have worried and fretted and cried herself into a state of lowered resistance . . . wouldn't have picked up the germ, wouldn't have — *died*.

That it was partly Letty's money that buried her he didn't know. That was one reason Carol had come, to ask Letty to help her to pay the bills. Merrick's business was still at a standstill, Tom, of course, contributed nothing now, and she, Carol, hadn't saved. "There's Snooks," she said defiantly, "but I can't ask him. We — had a row, there in Southampton. I — was wrong. It wasn't something for nothing. Not indefinitely. So — we had a showdown. I — thought of ma —— "

Letty gave her the money, drawing it from the savings account. And that was that. She was abstracted, these days. Doing her work, reading nights; the nights she didn't go out with Fisher. Fisher worried about her. "What is it, Letty? May I help?"

No, he couldn't help, no one could help. It wasn't all Dan Merrick's attitude toward her, its manifest unjustness that hurt. He couldn't help being unjust. When you're wounded, you strike out, at anybody, anything. But she was beginning to feel futile. She was beginning to question her own existence. She was beginning to wonder where, if anywhere, she fitted into the world. And why?

Drifting. Work, a job, a little money coming in, a roof over her head, a bed to sleep on; a man now and then to talk to, a man whose eyes caressed her but whose hands were cool and friendly. Dinner, dancing, a theater. How long would that last? There was Nelda. Sonia, too. But Sonia had fought her way up, Sonia had something to fight for, a child first and then a man, with blue eyes, and a way of laughing . . .

One night Carol arrived at Nelda's. She had not been at work all day and Sonia had spoken to Letty about it. "She's done this once too often," said Sonia, "if you hear from her you might tell her that. There are plenty of girls who would jump at the chance to be in her place."

Letty did hear from her. She answered the bell herself and fell back, astonished, at the sight of Carol, her small chin cuddled into a big fur collar, a suitcase in her hand.

"Will you put me up for the night?" she wanted to know.

Letty would. There was only a single bed in her room, but if that would do —— ?

It would do.

After a while, they were together in the small bedroom, and Carol, perched on the end of the bed, smoking furiously, lighting one cigarette from the stub of the other, was saying, "I'm through. *Through.*"

"Carol, why?"

Carol asked, "Why?" and looked at Letty with desperate eyes. Her father for one thing. Since her mother's death he had been — different. Suspicious, asking questions; things Tom must have told him had come back to him. Mrs. Merrick was no longer there to make excuses, to rationalize, to take Carol's part. He and Carol quarreled, increasingly. And last week his sister had come to keep house for them. Carol loathed her aunt.

"Snooper," said Carol darkly, "flat breasted, holier than thou! She makes me sick. Been going through my clothes, and telling Dad

116

what they probably cost. And my jewel case. *And* my letters. I'm through, see?"

Letty said, understanding, pitiful: "If Nelda only had a free room. Carol, where will you live, what will you do?"

Carol's chin was high, bright spots burned on her cheeks.

"Oh," she said, "I'll live."

"Sonia's sore ―― "

"She'll get over it. I won't need her long. Snooks — I called him — Snooks will stake me to a trip. To Paris."

There was a long pause. Then Letty asked low, evenly:

"He's going too, or — isn't he?"

"On a different boat." Carol laughed outright, then sobered. "Letty, don't — don't look that way. I tell you, I'm tired of grubbing, tired of — cadging for small favors. If," said Carol, "you want to go wrong you might as well do it in a big way!"

She jumped off the bed, went to perch on the arm of Letty's chair, ruffed Letty's hair with her hands.

"You'll be cutting me," she said, "and how!"

"Don't be a fool, as if anything you did would matter," said Letty. "But ―― "

All the buts were futile. She saw it; ceased to speak.

117

"But — but what? But, he's old? But — but he's this and I'm that? What of it? I like him," said Carol defiantly, "he's a prince, a real person. Snooks is swell," said Carol, unaware of the absurdity of the nickname in conjunction with the situation. "Swell. He — won't demand much. He'll give me a lot. Anything I want."

"Except marriage," said Letty.

"I don't want that," said Carol stoutly; and then after a pause, "Perhaps he *will* marry me."

"Carol," said Letty, and it was half a sob, half a laugh — "Carol."

"Well, perhaps he won't. But he's free enough though except for those high-hat kids of his. . . . Mrs. Seymour Masterton was seen last night at the opera — she wore cretonne, pearls and galoshes," said Carol irrepressibly, "and Mr. Herbert Gordon Junior is opening his shooting box in Scotland, he's gunning for Harry Lauder. . . . Well, if he doesn't marry me he'll do almost as well by me. He'll give me — security. If ma had lived. . . . Well, she didn't, so what the hell," said Carol, "it's my own life, isn't it?"

It was her own life. This was the end of one life, the beginning of another. The end, too, of Carol, Letty's Carol, the start of a new Carol, a little harder, a little more reckless, a

118

little more wary now that caution had been left behind her and there was less to be wary about; another Carol.

Chapter 7

Carol had sailed. Quietly, secretly, luxuriously. Letty didn't see her off. "Better not," said Carol, saying good-by up at Nelda's. "Don't complicate things for yourself, Letty, it doesn't pay."

She was extraordinarily well dressed, and if the wages of sin was death, death was not in her eyes, nor on her face. Her skin was a perfection of smoothness and delicate coloring, her eyes bright and wary. "Are you — happy?" asked Letty wistfully.

"Sure, why not? What a fool I'd be, not to be happy. He's good to me," explained Carol, with inflection.

A night or two later Letty sat in a very small, very swanky speakeasy, distinguished for its excellent liquor, its superb food and its air of subdued respectability. Mortimer Fisher faced her across the table. He spoke of Carol, lightly, amiably. Letty shrugged her shoulders.

"It's her life," said Letty.

"You don't approve," he asked, eyes veiled from her own.

"No," said Letty, without qualification.

Fisher considered a moment. His pleasant smile quirked the corners of his mouth. He asked, after an appreciable pause:

"Scruples, eh? Moral or emotional?"

That was shrewd. Letty's eyes widened and darkened. Then she looked across at him.

"A little of both, I suppose," she replied honestly. "I don't know, really. You must remember — Carol and I grew up together. It's hard to think that she might be storing up unhappiness for herself."

"Then the scruples *are* emotional," Fisher told her, laughing. But relief flashed in the glance he sent her, too swiftly for her to read its message.

"No, not entirely," Letty told him gravely. She added, "Please, let's not talk about it any more, if you don't mind."

"I don't mind. But — Gordon's a good egg," said Fisher, "and I hope your little friend realizes it."

He doesn't like Carol, thought Letty. She did not reply. Fisher regarded her silently and then said:

"Loyal, aren't you? A nice trait, and a rare one. Look here, Letty, let's talk about — yourself."

She smiled at him, with gaiety, and lifted her glass to her lips, looking over the rim.

"That's always an interesting topic," she agreed lightly, "to me."

"No, seriously. Look here, you've youth, brains, looks. Brains, and an inquiring mind. Youth, and a certain dignity, very unusual nowadays, a little impressive — please don't think I think you're a dowager!" he laughed, "but there it is. Looks — combined with charm. You're wasting yourself at Sonia's, Letty, getting nowhere. You'll never get anywhere, there. You have an interest in chemistry, a knowledge of it. And you've those formulas you've told me about. You have by now some experience in this beauty racket. More than the time you've put in because you've made it your business really to learn, whereas most of the girls in that business are content to skim the surface. Why not put your knowledge and your assets to work for you? Go in for yourself. That's the only way to reach independence, moral, mental, physical, financial. You'll make a go of it. And I'll back you."

He spoke quietly and insistently. Letty looked at him astonished. The astonishment came as a definite shock to her. Her heart thudded, pounded, and then slowed to a more normal temperature. Somewhere a little signal rang, a harsh, small bell . . . a note of warning, of danger ahead, danger very close.

"Why, Morty," she began, after a moment, inadequately. She looked fleetly around the speakeasy, at the people sitting in the dim corners, talking, laughing. A subdued place. He'd said, "You won't mind a speakeasy, will you?" He'd laughed, "I'm not likely to meet my wife at speakeasies!" he said.

"Why not? We'll put it in solemn legal form. We'll draw up papers and tie 'em with nice red tape. I'll be a silent partner, it will be very shipshape and regular. I'll see that you have an ample sum, on which to start, something in reserve, and an appropriation for advertising, and for laboratory experiment. You'll pay me a legal rate of interest; and some day you'll be able to buy me out and be entirely your own man. What's wrong with the picture?" he asked her abruptly.

She was looking at him with extreme gravity, and with some distress but her eyes blazed black with excitement. What's wrong with the picture? Nothing. Everything. She considered it, as it stood. Her own shop. She'd know how to run it, she could avoid the mistakes Sonia made. She'd make her own, of course, but she'd learn. She would put up her father's formulas in her own laboratory. Herself, at first. Then in bigger quantities and with expert help, always under her own supervision. She'd sell the preparations in her own salon, and later over the counters of the better department stores. Not too many, three perhaps in New York, one in each of the other big cities. And she'd never cheapen them, never lower the quality. That was the error too many made. Her own business, herself her own mistress ——

That brought her up sharply. The flame died. And she shook her head, still gravely, a little sadly.

"That's fine of you, Morty," she said soberly, "and tempting to me. But I couldn't."

"Why not?" he asked her again.

Under the table she clenched her hands. They were cold, the palms wet. Nervousness, a little terror, a little normal human sorrow at seeing a dream die aborning.

"I'm not a fool," she said quietly, "and neither are you. So — you *know* why."

Mortimer Fisher laughed, low, without amusement. He spoke, swirling the amber liquid in his tall glass until the ice tinkled a cool accompaniment to his words.

"Cautious girl, aren't you?" he asked, "and so afraid of strings! There aren't any strings. I'm not trying to seduce you, my dear. Seductions have never appealed to me and I'm tired of buying favors. Too old, and too young, for that, any more, I fancy. No. It's just that I — like you. Like is, of course, hardly the term.

But that doesn't matter, we won't go into it. Also, I know you know, I think, I didn't at first, I confess it freely. I thought — well, what I thought then doesn't matter either; as I no longer think it, we'll let it pass. Nothing, Letty, is good enough for you except marriage. Even that mightn't be good enough, I don't know. However, I can't offer you marriage. Therefore I shan't offer you anything else except a strictly business partnership, and my friendship."

That was disarming and a little touching. She answered him brokenly, her eyes misty, her defenses down, her generous heart ashamed, and — the warning bell silent. Or was it that she closed her ears?

"I'm so grateful. Please forgive me for —— "

"There's nothing to forgive. It was a natural assumption," he interrupted swiftly. "So, will you accept the offer?"

"The friendship, of course. But the other —— ?"

She looked at him hesitantly. He was a wise man, in his way. He said:

"Don't answer now. Think it over. That's the best way, isn't it? And now," he told her, taking a menu from the hovering waiter, "with your figure, you can afford a sweet, can't you?"

She thought it over, night and day. Nights

125

in her narrow bed at Nelda's, and days going her round of work. Hard work. Half the women in New York were demanding that they become platinum blondes. It wasn't her job, but she watched the men operators and took mental notes. An expensive process, ruinous to the hair in most cases, and very tedious.

Then one day in late autumn Fisher called for her at Nelda's and they drove a little way out of town to a simple, pleasant wayside inn which had not gone in for liquor and noisy dancing or crooners with a radio hook-up. They had dinner in a round, many-windowed room and could look from it over the river, and away from it to the great wood fire blazing on the hearth, in the lounge. The place was almost deserted but the service and food were of the best. After dinner, over the coffee-cups, he asked her.

"Have you — thought it over?"

He was friendly but detached, a little abrupt. It seemed to Letty that only in that split second was her mind really made up. For through all the days and nights that had passed since his original proposition she had fluctuated from mood to mood. Now she knew. It was her opportunity. She'd take it, make something of it and herself. She would trust him to keep that unspoken promise. She nodded her fair head, once, twice, quickly, like a child.

"I have. It's yes, Morty," she said. And when she had said it, her eyes danced and her entrancing mouth curved and she felt an excitement, deep within her, such as she had never before experienced. The past was past; the present was caught in a golden, glowing bubble of hope and dreams and glamour; and the future was ahead.

If he felt elation or triumph, he did not display it. He merely said gravely:

"That's good. I'm glad. I'll have the papers drawn up, everything attended to quite properly. You'd better start looking around for a location."

She told him, flushing a little, that she had looked around — tentatively. And there were one or two places — with his approval . . . ?

His gravity broke into laughter.

"Then — all along?"

"No," said Letty practically, "no, not at all. But I thought, if I *do* decide I may as well have something to go on."

His delighted shout brought the startled blood more warmly to her cheeks. He said, after a moment:

"I'll be practical, too. Look here, you have that insurance you spoke of, haven't you?"

"Yes, of course. Why?"

"Well, if anyone asks you, why not be vague? You had a legacy, you went to Sonia's for experience. You decided to use your stake and strike out for yourself. And if you want you can say you borrowed extra capital. Still vaguely."

That distressed her for a moment. She argued evenly.

"I'm not ashamed of our partnership."

"No, of course not," he said hastily, "but it will be best, won't it, not to go into details? Remember," he reminded her, "your own natural reaction when I first made you the offer. Other people will experience the same reaction especially those who do not know you very well. It's just being sensible isn't it?"

She was forced to agree.

Home that night she found a card from Carol. It read "So this is Paris" and that was all save for a bank address. Letty looked at it thoughtfully and put it away.

By the first of the year she was in business for herself. She had resigned from Sonia's giving Sonia her reasons. Sonia was enraged out of all proportion. "Such ingratitude," she complained to Nelda sharply. "Comes in here, learns all I have to teach her and then pulls out and starts in on her own. And expects, I presume, to take a large percentage of my clientele with her! I might have known I couldn't trust her, she was entirely too good to be true."

Nelda was loyal to Letty, despite her older loyalty. "How," she asked Sonia mildly, "do you expect her to get along if she doesn't go in for herself?" But Sonia was too indignant to be reasonable.

"Where'd she get the money?" she demanded. "Can you answer that!"

Nelda could. Letty, explained Nelda, had had some capital of her own, since her father's death.

But Sonia was not persuaded. "She told me about that," she said, "and it wasn't enough then to keep her from working here."

"She wanted experience," Nelda said.

"What kind of experience?" Sonia wanted to know. Nelda was silent. Sonia wrote Burt Barker all about it, out of her vast annoyance. He read the letter sweating under the South American sun. Things weren't breaking right for Barker out there. Plenty of trouble, dissatisfaction, annoyances. For a moment his mother's letter held him, and he grinned over it, a flash of white teeth in a face burnt black and much thinner.

"After all I did for her," the letter went on, "taught her the business . . . now butter wouldn't melt in her mouth. I understood she had no outside means . . . people are saying she's using capital her father, a chemist, left her. That's as may be but, personally, I wonder! Someone is backing her. Who? And, if you please, she has her own 'formulas.' She said nothing to me about them when she came in here." The letter went on for some time in such a strain; ended on a wail. "When are you coming home? I'm lonely," wrote Sonia fiercely, an admission hitherto never wrung from her, "and I'm getting no younger, Burt."

Barker's grin faded. He put the letter in his pocket. Thought, deeply, of his mother, her struggle, her endurances, her battles, her violent jealousies. Thought, more briefly, but with a curious intensity, of the girl he had seen in the reception room, with the very fair hair and the miraculous skin and the unusual, unlikely eyes. If Sonia were right? Sonia, women in general, were usually right. Too damned bad, a girl like that, thought Burt Barker, returning to his job, but one didn't blame them, in this catch-as-catch-can world. Still ——

The papers were drawn up. Fisher and Letty had a brief struggle over the trade name. "Lawson, Inc.," said Letty. Morty raised his eyebrows to heaven in horror. Harsh, almost brutal. It didn't, he told her, sound like a beauty salon, it sounded like a plumber's shop. But she was adamant. The Lawson remained. After all, if Fisher was a silent partner there was another partner too, her father, his formulas, his life work. She did not explain that to Mortimer. But she persisted. Finally they reached a compromise.

Letty Lawson, Inc.

Just that. No foreign faking, no languorous names, no attempt at indigent nobility in business and disguise. Just Letty Lawson, herself; and incorporated.

The salon she opened was small and complete. She had selected a location on upper Madison Avenue, a good district, easily available from both Park and Fifth. Not a ground floor place, but one in a business building. Ground floors and display windows attracted casual trade which might become permanent; it was harder to work up the trade several stories above the street. But less expensive when it came to rentals. Later, perhaps, a ground floor, two floors of her own. Not now.

Money was ample, as Fisher had promised. Letty was left to work out most of the details. She consulted him gravely over everything but he laughed at her. "Have it your way, Letty; you know what you can spend, what must be kept in reserve. I know nothing about the beauty business. You do. I leave it all to you, you have good taste, you are practical."

She found herself wishing that he would

show a little more interest in the building up, rather than in the completed project. But that was, after all, too much to expect.

She had only herself to rely on. Nelda was friendly and interested but Nelda's real allegiance belonged to Sonia. So she did not consult Nelda very much. When Nelda found her an experienced bookkeeper willing to double at the reception desk, Nelda's part was ended, or so Letty concluded. She found, for herself, two good operators, fresh from school, to whom she could teach her own methods, which weren't, exactly, Sonia's; and a man for the hair work. She herself would work as an operator and in the laboratory for the first few years. She wanted to. She had still a lot to learn, she told herself.

She installed ultra-violet-ray lamps, good ones, two of them, and learning to operate them in the office of a physician she knew, taught her quick assistants, pretty and practical girls. There would be sun-tan if you wanted it. Also there would be bleaching processes, if you wished to fade back to a normal pink and white. It would work both ways. Some day she would permit herself to dream of a bigger place, a health institute in connection with the beauty salon, with technicians and trained nurses in charge and courses in reducing and in putting on weight, in exercising and all the rest. Some day.

The salon itself was beautifully done, by a good decorator, an unusual girl once employed by a big department store, where Letty had met her, and now starting out for herself. She was modern, she had ideas, she was not too expensive. The result was charming, not too many angles but modern enough, and restful, relaxing, becoming. The operators' rooms were small, almost sedate, perfectly equipped, and the couches deep as a good night's sleep.

Letty wrote her own advertisements. They were clever but not too exuberant; eye-attracting but not too smart-aleck; and confined to a quarter column in one smart, widely read weekly and two expensive monthly magazines which had the mode as their watchword.

In the beginning she did not try to place her preparations in the department stores but by spring she was receiving inquiries. She held off, for a time. In her own shop the preparations were brilliantly priced: inexpensive enough to be within the reach of the medium purses which, with their owners, marched in, on the quest for beauty, but not so cheap as to appear inexclusive. And there were, of course, a few specialties which cost a good deal more and could be afforded only by the more extravagant customers.

Letty was busy; busy watching her girls, working, spending hours in the laboratory. She had, through the friendly physician, engaged a young chemist, a woman, to help her. A good chemist, a keen, interesting woman. There would be a time, she reported to Mortimer Fisher over a dinner-table, when the laboratory would have to be moved downtown to quarters of its own. In a year or so; maybe less. By then it would be time enough to place the preparations in carefully selected shops.

She was full of her business; and she had never looked prettier. Letty Lawson, Inc. was doing well. Almost from the first she had broken even with her expenses, and now was beginning to make money, a little, not much, but still a profit. Astonishing how the women came in, some through the advertising, some through word of mouth publicity, and others from the Sonia group, women she had known there and who had always asked for her.

This she neither encouraged nor discouraged. She had made no bid for their custom while she remained at Sonia's, knowing she would soon leave. But they had come in and asked for her, and later drifted in to see her, her own following, small at first but later increasing, as the women brought their friends. In such fashion was trade built up.

It wasn't all roses. There were days of discouragement and days of fear, of wondering if after all she had attempted too much. But for the most part the hours passed quickly, too quickly, in the quiet pleasant atmosphere, with its odor of cosmetics and its light laughter and pleasant talk.

The operators wore white; Letty wore white. There was no attempt to mimic the uniform of a trained nurse, as is done in so many places. The white uniform at Letty Lawson, Inc. was merely a fresh, starched, white smock, and pretended to be nothing else. Time enough for the frills and furbelows later.

Early in the winter Letty moved from Nelda's. She felt some compunction at so doing but it vanished when Nelda told her frankly:

"It's all right. Better, in fact. I can find someone to take your room, and I won't lose by it. Then there's Sonia. She hasn't liked your living here, although she hasn't said so in so many words. And of course she tries to pump me. Who goes to you, anyone she knows, is that the reason Mrs. Nelson is no longer on our books, and Mrs. Carman and a half dozen others? It will be more comfortable for me if I can say I know nothing of your business affairs. Of course, I don't know much as it is, but she won't believe me."

Letty was relieved and said so frankly.

"You've been dear to me, Nelda, and I won't forget it."

"Nonsense," said Nelda briskly. She added, "You did the right thing. Wish I had — years ago." Her small face set in aging and stubborn lines. "Well, it's too late now. And I owe Sonia a lot," she added.

Letty moved over on the East Side, near the Sutton Place district. She found a very small, comfortable, furnished apartment which she was able to sublet on a long lease. She lived there quietly and alone, getting her own breakfasts and depending on a good part-time maid for cleaning and dinners. Now and then people dined with her: Nelda, the decorator who had done the shop, the young chemist employed by herself, and others; for she was making friends, not many but they were pleasant acquaintances and while her social life was slight and circumscribed it was relaxation for her and pleasure.

Fisher came occasionally. She debated with herself for some time before she asked him. Finally, she did so, wondering if it were in the nature of an ignoble experiment and how it would turn out. The part-time maid cooked well and simply and served adequately. After dinner, over coffee and cigarettes, she produced books and sheafs of papers and went over the details of the shop with him. He was interested and congratulatory. If he did not understand the trappings of her business, he understood figures and facts. When they had finished talking and a slight awkward silence had fallen, he broke it by suggesting, naturally, that they walk to a near-by motion picture house, a small one on Lexington Avenue, and see a picture that had been well criticized and which neither of them had seen. And so the evening passed off pleasantly and was followed by others at discreet intervals.

In the spring Carol came home from Paris and established herself on Park Avenue. She was thinner, and better looking. She had trunks full of very good clothes and some, but not too much, excellent jewelry. The apartment she selected was not too large, it was well furnished and she had a good, close-mouthed maid. Letty dined with her — alone, Mr. Gordon effacing himself to eliminate any real awkwardness, and Carol chattered in a slightly feverish manner, telling her about Paris, Vienna, Budapest, England. It was fun, the trip, she said defiantly. A great deal of the time she was alone, of course. Naturally one made amusing acquaintances among traveling companions. Herbert, she explained — and Letty realized suddenly that there was a

137

pathetic little false front effect in the dropping of the absurd nickname — hadn't traveled with her, not openly. He had been busy, too; and when he did send her ahead of him to one place or another, with a letter of credit and carte blanche, their eventual meetings were discreetly arranged.

No, she said briefly in answer to Letty's question, she hadn't communicated with her father nor with Tom. She didn't know where Tom was; didn't, she said, care. "Good-by to all that," said Carol gaily.

She was interested in the business. "Where did you get the money?" she wanted to know. Oh, she knew, of course, that Letty had gone in for herself, although they had written each other infrequently; but she wanted details. Letty explained. There was no sense in not explaining, to Carol. Carol sat very still, regarding the square-cut emerald on her left hand. "Morty?" said Carol. Then, "Well, you know best," she told her friend, a trifle wearily and in an accent which was not at all of Bay Ridge. She had acquired a veneer, these past months, had Carol.

"It was purely a business arrangement," Letty told her a little hotly.

"Oh, yeah?" asked Carol, reverting to type.

Letty flushed, wounded. Carol laid a hand on hers.

"I know, on your part. But on his? And how long will it last?" asked Carol. She looked at Letty with wise, tired eyes. "Men are all alike, in the long run. It's eventually, *if* not now, with them," she said, twisting the old phrase a trifle.

"I don't believe it. I — I took a long time to think it over," said Letty. "I wasn't sure," she told Carol frankly, "but I am now."

"That's good," said Carol ambiguously. She said wistfully, "It would be fun to be together — the four of us, wouldn't it — dinner, some place."

Letty said, yes. Later she spoke to Fisher but he shook his head. "I don't think so," he told her, "it — it wouldn't do. You'd put yourself in the same category at once. Originally, it was a little different, wasn't it? But now — well, Carol has definitely made a choice and such choices do not pass by without outside comment. So, better not," said Fisher, "unless some time, perhaps, a quiet dinner, here, in your place."

Letty was forced to agree with him. She found herself sickened, a little, at all the circumlocution, the care, the discretion. But she couldn't let Carol down. Carol and Herbert Gordon and Mortimer Fisher came to dinner with her in her apartment. Gordon looked younger, she thought, and more alert than she had ever seen him. He was obviously devoted to Carol but his behavior toward her was a model of discretion even in that quiet little place, with no white light of publicity threatening them.

Carol came to Letty Lawson, Inc. And she did more than that. She sent other people. Pretty girls, for the most part, so pretty that one did not inquire whether they were as chaste as they were beautiful. They made a little hum of noise and color and laughter through the shop, they prattled in and out, needing very few artificial aids to a natural beauty but fearful lest they reach the day, too soon, when artificial aids would no longer be of use. Business, for Letty Lawson, Inc., increased.

"I don't," Letty confided to Mortimer Fisher, "want to attract solely that trade."

She spoke firmly. She was grateful to Carol, and she was a good business woman. But Carol's friends were kept; and well kept, too, considering the times.

Fisher understood and consoled her.

"Never mind," he said, "it's well known that where the bad girls go, the good girls follow; hats, frocks, hairdressers, beauty places. Sit tight and offend no one."

She nodded and sat tight.

A sprinkling of stage women began to come

to her. From that moment she was really established. Some drifted away, others became permanent fixtures; some were poor pay and ran big accounts; but all who came regularly were marvelous advertising. They sent their friends, of the stage and not of the stage.

Letty took on another operator and sacrificed part of her good-sized private office for another treatment room. Later she would have to rent more space. Just now, however, it was better to have a small place, with every hour in the appointment book filled, than a large one with rooms and operators idle, and the burden of a big establishment to carry.

She was becoming a personage. Articles began to appear about her in the women's sections of the newspapers. Reporters came, and looked and watched. The beauty editors of weeklies and monthlies and newspapers came too, and had treatments or sent their assistants. And wrote about her, "The remarkable young girl who is making such a scientific study, and with such success, of skin care." Name, of course, on request. Requests poured in. And Letty, encouraged, branched out and engaged a clever specialist in advertising to prepare a brochure, with a picture of herself, a picture of the establishment and a little brief history, with emphasis on the formulas "which have been in the Lawson family for years."

She paid well to have the booklet written, and sent out. She managed to find a haven for it in the dressing rooms of smart restaurants which had, of course, no beauty salons of their own. There were samples of face powder, of lip rouge, of rouge, on the dressing tables, and the booklet near at hand. This brought more clients.

In the trade and out she was making friends. That summer she permitted herself no vacation. Business slackened but she devoted all her energies to the laboratory end of things, evolved a mild skin bleach and a tonic that was as soft as milk and as stimulating as a side-car. When fall came again she sat and waited breathless. Would the people come back? They came; and brought others with them.

Less than a year after she had launched the venture she was a success. Not a spectacular one, but a success nevertheless. She was seen lunching here and there, always in good places. She wore good clothes, for business reasons. She permitted herself a drawing account, one which would cover her rent, her living expenses. The rest went back into the business.

People looked at her across dining rooms. "Who is that extraordinarily pretty girl?" "That? Oh, that's Letty Lawson. You know, has the beauty place. I've been thinking of going to her. She did wonders for Nancy Manners —— "

"Is *that* Letty Lawson? I saw an article about her somewhere. Twenty-two, isn't she, or twenty-three? Amazing!"

"She doesn't look that. But I have it on good authority she's really forty-eight."

"No! My dear, I must go to her. Not forty-eight! Well — wonders will never cease!"

So ran the rumors; twenty, they said; no, thirty, forty, fifty, even perhaps sixty. "She's had some gland treatment, in Vienna," said the sixty rumorists. Letty heard the legends and made no effort to stop their spread. Better so.

It didn't matter what people said as long as her personal reputation remained unblemished and as long as she was a success — a success.

Chapter 8

During that same autumn Burt Barker returned from South America. He did not
return as one who has triumphantly carried a
big job to its proper conclusion. He returned
with a grievance, one which he considered
perfectly just, and with a chip on his shoulder
which must have been hewn from a giant red-
wood. He left his job — such as it was — in
charge of a jaundiced, malarial but loyal assis-
tant, and came back to New York unexpectedly, without permission, and paying his own
expenses. No doubt word of his desertion
would reach the powers that be before he did,
but Burt Barker didn't care. He was fighting
mad.

The job had blown up. It was at a standstill.
It had all sorts of offshoots and intricacies
for which he hadn't bargained. Burt Barker's
work was railroad construction and he was
perfectly equipped for it. He had been sent
out, so he thought, to a remote part of a
strange country in order to build a railroad. A
big task, a hard one, the sort of task he liked.

Instead, he found nothing as simple as that. He found himself involved in tin-pot revolutions; oil concession deals, government interventions, official briberies milled all about him, much more troublesome than bad liquor, dissatisfied workmen, earthquakes, disease, warm-blooded, half-breed girls, and terrible food.

So he returned to New York, thinner, very brown and edgy, in order to have a heart-to-heart talk with promoters for a railroad that was being built, as Burt had discovered, for more reasons than the plain matter-of-fact one of carrying passengers and freight.

He came back, therefore, to see Mortimer Fisher.

On the day when, after business hours, Burt stormed into Fisher's offices, Letty was just leaving. No one was about save Mortimer Fisher himself and his confidential secretary.

The confidential secretary was a thin gentleman of uncertain age who knew more about Mortimer Fisher than was good for either of them but who was magnificently reimbursed to forget any inconvenient knowledge. Letty Lawson, Inc. did not come under this heading. The confidential secretary knew all about that, his name in fact appeared upon the incorporation papers. He was, in this and other matters, an obliging and well-paid dummy.

Burt had made no appointment. He had just about landed. He hadn't his land legs yet, or so one would think, as he slammed open the door and slammed it shut behind him and rocked across the reception room.

He looked very much the way he felt. The change in his expression was almost ludicrous as the first — and only — person he saw was Letty walking lightly across the space between them.

It was her second visit to Mortimer Fisher's office. The laboratory demands were already taking her limited space. She had found a place downtown which she could rent at prevailing low prices; and an even better one in Long Island City. Fisher was leaving town that evening and she had telephoned she would come to the office to talk to him about the projected lease before he left. It was all very simple . . . to her.

She didn't at first recall Burt Barker; not that she did not remember him. But now he had changed. He had a prowling look, dark, intent. But, amazed, he recalled her at once, and smiled, as if unwillingly. The smile interpreted him to her. Her own lips curved, in unbelief and friendliness. Barker held out his hand.

"Surely I know you," he said, and it seemed to him that his voice was rusty, it had been, as far as lip service to beauty went, in disuse for so long. "I — I saw you at my mother's — at Sonia's. . . . You're . . . " he groped, but for a moment only. "You're 'Miss Letty,' are you not?"

Letty nodded. Her responsive hand was cool and slim in his own.

"Yes," she answered, "and you're Mr. Barker. I've my own place now," she told him. She added, withdrawing her hand, "Remember me to your mother, won't you? She's angry at me, a little," Letty admitted, and her smile faded.

"Competition," said Barker foolishly, "is the life of the trade." He watched her start to walk to the door, walked with her. "I hope you're having a great success."

She nodded, smiling. The door closed behind her. She on one side, he on the other, considered matters. Sonia was angry with her — a little, justified, as Letty knew for Letty Lawson, Inc. was doing far too well. The Sonia clients who had followed Letty were remaining with her. "The girl with the hands," they had called her. Successful hands. They were insured now, partly as a publicity measure. It was good business; it had been done before, of course, and would be done again.

Letty, on her side, was flushing a trifle. Awkward, perhaps, to meet Burt Barker there. He would mention it to Sonia. She had, in fact, seen to it that he would mention it, idly enough, for something to say. He'd been away. She knitted her brows, recalling. South America, wasn't it? That was why he was thinner, and so very brown. She wondered what he was doing in Fisher's office? But it was none of her concern. Fisher — and railroads in South America. That, of course, was the connection. She pressed the elevator button, and waited a moment for the cage to ascend. She had plenty to think about, she couldn't waste a moment on Burt Barker. The lease, for instance. Morty had advised the Long Island City place. Tonight she would talk to Kate Miller, the young chemist; and tomorrow they would inspect it together. Kate was practically her right-hand man.

On his side of the door Barker was frowning again, thinking not of himself but of the girl who had just left the office. He had little time for thought, however, for the confidential secretary catapulted out of the inner office, having heard voices. In the reception room he met an immovable object. He was astonished and outraged.

"Who are you?" he demanded.

"Barker. Burt Barker, I'm to see Mr. Fisher," Burt replied.

"It's after hours. Mr. Fisher is leaving for

Washington. Did you have an appointment?" inquired the secretary.

No, no appointment. Burt had had his fill of appointments, of cooling his dusty heels in the curious and ornate offices of potentates, brigands and other fry. He brushed by the secretary. It was more than a brush, for the secretary, small and slim, stoically stood his ground as long as he could. It did him no good, it amounted to a flying tackle. Almost you could hear the voices from the side lines. . . . Hold 'em, Harvard! And the long thrilling cry — Barker — *Barker!*

The secretary recovered his balance and started after the intruder. The door of the inner office banged in his face, almost catching the end of a long thin nose. Racketeer? Such had been known before to invade these offices, gentlemen with elegant shake-down schemes. They had come flying out of doors on their insulted behinds. Blackmailers? They were known to Morty Fisher likewise. "Just a minute, while I telephone the District Attorney."

Perhaps Mr. Fisher would need a witness? Shakily, but game, the secretary knocked, turned the door knob and entered.

In the inner office Burt was standing at the desk, his hands sunk in his pockets, his head thrust forward. He was not frowning, he was scowling. Morty at the desk, seated, leaned back and smiled.

The opening gambit had been short, if not sweet.

"And who the hell may you be?" Mortimer Fisher had inquired.

Burt had told him. And a moment later had asked in his turn:

"What's the idea of these damn double-crossing political shenanigans? I was sent out to build railroads, not to spy out oil, and instigate revolutions."

Now, Morty looked up and perceived his secretary, clinging close to the threshold. "I shan't need you, Watts," he said, and Mr. Watts departed, thankfully. But not until he had seen that his employer was a little jittery and the smile not all it might have been. Loyal as he was and superlatively rewarded, a small thrill of hero-worshiping admiration shot through his meager and marrowless frame, a tribute to a strange young man who bearded lions in their dens and didn't, apparently, give a damn.

Watts would have preferred to wait to be in at the finish, but instead he departed, following his former instructions, to eat his lonely dinner and later to meet Mortimer Fisher at the train.

In the inner office the interview continued.

It was brief. Burt told Mortimer Fisher what he thought of him and his job and that was that. And Mortimer Fisher told Burt that there wasn't any job, not any more. And that was even thatter. There were a great many good engineers, drifting about the universe, Fisher explained, who weren't quite as scrupulous . . . or insane.

Burt Barker left the office of Mr. Fisher. He was still considerably annoyed, but he had spoken his mind and that had done him a world of good; it had been a violent and beneficial catharsis, clearing and purging his system of a lot of stored up anger, and amazement and disgust.

He went directly to his mother's apartment, whither he had sent his bags. He'd put up there for a day perhaps, and then pull out. Over dinner he explained matters to Sonia, who had been flushed and a little unsteady ever since his laconic wireless had reached her. He was, said Burt, one of the unemployed. Well, he'd been that way before. It wouldn't last long.

She said, the flickering candlelight very kind to her,

"If you need money, Burt . . . ?"

"No, Sonia." He always called her Sonia. At first it had been quaint and amusing, from a child's lips; later, it had been flattering and good business; now it hurt, a little, and obscurely. "No. The salary was elegant while it held out. I didn't spend much down there. I could have, of course, if I'd wanted to go in for the usual entertainment. But I didn't. So there's a lot left. I'll dig out in a day or so and go out to Pennsylvania and see the old folks and maybe come back and take a room somewhere and look for work. I'm O.K. Don't worry."

They had their coffee in the pleasant living room, cluttered with beautiful Copenhagen ware, figurines, dogs, bunnies, squirrels, deer, everything; Sonia's collection, a minor passion with her.

She was talking about her business. Fair, she said, she couldn't complain. But her voice complained, a little. Barker, remembering, looked up, and across at her where she sat facing him on one of the twin tub-sofas.

"By the way, here's a funny thing. I ran into that tall blonde girl of yours today. The one who's in for herself now. Letty —— "

"Letty Lawson?" Sonia interrupted. Her eyes narrowed. She asked for details. "Where?" she wanted to know, "and how?"

"At Fisher's office. She was just coming out as I left," Burt answered. "She asked to be remembered to you. She said you were angry with her."

"Oh, she did!" Sonia snorted slightly. "Like her impudence," she remarked. She was silent a moment. Barker laughed.

"I remember, you wrote me." Up to that moment he hadn't realized the letter in detail, now he did. His brows drew together. He said, "After all, you can't blame the girl for wanting to be independent."

But Sonia wasn't listening. Mortimer Fisher! And Letty coming out of his office, after hours. Was that the explanation? It must be. A long shot but not entirely in the dark. Letty had been seen with Fisher, here and there. These things came back to Sonia. Her business bred gossip as honey breeds bees, as jam breeds flies. She laughed outright and slapped her velvet-clad knee. A vulgar and forthright gesture, one which was native to her and which she restrained during business hours. "So that's it," she told her son; "I knew she had backing from some source. It's simple, isn't it? I can see through a stone wall as well as the next person. Of course, Fisher."

Burt was slightly taken aback. He had, also, an unpleasant feeling at the pit of his lean stomach. That girl . . . with that direct look of hers, sagacious enough, of course, not one of silly ignorance. But a look of integrity, honesty and . . . he groped mentally for a silent phrase — armed virginity. He shook his head as Sonia went on talking. He supposed his mother to be right; she was, as a rule. Hell, thought Burt, women were all alike. All save Sonia. He changed the subject. "That pain of yours, your arm, hadn't you better see a doctor?"

He stayed on a day, two days; grew restless, and departed for the home of his grandparents. They were very old now. He would not be coming home to them much longer. He knew this, commanding his patience in the small, shut-in atmosphere, entertaining them with wild stories of alien countries, listening, smiling, to their shocked, amazed exclamations. . . .

Sonia, meantime, was talking too. She talked discreetly to some of her clients, and her friends in the trade. She mentioned no names save Letty's. That could wait.

Everything is talked over sooner or later in the comic, the tragic, the muted and perfumed atmosphere of the beauty shop. It's a pity the major gossip columnists aren't women. Relaxing, on a deep couch, with pads over their eyes but their ears wide open, they could hear enough to tear the town wide open and topple penthouses from their costly heights.

Carol, coming in to Letty Lawson, Inc. for a sound muscle strapping — "See, how it sags there, Letty, just a little — ?" warned her friend. She felt the cool, fine hands on her dry and fevered skin and closed her eyes, sighing. She said:

"Sonia's got her knife in for you, Letty. She's telling everyone you're being backed."

"Well, I am," Letty said, laughing, "and you know it."

Yes, Carol knew. She frowned, and then relaxed her face into prescribed blandness. She replied,

"Sure, I know. But the tone in which she says 'backed'. . . . You can imagine, can't you? It's dangerous, she's dangerous, Letty, be careful. Don't be a fool."

Letty's smile had vanished. She said, smoothing in creams, oils, "You know it's on the level, Carol."

"Hell, darling, yes. But who else knows it?"

"I do; and Mortimer."

"Of course. But who'll believe it — except me?" Carol asked her. She asked further as Letty did not reply, "You like Morty Fisher, don't you, Letty?"

"Naturally."

"Don't like him too much, honey. It doesn't pay."

Letty brushed that aside. Something in Carol's voice, in the twist of her mouth, wiped clean of its heavy lipstick. . . .

"Carol — you're not unhappy?"

"No, I'm not. I'm not happy, either. What's the odds? I — I was wrong about old men," Carol said. "My error," she remarked and tried to laugh. "What difference does it make?" she went on, "it may not be a bed of roses, but it's got a damned good mattress!"

"Oh, keep quiet," cried Letty, a little out of control. Then she said, professionally serene, "Don't talk now. I'm going to strap you up."

Later, Carol lingered a moment in the small reception office. The bookkeeper, Mrs. Burnet, looked at her sourly. Carol spoke, standing close to Letty, her voice well down:

"Tom's back. I just heard. Father's wild. You watch your step, Letty."

Then she was gone. Perfume at heaven knew what an ounce spoke of her departure, a breath of it still on the air. The bookkeeper reminded her employer.

"Miss Coleman — " which was Carol's new nom-de-duplex — "is behind, three months."

"Let the bill run," Letty told her absently, "she is one of my oldest friends. She'll pay, eventually."

Mrs. Burnet shrugged. Too many old friends on the books was bad business and put you deep in the red. But Letty Lawson hadn't many; hadn't in fact any except this Coleman person. Person, repeated Mrs. Burnet, who was violently and reluctantly respectable.

Letty went back to her work, thinking. Tom back? But he wouldn't, she thought, bother her now, after all this time. She knew that Carol saw her father occasionally and had since summertime. She had told him that she was now a buyer, in a big way. Cosmetics, for a chain of shops. Lots of money in it, she had assured him. Mr. Merrick didn't believe her. He couldn't. He wasn't that much of an idiot, listening to her light voice weaving its tissue of lies under the extremely soiled glances of the hostile aunt, his sister. But he had to pretend to believe her. He was old, he was alone, he was broken. The business, which he had built up with such infinite pains and pride, was gone, swept away. There was the house left, with its only occasional tenants to depend upon, the complaining holier-than-thou sister, and his own failing health. He couldn't even get odd carpentering jobs, these days. And now Tom was back, a bitter burden, drinking too much, petulant, given to terrifying bursts of temper, lacking all control.

But Carol had come to the rescue; Carol and her open purse.

Merrick loathed taking her money; but he took it. These were strange times, you were down and out, you had no control over your kids; the child with the pay check and the bank account obeyed no rules, laid down laws, dictated to you. . . .

He had promised Carol to tell Tom nothing about her. He had telephoned her on Tom's return; and she had said:

"I won't be over. I'll send a money order. Look here, Pop, don't tell Tom where I am, the address or anything. I'll not be bled by him," said Carol.

But it was not entirely of herself that she thought. She thought of Letty, too. Her father had told her enough about the prodigal's return to make it clear to her that Tom, wherever he had been and whatever he had done, had returned in an ugly humor. She could, she thought, handle him if ever he did manage to find out where she was. But, if he should look up Letty too and, by some wild mischance, find her? It would be the simplest thing to find her. All he had to do was look in a telephone directory. But, of course, that was probably the last thing he would do, thought Carol. Carol rang up Nelda, whom she saw occasionally, that same evening.

"Be a good egg, Nelda, and if a nut professing to be my brother comes into Sonia's, you don't know where I am or anything. And you don't know anything about Letty either, see? He's a bad egg, and would ruin any picnic," said Carol.

158

Nelda promised, not particularly curious. She knew that Carol had a brother somewhere. No good, most likely. She didn't blame Carol for not wanting to cut in with him.

The warning was timely enough. A few days after Carol had had her muscle strapping, Tom Merrick swaggered into Sonia's. He swaggered because he was very drunk and it was easier to swagger. He marched himself up to the reception desk and hammered on it. He wanted, he said, to see his sister.

Merrick had told his son nothing. In reply to all his questions he had said, "I don't know where Carol is, she doesn't come here any more." The aunt had sniffed under Merrick's warning glance. As a matter of fact, *she* didn't know; Carol had never favored her with a telephone number or address.

Well, thought Tom, broke to the wide, they'd know at that beauty place — Sonia's, wasn't it? He remembered. God knew he'd heard enough about it, in the old days.

So here was Tom, odorous of liquor, drunk, good-looking still because youth remained to him and a certain amount of strength, if not the kind which would do him much good, frightening the appointment clerk into a frenzy.

Nelda came out just then. She took charge. She informed Tom that Miss Carol and Miss

Letty had not been in Sonia's employ for over a year, and then she attempted to guide him to the elevator.

But she couldn't manage him. His voice grew louder. Clients in the little rooms stirred and looked — if physically capable — with inquiry at the operators. And Sonia herself came out.

"What's all this?" asked Sonia, low; and very angry.

Tom was harping on Carol now. He swung around on Sonia. "Where's my sister?" he demanded.

Sonia regarded him. A type one didn't encounter in beauty parlors. Nelda explained hastily. Miss Carol, said Sonia coldly, hadn't been in the shop for a good many months, and if her alleged brother didn't go, and quickly, she would call the police.

The appointment clerk had her hand on the phone. Nelda ran and pressed the elevator bell. A hold-up, a drunken man? The operators who were idle crowded to the doors. One of the men appeared, hot marcel waving irons in a rather tremulous hand. You were pretty well isolated on the eighth floor of a Fifth Avenue building. You couldn't dash into the street and shout for a cop. . . .

The elevator came up at that moment. Burt Barker got out of it. He had just returned to town, and was coming to take his mother out to lunch and to the doctor's. She hadn't been well for a long time; and he'd insisted.

Tom was still standing by the desk, hammering on it. Burt regarded the scene. His mother stepped toward him, Nelda fell back. The appointment clerk dropped her hand from the telephone and breathed an audible sigh of relief. Mr. Barker would take charge.

"Here, you," said Burt briefly.

He took Tom by the shoulder. "Better come quietly," he warned, grinning.

Tom Merrick was still very drunk, and very angry. The entire world conspired against him. He put his hand in his pocket. One thing he had acquired in his recent travels was a gun. He displayed it now; half bravado, half business.

Nelda screamed, watching; and Sonia made a strange sound in her throat.

Burt wrenched the gun away. Tom was still talking; if he couldn't see Carol, he'd see Letty. Letty, said Tom, was his girl. He had a right to see her.

Nelda was ringing the elevator bell again, keeping her finger on the button. And Tom found himself presently in the elevator, with an escort. And then, out in the street.

Burt ran back, laughing a little, and went on up to the eighth floor. He was too late. The

161

sobbing girl who had been sent to fetch him, missed him, was on her way up in another elevator. For Sonia was dead.

She had lived to see all she had ever loved, all she had lived for threatened. She had stood there watching, while the gun was rendered harmless; stood there long enough to know her son safe, laughing a little, even, marching that insane young hoodlum into the elevator. But she had been desperately frightened. The occasion for fright was over, but the few swift, crowded moments had had time to do the irreparable damage to the overtaxed heart. The heart she had strained by dieting, by overexercise, by God knows what. The heart which had suffered in the years of anxiety and undernourishment. Her magnificent vitality had carried her through then. Not any more. . . .

So Burt came back to find her where they had taken her, in the inner office with as little confusion as was humanly possible. Nelda, looking eighty years old, had kept her head. People mustn't be frightened, mustn't know, not until someone in authority came.

A doctor came. Sonia wouldn't go to a doctor now, at Burt's insistence. One would come to her. Too late.

End of Sonia, and a curtain rung down. And here was Burt, without a job, and on the very private and important blacklist of one Mortimer Fisher, standing beside a couch, looking down at a face suddenly serene and indifferent, and seeing it dimly.

Sonia gone; but her business remained; Burt Barker had inherited it, at the careless hands of Tom.

Chapter 9

Sonia's funeral was private; just the few people who had cared very much for her. Nelda
brought Burt the cards from the flowers.
There had been so many flowers. "Sonia?"
said people, rivals, salesmen, old customers,
"Sonia! Why, I can't believe it! I must send
flowers." And the customers said, "A son? I
can't imagine Sonia with a son!" It was the
first time a good many people had heard of
Burt Barker.

But Sonia was well known in her fashion;
she rated a few lines of obituary in the papers.

One card which Nelda brought Burt was
Letty's. Her flowers had been quite lovely,
nothing funereal, gay and bright and full
blown, with a special beauty. Sonia would
have liked them. Burt flipped at the card with
his finger, thinking.

Nelda was haggard. It wasn't that she had
been emotionally involved with Sonia. Their
friendship hadn't been, exactly, love. But it
had been a long association, a habit, a growing
together; and Nelda was grateful.

"These are from the girl who — ?" Burt stopped, slurred. In a roundabout way, Sonia's death lay at Letty Lawson's door. If it hadn't been for that drunken madman ——

Burt didn't know his name. Now, he inquired it of Nelda. Nelda nodded, Carol's brother, Carol Merrick.

Burt sat at his mother's desk in the apartment she had owned and which was now his and drew idle lines on a sheet of paper with a fountain pen. To think of Merrick was sheer melodrama. Useless, futile to look him up — as if one could, there were how many million people in New York City? — and demand a reckoning for what he had done. He had been, reflected Burt, an instrument rather than a conscious destiny.

Burt felt his mother's death deeply, in a curious way. He had been very fond of her, he had appreciated her rooted, sturdy qualities, which included her savage, inarticulate love for himself, and her real fortitude. Yet he hadn't, after all, known her very well. He had neglected her, he pondered, seized by the painful regret which comes to most of us at one time or another. Yet, she had wished to be neglected, for the sake of her business.

His business now.

He laughed a little, shortly, and without merriment. Nelda, calling at the apartment to help him, to interpret the — to him — strange maze of names on the many cards and signed to the letters, looked at him anxiously. "What are you going to do?" she wanted to know.

"I don't know," Burt answered. "Sell, if I can, I suppose."

Nelda went yellow-white under her rouge. The salon sold, to a competitor, to someone new, to a chain — it would mean the end of her working days, she thought. Not so easy to find a new job, at her age and in these times, despite her experience and her efficiency. Burt glanced up from the desk, the sunlight fell, slanting, from a window, across the note-paper and blotter. "Don't worry, Nelda," he said kindly, abstractedly, "you'll be taken care of, you know."

She flushed, content with that. She had always liked Sonia's boy; she remembered him when he was very small. He was no longer small. He was a big, a competent man, sitting there at the too ornate desk, frowning up at the Copenhagen group which topped it in gleaming porcelain.

He saw his lawyers, Sonia's lawyers. He saw people who knew what they were talking about. To sell, to attempt to sell Sonia's business now would be insanity. It was doing well enough, it had a reputation, but money simply wasn't available. If he sold at all, it would be at a loss, a tremendous loss.

He took Nelda to dinner and told her, over the coffee. He asked her gravely, "Sonia cared a lot for her business, didn't she?"

Nelda's reply held an emotional quality rare to her. "It was her life, Burt — except for you."

Burt was thoughtful, regarding the ash on his cigarette. "She'd hate it, wouldn't she, if I sold it to the first comer and pulled out for the Antipodes with whatever stake it provided and the rest of her savings?" His mouth twisted a little. Sonia, he reflected, hadn't had the good time to which she'd been entitled, after all the years of work. Her lawyer had said, "She spent nothing on herself save what seemed good policy to her."

A decent apartment, good clothes, for business' sweet sake, and that was about all. One would have said, not knowing, that she had been almost a miser outside of her adequate business expenses. Not a miser, thought Burt, frowning. Saving it all, for him.

There was considerable money, some of it tied up. The stocks, most of them, had cut their dividends, one or two had stopped paying, but they were good stocks, they would come back, they were bound to. The bonds were government bonds. There was some insurance, not very much, taken out in an earlier time of life. Later, when she could have afforded more she wouldn't have been able to get it. There was cash in her current private checking account, several thousand dollars, and more in the trade account. There was enough in reserve in the savings banks. There were several good mortgages. And the apartment.

Burt crushed out his cigarette. He felt like a fool. Every square inch of him. He straightened his broad shoulders and drew a long breath and Nelda, watching him, saw his unique grin, fleeting, a little wry. He'd reached a decision.

"We'll go on with it," he said. "I — I'll run the business, Nelda. I'm a good engineer and I know figures — in books," he added hastily. "And — could you take over the management?"

While she stared at him, her heart pounding, he explained that she, next to his mother, knew best all there was to know about the policies and running of the shop. There would be, of course, a salary adequate to her new job. Nelda flushed painfully and thanked him. Then she said thoughtfully:

"Yes, I can manage. I know how she did things. But I must manage from the office." She hesitated. "I haven't the 'front,' " she went on, and smiled at him, more wryly than he had at her. "I haven't Sonia's appearance," she explained frankly, "and that's important to this business. We need someone young, good-looking. If only," said Nelda, thinking aloud, "if only Letty Lawson hadn't left!"

His eyes were vividly blue, interested, on her own. Letty Lawson. He asked, "She has her own business, hasn't she?"

Nelda said, "Yes." She added, without grudging, "And a good one; she's been marvelously successful considering the short time she's been on her own. And her formulas are really excellent."

"Well, let it ride for a while," Burt told her, "perhaps she can be persuaded to come back. This is, of course, in confidence," he reminded her.

Nelda had her own thoughts. And as for confidence, she'd keep it. She did so. And so it was without warning that Letty came to the telephone one day to hear Burt Barker's voice. Might he see her — on business?

She set a time, and replaced the receiver, wondering. She saw him, when he came, in her private office, early one morning before the customers had started to come in. The office was less imposing than his mother's but impressive enough. It was a background for the fair hair and the lovely skin and the dark eyes. And a background too for the wool frock she wore, the color of the purple bloom on grapes.

He explained briefly, courteously. He had taken over his mother's business. Nelda would attempt the business management, under his guidance. He laughed a little, "I'm pretty new at this," he explained, "I'd better say, I will attempt it, under her guidance."

Letty listened, leaning back in her chair and watching him, his thin brown face still as a mask. He asked, after a moment:

"Would you come back? That is, sell out, to us? Merge, if you like it better, and bring us your formulas and your knowledge, and take over the customers' end of things, the personal contacts, the advice? I would be willing to pay you a good price for your business, a salary, and a percentage of proceeds. That is, I think," he told her, "a fair offer."

"A very fair offer," she agreed. But she shook her head. She said gravely:

"I appreciate this very much, Mr. Barker. But I am doing very well as I am."

Her voice was smooth, there were no rough edges. As if irony had been sandpapered off — she "appreciated it very much." The hell she did! He asked bluntly:

"Hadn't you better think it over? It's a good proposition. After all, you've only just started, and my mother's business has been established for years."

"Were you thinking," she asked, "of a partnership — later?"

Her eyes were very dark, mocking him. He disliked her intensely. She was hard, avid. She was lovely, infinitely desirable. He had never forgotten her. She had remained in his memory, from the first day he had seen her. He thought of the things his mother had written — and said — about her. Looking at her he was unable to believe them. Yet, he must believe them, they added up, they made sense. If she had consented, if she had come in with him, if he had been able to see her every day, to get really to know her — ?

He said, "I hadn't gotten that far."

Letty looked at him. The interview was terminated and he knew it. She said:

"Even a partnership would not tempt me, I think — provided you had 'gotten that far.' You see, I'm independent. That's what counts."

He repeated "Independent?" and found himself using a rising inflection. His glance at her was direct, straight, and spoke of his dislike and not of his illogical desire. Letty flushed faintly. Rumors . . . and he had heard them, she thought. Well, what did it matter? He didn't matter to her, not an iota.

She rose, and stood beside her desk, grace in every line. She said, "I'm sorry. I can only repeat that I appreciate your offer — and decline it."

He rose, too. He said, after a moment, losing a temper worn to a fine edge by the recent events, "I understand that Mortimer Fisher has an interest — "

Letty interrupted evenly, "Mr. Fisher is my business associate — " She could have bitten out her tongue. It would be all through the trade, she reflected, in a few days. But Burt said nothing, shrugged his shoulders and turned toward the door.

At the door he said suddenly:

"I'd advise against Mortimer Fisher as a — business associate." Then he asked, remembering, wanting to startle her into some sort of emotion, "Do you know a man named Merrick?"

"Merrick?" She was so taken aback that she did not remember that she had ever known anyone of that name. Then her mind cleared and she said, "Yes . . . two — the brother — and the father — of a friend of mine." She looked at him, puzzled. "Carol Merrick was once an operator at Sonia's," she said.

He had his hand on the door knob. He twisted the round piece of metal, the door opened slowly. He said:

"It might interest you to know that it was Miss Merrick's brother who came to the salon, drunk, and flourishing a gun like a cheap gangster, demanding to see his sister — and *you* — which caused the heart attack which resulted in my mother's death."

An absurd thing to say. Absurd and cruel. But he couldn't help it. Why? He had gone to her, not really expecting that she would take his offer. And he had found that, unreasonably, he wanted her, that he was in love with her, and that he disliked her out of all proportion. *Here* was something that didn't add up, and didn't make sense! And a certain imbecile fury had overcome him when he saw her flush when he mentioned Fisher's name, when he heard her grave, sweet voice making that palpably false explanation.

She had paled. She said, "Tom — came to the *office?*" She couldn't believe it and told him so. She said, "I haven't seen him for some time. Nor has his sister. He's been away. I can't understand it — "

She was shaking, a little. He saw her put her hand on the desk to support herself. He was sorry, desperately. He'd had no right. And yet, it had been obliquely her fault, why not let her know about it?

"I'm sorry, I shouldn't have told you. But when I think about it — "

She had no answer for him, only a wordless gesture of the small, fair head and the trouble

173

and distress in her eyes. He went out in silence, and awkwardly, knowing himself defeated in more than her refusal. Knowing also that he had done a cowardly thing. But, he assured himself, a human enough one.

Back at the office he told Nelda flatly that Letty would not consider his proposition. Nelda nodded. She hadn't believed in any other outcome. But now the pledge to confidence was over, perhaps she could phone her, go to see her, persuade her, she suggested.

Barker steam-rollered that idea, at once. She'd had her chance, he said with rancor. They could get on without her. Wasn't there someone who could be promoted to the reception room end of things, some girl now in their employ who had the appearance and enough knowledge to offer advice? "After all," agreed Burt, "what does the advice amount to? Just a sales argument, in the end!"

Nelda was thoughtful. Yes, she said, a girl might do. She considered it. There was one, Sonia had taken her on a year ago, a girl who had once had her own shop up north. Handsome, dark, about thirty and with sufficient manner. She'd do, said Nelda.

At home that night, alone, in the apartment Sonia had furnished for herself and which was too cluttered and ornate for a man, Burt prowled about the rooms thinking. He'd live there, of course, it was the sensible thing to do. But he'd eliminate some of the furbelows. He knocked a Copenhagen seal from a bookcase with a sweep of an elbow and cursed as he stooped to pick up the pieces, and the excellent maid Sonia had had for years came running in with exclamations of sorrow. He must, he thought, give away most of the porcelain. Nelda might like it. He felt compunction at the thought. Sonia had cared a lot for her little static animals. But he had to have room to stretch and breathe. It had been some time since he had had the house habit. He was accustomed to living where and how he could, to discomforts, to curious climates, to long journeys. He went to the window and looked down at Central park, the lights shining up at him in the crisp late autumn air.

He was a builder of railroads and he was about to run a beauty business. That was funny; it was very funny. But, by God, it would cease to be funny. He'd stay in the background but he'd learn his subject. Nelda would teach him. He would study, read. He'd interview salesmen, he'd get to know and be known in the trade. He'd have six new ideas a day and one of them would be good. He'd make this a real business, one in which he could find some satisfaction. Bigger than Sonia had ever dreamed, he'd make it. And he'd give Letty Lawson, Inc. a run for Mortimer Fisher's money. There were, of course, hundreds of beauty places in New York City but for Burt Barker there were only two: Letty Lawson's and Sonia's.

Everything that Letty did, they'd do better. There were ways of finding out. He forgot his anger and disgust at the curious and devious methods of Mortimer Fisher's men down in South America. He thought — if I could plant a girl in there — ?

He was ashamed of himself. But all's fair in love and the beauty business and this was, after all, his private war. Nelda? That was one time when Nelda wouldn't be taken into confidence. She was out the morning he interviewed the new girl, a clever little thing, pretty, a red-head, who had come to them from one of the bigger hotels and hadn't been with Sonia's long. Her name was Sally.

He saw her privately. It was arranged, quickly. Sally had a very agile mind. She was to resign, to quit, to leave; and at once. She was to try and get a place at Letty Lawson's. She was to report to him, all for a considerable consideration.

It worked. Letty could use a new operator and this one had had considerable experience; a pretty girl, and bright. Where had she been last? Sally named the hotel, and made no mention of Sonia's. Safer that way. Letty engaged her; and no one was the wiser, not even Nelda, annoyed at losing a promising employee and looking for one to take her place, or Letty, brisk, friendly and businesslike.

Letty had other things to think about. She had rung up Carol as soon as Burt left the office. Carol came to see her that evening. "I can't discuss it over the phone," Letty told her. Carol came in silver fox and black broadtail. She listened to what Letty had to say to her, incredulous.

"You don't believe it?" she said. And when Letty said that she did, Carol was forced to admit that she believed it too. Her dark, small face hardened. "I'll see Tom," she threatened, "and what I'll tell him won't be fit to print."

"What's the use?" Letty asked her wearily. "I just thought you'd better know. He — Burt Barker — he's — oh, I don't know what he is, angry, crazy with resentment. If ever he sees Tom again! It was a terrible thing," she said somberly. "Carol, did you ever know that Sonia's heart was bad?"

Carol hadn't known it. She knew it now. She went to Nelda first before approaching her brother. Nelda told her all she knew. It had been Tom, of course, there hadn't been the faintest chance that it could have been anyone else.

Carol went to Brooklyn. She dismissed her car and went by subway, vaguely wondering how on earth she had ever traveled that great distance all those years, in the press and jam and confusion and smells and noises. So quickly does one become adjusted to ease and luxury.

She had telephoned her father first. "This time," she told him, "I want to see Tom, it's important."

In the little house Tom awaited her arrival without much interest. She walked over from the subway, trying not to think the thoughts which came to her, trying to keep her heart from twisting, pacing the few steps between the street and porch. She regarded Tom, there in the shabby familiar living room, with something more bitter than scorn.

"Oh," said Tom, "so you've condescended to come back to the old manor."

"You needn't," Carol told him sharply, "take that tone with me."

"You look pretty damned prosperous," he told her, ignoring that, "I suppose the beauty business is flourishing — depression or no depression?"

"I'm all right," said Carol shortly.

"Good for a touch?" asked Tom, turning his pockets inside out and smiling. He had his engaging moments still; he was too young and

178

too vital to have lost all his charm in a few crowded miserable months.

But Carol was impervious to charm; to his, at any rate. She said. "No, I'm not. I didn't come here for that."

"Why did you come then?" Tom wanted to know. His father turned uneasily in his chair, in which he crouched lax like a very old man. Carol had insisted that he be present at this interview; and he had promised while disliking the idea very much, terrified of it; of what he might be forced to hear — to witness.

"I'll tell you why I came," Carol replied tartly. "I don't suppose you read in the paper of Sonia's death?"

"Who — oh," said Tom, remembering. He was ludicrous in his astonishment. "No, I didn't, what of it?" he inquired.

"Just this. You went in there, drunk, storming around, looking, you said, for me — and Letty. And when no one could give you information you grew ugly, Sonia's son had to put you out. When he got back to the place Sonia was dead. A heart attack. Your fault," she flung at him.

"That's damned silly." He began to laugh; stopped. He heard his father's startled exclamation. He said sullenly, "How could it be my fault? How'd you know it wouldn't have happened if I hadn't gone there? He — "

179

he jerked a hand in the direction of his father
— "he — swore he didn't know."

The thin, rather mangy aunt was listening
now, looking around the doorway, her spite-
ful eyes on Carol, on her good clothes, but not
too good, Carol hadn't worn the silver fox and
broadtail . . .

Carol said: "That's neither here nor there. I
told you so you'd think twice next time. And
keep out of Burt Barker's way. You had a gun,
didn't you? Oh, don't trouble to deny it. He
took it away from you. Gave it back, I suppose. Well, there's a Sullivan Law. If Barker
ever sees you, wants to make an issue of it — "

Tom said quickly:

"I haven't the gun. I — I only borrowed it.
I've returned it."

"It would be a good idea," said Carol, "if
you'd clear out again and stay out. You aren't
helping pop any, you're just a burden to him.
You haven't work — "

"I've tried, I can't get any," he said angrily.

Carol took out her purse, opened it, and
under his eager eyes removed and folded
together two fifty-dollar bills.

"I'll stake you," said Carol, "to a long train
trip."

His hand went out. Then he put it in his
pocket and stood looking down at her. She
put the money on the table between them.

"Take it or leave it, it's the last cent you'll get from me," she said, and rose.

Tom said:

"Generous, aren't you? After all, with business so good you could afford a little more. A grand," said Tom, "wouldn't be too much."

Carol said briefly, "That's all. Not another cent. I want to talk to pop," she said.

"Wait a minute," Tom told her. He came up close, walking with that strength and vitality native to him and undimmed by his careless slouch. "You want me to get out of town, don't you? Afraid I'll find out who you're living with and ask him to increase your allowance so you can help your family more — ?"

"Tom!" said his father, in anguish.

But it had been said. Tom turned on his father a moment, flashing into sullen anger.

"You know," he said, "you know what she's doing. Buyer!" He laughed. "Seller, that's more like it. You knew," he repeated, "and pretended not to, so you could take her money. Oh, I'm on to that, saves your face. Well, *I* don't care how she gets it," said Tom, and snatched up the bills on the table and thrust them into his empty pockets and was gone, slamming the outer door behind him. The listening spinster aunt clucked and withdrew, her nose sharp and uplifted. Mr. Merrick sat quite still.

181

Carol said, uncomfortably,

"Why pay any attention to him? He's just no good, pop."

Merrick thought, dully. Both of you. No good. He said something, anything. A sop, thrown out to the decencies. "Oh, that's all right," he said. He sat there still thinking long after she had left. It had all been said between them. She had denied nothing. Even had she denied it, what was the use? He couldn't take any more money from her now. A check lay between his fingers, a slim green slip of paper. Every week or so, the money came, money order, check, cash. He wouldn't take it. As long as he had blinded himself, deafened himself. But now . . .

He had to take it. There was no other way out. His stubby workman's fingers which had poised the check to tear it, fell listlessly apart. The check fluttered to the floor. He sat there staring at it. Later he would stoop painfully and pick it up. Stoop. He was old and frightened and bitterly ashamed.

Chapter 10

Tom had, Carol reported to Letty, finally departed. The little house in Bay Ridge was the happier for his going, although the sour aunt, with the curious and unexpected perversity of her kind, suddenly took his part. "If it hadn't been for that girl, in the beginning," she said, "it wouldn't have happened; nothing would have happened." "That girl" was Letty, on whom she had never laid eyes save for fleeting and uninterested glimpses when Letty had been a long-legged, blonde kid racing about the Merrick yard with Tom and Carol, during the aunt's former, infrequent visits.

Winter was not winter that season. It was warm, and strange, with always a sickly suggestion of spring in the air; in the suburbs and even in parts of the town, roses were blooming into January and great fat robins hopped on grass that was still green. Carol went South for the season, as Herbert Gordon would be with his family. She tried to persuade Letty to come with her "for a rest," but Letty shook her small head stubbornly and stayed where she was, the shop working overtime to get its customers into shape for their seasonal parties and activities, to make them lovely and to keep them lovely despite late hours, rich food and indifferent liquor.

Letty had instituted a "traveling operator," one who went to houses on party evenings to give facials and arrange make-ups and generally make herself useful; a clever girl who could marcel as well as finger wave. This operator was in great demand, evenings. The charges for these services were higher than in the shop and the other girls envious as, although the work was after hours, the tips were also larger than the salon tips and Letty permitted a percentage of the proceeds to the girl. The other girls begged for the chance and if the season kept on as well as it had begun, thought Letty, there was no reason why all of them should not be on call, so to speak, unless the hair work was definitely desired. Most of them could finger wave, but marcelling was another matter.

The season did go on well, much to Letty's relief. She was, of course, greatly in demand at the shop and, as she had at Sonia's, she found her clients for the most part querulously confidential. Strange stories were told in that atmosphere and Letty saw and heard a good deal. She was daily learning something about life and a side of life that dealt with ugly things, fear, greed, jealousy, envy . . . these were the emotions which brought fine lines to the skin about the eyes and deepened the parentheses at the sides of pretty painted mouths. Most of the women who came to her were afraid of something, of age, of the loss of beauty, of the failure to win or to hold something, love, social position — most of them were greedy, greedy for beauty, for life, for the passing hour; most of them were jealous, of the years, of each other, of the stranger girl passing by on the street with unclouded eyes and a light step; and most of them were envious, of the prettier woman, the woman with the bigger bank balance, the sable coat, the larger string of pearls, the most attractive lover, the most complacent husband . . .

She spoke of these things to Mortimer Fisher whom she had continued to see, discreetly, but often.

"You get to know too much," she said.

"That's grist to your mill," he laughed; "it's lucky that girls in your job don't go in for blackmail."

She recalled the things Carol had told her when she was first at Sonia's.

"Some do," she said, "in a veiled, small sort of way." She sighed. "I suppose they feel they have to live; and if a woman has been indiscreet in her confidences the girls make no bones about why the bigger tip is given next time. It's all pretty sickening," she added, "and it troubles me, a lot."

"Don't let it," he urged her, "that's a foolish way to look at things. No one's job is all roses, you know."

"I know," she said with her sudden, lovely smile, "and, of course, I do like the work. I like my own place, the authority, all of it. I like working with oils and honey and perfumes; and with Kate. Kate's a great girl. I don't see much of her now that she's over in Long Island City, but she's doing a good job. Too good, and not, really, worthy of her. I'll lose her soon I suppose," she complained.

"You can get someone else," he consoled her.

She regarded him with wide, dark eyes.

"I suppose so. It's a little terrifying to think that no one is really indispensable, isn't it?" she asked him.

"What a humor you're in tonight!" he said lightly, gently.

"I'm not, really. I like a lot of the people who come in to me. The débutantes in their first season. Many of them are so pretty and eager and have such lovely unspoiled skin, and eyes. I keep wondering how long that will last. Then there are some of the successful career women, they're fun too. Mary Dart, the novelist; she's a real beauty if you like, not just features but expression, animation, intelligence. She'd never come to me if her sister didn't drag her to the shop every couple of weeks. Her sister guards her like — like a bit of china. And is so proud of her, her red hair and her creamy skin. Then I've several young married women, Westchester, Long Island, New York. They're sweet, with their talk of houses and babies and gardens and bridge lessons and keeping up with the Joneses."

"It sounds intolerably dull," Fisher told her.

"I suppose so, to you; to a lot of us, if we stop to get cynical about it. We don't think people are really living," said Letty seriously, "unless they are making careers or experiencing great tragedies or romances. Bridge, babies, gardens, husbands coming home on the five-fifteen. It does sound dull. But it's not all surface, it has roots, somehow."

"*You* sound," he said, and his eyes were anxious, "as if you were wishing — ?"

"Perhaps I am, perhaps I do, sometimes," she said, laughing frankly. "But then, again, I'm quite content as I am."

"I'm glad. . . . No, I'm not," he muttered after a moment. His eyes were possessive now, jealous. But just for a moment. Then he said slowly:

187

"You can't stick this pace long. Just work. And no — no men friends except me, and I don't count."

"Of course, you count," she contradicted him, a little frightened.

They were having dinner together in her apartment. The competent maid came in and cleared away. The candles flickered, casting eerie dancing shadows. The roses Fisher had sent were dark red velvet in a pewter bowl between them. From next door the sound of a radio came faintly to them. A child ran staggering across the floor above, its small triumphant feet beating an uneven rhythm over their heads.

"Only in business . . . that's as it should be. You aren't — you don't see other men, do you?" he asked her.

"One or two people I've met. They don't matter," she said carelessly.

He sighed. He said:

"So you're content? I'm glad, and I'm sorry."

She said nothing; wiser not to ask him why. Obviously he waited, as obviously he was disappointed when the question did not come.

She reached out her hand for a cigarette, lifted it from a box of old rose-colored china he had given her, a pretty thing, and quaint, and far costlier than she dreamed. Lighting it, she said:

"I've been worried, you know, for fear that — that I could not discharge my debt to you, properly. I couldn't, of course, not the real debt; but I mean the money part of it. But if things keep up — "

"If they keep up, you'll buy me out," he said, laughing. "Meantime the interest comes in on the nail. I don't mean to drive you that hard. I'd give you some leeway, my dear. You've been a very good investment. When you do buy me out I'll be sorry — and glad."

There it was again. She couldn't resist it this time. She asked, "Why — glad?" and regretted it instantly.

The candlelight flared between them, and died to a steadier glow. He looked at her across the small table set up in a corner of the living room.

"It isn't easy seeing you," he said quietly, "but I couldn't endure it, if I didn't."

She said, low:

"Please, please don't talk like that. If you do, it will spoil everything."

She was right and he knew it. If he "talked like that" she must send him away, must refuse herself to him; the business arrangement would remain, awkward, a burden instead of a bright secret between two good friends.

He said:

"Very well, I won't. I know when I'm well

189

off — better off, that is, than I would be if I made a fool of myself. . . . Things aren't so pleasant at the place I call home," he admitted after a moment, "and I've grown to depend on this little haven — and you."

That was true and she knew it. They were silent a moment, in the spell of candlelight and the drift of slow blue smoke and the scent of roses piercing through, and then Letty reminded him.

"If we're to be on time for the theater, hadn't we better go?"

They were going downtown to a remodeled barn to see the work of some frustrated genius. Now and then they went to an uptown theater together, but not too often. It was rather fun discovering the "little theaters" during the summer a few miles out of town, winters down in the village, and sitting through what were usually dreadful productions and long-winded, very bad plays, and amusing themselves watching the eager, vivid, generally foreign audience, who enjoyed itself, quarreled and argued and was terribly articulate on the subject of art.

During that winter they grew imperceptibly closer. Their speech together was more intimate, more dangerous, their silences full of peril. Little by little, as he had done when they first knew each other, Mortimer Fisher was building up in Letty's mind a picture of himself. He did it by brief sentences, broken off, by fragments, phrases, a word here and there.

Eva Fisher was more than ever a stranger to him, aging rapidly, very nervous, feverishly immersed in her makeshift activities. The three children were more than strangers, careless, indifferent, armed with a deadly courtesy, and giving him no confidence. The two boys were already beginning to be an anxiety. One was, that winter, expelled from his preparatory school for no trivial offense. The other was given to fits of sullenness and temper which would one day get him in serious trouble. The girl, said Mortimer, was impossible. "Pretty as paint and twice as fresh."

Money, that's what they cared most for. As long as he made the money and was generous with it, nothing else mattered. He was a machine to them. Money for his wife's charities, money she gave away because it made her feel important to give, and money for the children to squander, he told Letty.

When spring came he said to her one night, walking with her back from the corner where he had left his car:

"I won't come in, tonight."

It was early. They had been to an exhibition of costumes, in which she was interested, at one of the galleries.

"It's not late," she said.

"I know. But it's too late for me. I'm too damned lonely, Letty," he said abruptly.

They stood in front of her apartment house. Her eyes were dark with pain and questioning and his were veiled. Hatless he stood there, and then after a moment turned abruptly and walked away. He did not say goodnight.

Troubled, she went in alone. The part-time maid was there, she always waited the nights Fisher was expected. Now, Letty told her she might go, and the girl went, wondering in her shrewd discreet mind. Letty walked through the living room to the windows and stood looking out. After a time she switched off the lights and went to bed. Impossible to sleep. Impossible to tell herself that Fisher's changing attitude — or had it always been the same? — did not trouble her, did not set up a disturbance in her blood. She thought of what Carol would say, Carol back from the South, restless, going North, more restless still, taking a little house at Long Beach, coming back to town now and then for treatments, chattering, saying very little, losing much of her impulse toward confidences, talking very rarely of Herbert Gordon.

Of course, it had been too good to be true, this friendship. Things didn't go on like that.

He'd been attracted to her from the beginning. If he hadn't been, she told herself frankly, he wouldn't have done for her what he had done. Men weren't made that way. They had to be interested — first.

He asked nothing of her, demanding nothing. But the import was plain enough. They weren't drifting blindly, they were drifting consciously, with their eyes wide open. Letty was intelligent enough to know that.

He did not come near her for several weeks. Once the confidential secretary telephoned her on some matter connected with the business. He made up the income tax reports, did Mr. Watts, and kept in touch with every phase of the business. At the end of his conversation he told her, briefly, that Mr. Fisher was out of town.

Well, it was nothing to her, or should be nothing to her. She missed him, of course, but that was quite natural. Among a hundred acquaintances he was certainly her closest friend.

Lunching one day with the interior decorator who had done her shop, Letty was amazed to see Burt Barker and Sally Richards, the operator in her own employ, leaving the restaurant together talking animatedly.

It was a small, uncrowded place, near the shop where Miss Morgan wove her wonders with chintz and polished wood and bits of brocade and all the rest; that was why they had selected it, and in order to talk business, for Letty was taking on more space and Frances Morgan was to have charge of the decorating. "What's the matter?" asked Frances as Letty laid down her fork with a little clatter.

"Nothing."

But she was disturbed. Sally — and Burt Barker? But it wasn't really incredible, she supposed sensibly, when she was back in her office. Sally was pretty and pert and Burt was a man and they might have met in one of a hundred different places.

But suddenly it became important to her to know where they had met.

Calling up Nelda, she asked her carelessly, that evening, during the conversation and an invitation to dinner and a theater, "By the way, have you ever heard of a girl called Sally Richards?"

Nelda had. She'd been, replied Nelda, an operator at Sonia's. A good one. She'd left them abruptly, oh, very abruptly, some time ago. About the time Burt took over the place, Nelda said. "Why?"

"No reason," said Letty, "except that I have her. She is clever, I think."

Not clever enough. She asked Sally the next

day. "You were at Sonia's place, weren't you, after you left the Lawrence Hotel?"

Sally made an error. She said, "Why, no, I wasn't. I came, direct."

She lied, obviously. A few days later, after seeing Nelda, Letty knew definitely that she had lied. She dismissed the girl, without further ado.

"But — haven't I given satisfaction?"

"Certainly," said Letty without rancor, "you're a very good operator. But you lied to me. Why, I don't know. You were at Sonia's for some months after you left the Lawrence. You made no mention of this to me when I engaged you. You denied it when I asked you. Why, I haven't the faintest idea. But I won't have a liar in my employ."

The girl flushed to the strong springing roots of her lovely red hair. She said something under her breath which Letty didn't catch. And left the room, swinging about on an impertinent high heel. Letty sat back watching her. She could be replaced, of course.

But it was too much of a coincidence, her leaving Sonia's after Burt came in as its owner, her being seen with Burt. . . . If they were such good friends, how illogical of her to have left his employ. There could be but one explanation.

This was made clearer to her as the rumors

which had never ceased to reach her reached her in greater numbers. They were not all concerned with her association with a "backer." Some were concerned with her shop and its methods, the "inferiority" of her formulas, the basic materials with which she worked. And absurd stories about women who had been "ruined, my dear, absolutely ruined" by her method of face culture. And about one who had had her scalp badly burned by a careless operator, and another whose permanent wave had resulted in dire things.

It lost her few, if any, customers. Her customers, if they heard, denied, and came to her. "I think you should know, Miss Lawson, that there is a good deal of malicious gossip going about."

Letty was unhappy about it. There was nothing she could do but fight back, her weapons being merely her integrity. But that the rumors came from the girl she had dismissed she was certain; a girl, she thought, in Barker's pay.

The girl was, therefore, merely an instrument.

Letty was partly right. Sally spread the rumors. She had gone back to Sonia's where Nelda refused to engage her. She had appealed to Burt. Without disclosing his transaction with her, he couldn't go over Nelda's head. He overpaid Sally for her work and gave her a recommendation. Eventually she was taken on again by the Lawrence Hotel. To do him justice, none of the ugly legends had been spread by him; he had never even heard them. Sally had been paid merely to watch Letty's methods and any innovations she might make. This much was proven by the establishing of Sonia operators who went out evenings to private houses just as Letty's did.

But Sally had fallen in love with her comrade in intrigue, with all of her shallow, jealous little heart. It did her no good, she made it too plain and Burt, uncomfortable and astonished, had seen it and had also seen to it that he did not see her again.

The rumors died, cropped up again. Lonely, and a little frightened at the harm people did, consciously and with malice, Letty found herself looking forward to Mortimer Fisher's return to town. He seemed the one stable thing in a very uncertain world. On the night he returned she motored a little way out of town with him to dine in the old inn which was quiet and pleasant and to which they had often gone before.

"I missed you," she said frankly.

"Don't say that if you don't mean it," he told her somberly.

"I do mean it."

"Things been going wrong?"

"No. Yes." Suddenly she told him of the talk, the gossip. She betrayed no names and noticed no suspicions. "But," she ended, "it's all pretty disheartening."

"I know. People hate others to be happy. As — as happy as I could be, with you, Letty. But we'd never let them know. We'd be partners, as we are now. Secretly."

That was all, but it was enough. She trembled and did not speak. Later, going back in the car, he caught her to him in that dark, intimate cell as they purred along a lonely road and kissed her not once but many times, hungrily and roughly. Then he pushed her from him suddenly and said, his voice out of control:

"That mustn't happen again."

He asked no pardon. He was exultant, not abject. Letty said, "No," in a small voice, her face, her mouth burning.

She was tempted, terribly. Lonely and young, and her body awakening to its demands. She had no one, no one who cared enough about her to be hurt by anything she did. She might make for herself and Mortimer Fisher a very quiet, a very secret garden of happiness . . .

She was earning her living. She was under no obligation to him financially which she wasn't paying, couldn't pay. She was free, not bound. If she chose to take her friend as her lover, no one need be the wiser. The few people who knew of their association probably thought he was her lover anyway. Except Carol. Perhaps even Carol thought so now. She had said things, certain things, and smiled a little at Letty's hot denials.

She couldn't decide now, overnight. She must come to her decision slowly, she must turn it over in her mind, must think it out from every angle. Then make up her mind, once and for all; and whatever she did she must not have any regrets. She loathed people who did what they wanted and then whined about it.

He understood, she thought. They had spoken no word the rest of the way home. Leaving her at her door he had asked her:

"You aren't angry with me, Letty?"

"No," she had responded slowly. "No, I'm not angry, Morty."

"Then — ?"

"Please . . . " She put her narrow hand in his own. "Please. Don't ask me anything. Not now."

For a moment triumph was naked in his eyes, and unashamed. But he had waited so long he could wait a little longer.

"All right," he said, so briefly, so practically, so without emotion, in so commonplace a phrase and tone that she could have laughed and blessed him. He would give her, she thought, all the time she wanted. But did she need it? She thought, trembling and alone, that she loved him. Was it necessary to argue further with herself?

Was she a coward because she could not tell him at once that, as frankly as she had laid her hands in his so would she entrust her life to his devotion and his protection.

She did not know. Perhaps she was. Perhaps something in her blood, unmoved by the disturbance of her pulses, was both coward and conscience.

Chapter 11

True to his word, to that brief "All right" which constituted a promise, Fisher's attitude did not change toward her. There was no demand, no urgency. Yet sometimes she felt as if he were very sure of himself, of the outcome of the issue. He went away again on one of his trips and, returning, stopped off at White Sulphur for golf.

He did not write her. He had never written her, not a line. There was an element of caution in that which offended her when she thought about it, which was rarely; she did not permit herself to think about it. Better so.

She spent a week-end at Long Beach with Carol. They were alone, in the absurd bright pink little cottage with its flat, oriental roof and gay flower boxes. The ocean was bright and blue and immense from the windows and the air, undaunted by the myriad cars breathing their defiant carbon monoxide, was salt and keen.

Except for a too-knowing mulatto maid Carol and Letty were alone. They bathed, sunned themselves on as quiet a corner of the beach as they could find, walked on the boardwalk, went to bed early. Herbert Gordon, said Carol briefly, was in Southampton.

Carol had changed. Curiously, indefinitely. If she was harder in one sense, fine lines about the delicate skin of her eyes and petulant mouth, she had also softened. She flung out strange emotional sentences which disturbed her friend. She said, once, "Lots of people would think I was damned lucky. I thought so, too — once."

Letty asked her again, "You're not unhappy?"

A difference in phrasing, slight but telling. This time Carol's answer was different, too.

"If I am, what of it? You can't have everything," she said.

Before Letty left she knew; not much, but enough. Carol had fallen in love for the first time in her life. With a man she'd met casually enough, somewhere. A young man, goodlooking, vital. No money, of course, and plenty of scruples. He didn't know about her and Gordon — yet. He would know. It was only a matter of time.

"You think you can get away with it," said Carol morosely, "you can't."

Letty's heart twisted and her mouth set a little. But she thought, it would be different with her — and Mortimer Fisher. They really cared for one another. Carol — Carol liked Herbert Gordon, was fond of him even, grateful, perhaps. But she did not love him. And what Gordon felt for Carol was probably not love, but a jealous possessiveness, a vicarious snatching after youth, thought Letty, not really knowing. In a sense it was a business arrangement. . . .

She went back to town, rested but unutterably depressed. On her first evening at home, Fisher telephoned. Could he see her? Could she give him dinner quietly, no fuss, no furbelows? He had something to tell her, wished, he said, to consult her.

His voice sounded changed, strained. As she replaced the receiver various wild thoughts invaded her brain. Had Eva Fisher discovered their association, did she threaten trouble? Would it lead to a divorce and resultant scandal? She faced that thought sitting there by the table on which the telephone stood. Could she endure it, the dragging through headlines, the gossip sheets? Was it too big a price to pay, would there be ultimate happiness if it came in that way?

If he could endure it, she could, she told herself bravely. Rising and going into the kitchen to order dinner, walking back slowly, thoughtfully, to her bedroom to change, she thought further, perhaps it wasn't that, perhaps Fisher had persuaded his wife to a quiet divorce. In that case ——

She did not, for one instant, doubt him. That he would marry her, if it were possible, she was sure. She was spared the anxious speculations which might have come to another woman.

But when he came she saw swiftly, looking at him, feeling his hand on hers in a hard grip of greeting, that whatever bothered him, it had nothing to do with their friendship. His face relaxed from its drawn lines, he looked about him gratefully.

"If you knew," he said, "how good this is, after all I've been through!"

It wasn't until after dinner that he told her. They were alone in the living room. The good, strong, black coffee grew cold in his cup while he talked.

It was his daughter, he said.

Letty's mind leapt to all sorts of dreadful possibilities. Was she ill, had she eloped, what on earth had happened to her? It was the first time she had ever heard Mortimer Fisher speak of any of his children other than dispassionately. He complained of them to her but in a cool, detached manner. She had had a feeling that he tolerated, rather than cared for them deeply.

Even now, listening, she found herself wondering vaguely, and disliking herself for it, if Fisher's present anxiety and anger rose from his pride or his parental affection.

Briefly, the youngster had become involved with a life guard at a public beach.

"But *how?*" asked Letty, astonished beyond measure.

He sat back against the shabby pleasant upholstery of the divan and looked at her quizzically. He was aware of her, she thought, despite his preoccupation with these things which had so little to do with her. Her pulse quickened.

"*How* — you ask," he said smiling; "you don't ask — well — *why?*"

Letty considered this gravely.

"No. Why should I?" she inquired. "I can see why."

"You can? That's more than I can manage," he informed her.

"Morty," said Letty, "don't for heaven's sake be a stuffed shirt!" And as he looked at her, amazed and amused, she went on, astonished at her own vehemence; "Isn't it perfectly natural, if the boy, whoever he is, is attractive? He's out of her world, I admit that; probably out of her class, I suppose I must admit that too, but I don't know why I should," she added thoughtfully, "until I know some-

205

thing more about him. Lots of perfectly nice boys become life guards during the summer, boys from universities, boys with wholly possible families and backgrounds. At all events from the little you've told me of Gerry, she's spoiled, she's bored, she's looking for new adventures, new people. Probably she's fed up with her own crowd; and from what I've seen of the boys of her own generation," remarked Letty, as if she were forty, "I can't say I blame her. I've seen them around, at hotels and restaurants, vacations. The majority of them are a spineless looking lot," she said scornfully. "I think I understand Gerry and her life guard — if, at all events he's anything like the life guards you see on magazine covers," she ended, smiling.

"My dear child!" exclaimed Fisher. He laughed, and his face relaxed into lines of pure merriment. "What a grand pleader of a cause. Am I to take this lad to my bosom and give my blessing?"

"No, of course not," said Letty rather crossly, "that is, unless he turns out to be —— "

"You read too much fiction," he interrupted her, still laughing.

"I suppose," said Letty as if she were just making a discovery, as indeed she was, "I suppose I'm incurably romantic. No, I don't plead Gerry's cause. But you asked me why I didn't ask why; and *I* answered. *You* haven't answered the how."

"Oh, that's simple," he said, grave again. "Eva — her mother doesn't pay much attention to her; or to the boys, for that matter. She says she can't control them and she rushes off to another directors' meeting in order to play God to a bunch of slum babies and lets her own run wild. That's modern motherhood for you," said Fisher. "The family is officially at Southampton. The boys aren't there much, they visit around a lot. Gerry doesn't stick to anything more than six minutes but she's taking some kind of a course, heaven knows what, interior decoration, bathtub gin making, short story writing, tap dancing — I don't know. I simply pay the bills. At all events she told her mother that she didn't want to come down to the Island yet, she'd stay in town with some friend of hers, a young married woman, who has closed her Nantucket place because of the depression and is 'managing' in a penthouse. Her mother consented, I suppose — always provided she was consulted. And that's that. Apparently Gerry betook herself to the beach with a crowd, on a lark. Another adventure. And that's that."

"I see," said Letty. She didn't see, really. If Eva was lax, so was Mortimer. He had seemed uncertain about the woman's name with whom

207

Gerry was staying — if she was. Her heart sank a little. "What beach?" she asked.

He told her.

"Where is Gerry now?" Letty wanted to know.

"At Southampton. And she'll stay there," he said grimly. "I heard all about it as soon as I came home. By hysterical telephone, so I had her mother meet me in town and take Gerry back with her."

"Does she — does she think she's in love with this boy?" asked Letty slowly.

"Oh, of course! She thinks he's 'marvelous.' She doesn't even know his name," said Fisher, "or if she does, she won't tell me. She says she'd 'follow him barefoot over the face of the earth, hunger and thirst with him,'" he repeated incredulously, while Letty stared at him. "She's always been pretty extravagant in her affections, if you want to call them that; as well as in her speech. This isn't the first time, there was a riding master at her school. He was married, as it happened. This new Romeo may be, for all I know. She swears he isn't. She says he doesn't know who *she* is and therefore loves her for herself! Fat chance!" He laughed shortly. "It won't last with her, it can't. Once she was set on being an opera star. She has a voice, a good one, I spent thousands on her, was willing to spend as much more when she was older. But the craze died. This one will too. Meantime, it worries me. She makes threats, she'll run away, she'll kill herself —— "

Letty sighed. She was very young, not much older than Gerry Fisher, but she felt as if she might have been the child's grandmother. Undisciplined youth, wearing itself out in phrases and fantasies, beating its white breast against the cage of average existence ——

"Have you seen this boy?" she asked practically.

"No. But unless I can get her promise not to meet him again, I shall. He — he can probably be bought off," Fisher said cynically, "as the riding master was."

"Do you really think everyone can be bought — or bought off?" Letty asked him. She did not know her voice was, at that moment, as cold as her heart had suddenly become.

"Why, no," he replied swiftly, "of course not. I meant — You know what I meant." Abruptly he lacked ease, poise. To cover a momentary awkwardness he reached in his pocket and took out some snapshots.

"I've these to go on. She fought before she'd give them up," he said with a certain satisfaction.

Letty took them. There was a beach, black

with people; a listless ocean with more bathers in it than water; bright sunlight; and Gerry Fisher, pretty, pert, posed cheaply with a young man, both of them wearing brief bathing suits. Hers was a mere shellacking of material, for the final decencies' sake, over her shapely limbs and young torso; his was the prescribed affair for life guards, with his authority in great letters across a broad chest.

"Good-looking youngster," said Fisher indifferently.

Letty stared at the little pictures. She dared not raise her eyes. She thought her face must betray her.

The man was Tom Merrick.

In the instant it took to look at the pictures again and return them to Fisher, she had made up her mind. She would see Tom, do what she could. She would not tell Mortimer of her decision or her knowledge of Tom. No sense in that. One became too involved. If she could see him and persuade him to discourage Gerry, to go elsewhere, to do something, for once in his life, honorable, sensible, decent . . . then she would have in some small measure repaid a part of her debt to Gerry's father, and Fisher need never know.

"What do you think of him?" asked Fisher casually.

"I don't know what to think," she answered

truthfully enough.

"What do you advise me to do?"

That sounded strange to her; even to him, a little. He laughed. "You aren't very much older than Gerry," he apologized, "but, Letty, you're so sane. Too sane sometimes," he said under his breath, on the heels of a sigh.

She shook her head. She said:

"If you want to know what I think . . . Let it ride, get her promise not to see him for a week, two weeks. If that doesn't work — well — by then you will have found a way out."

He nodded abstractedly.

"I can't," he complained, "keep her locked up. She's too old for that, now. I can't even send her to Europe with a chaperone as I did when the riding master affair was at its height. You can't be forever chasing girls off to Europe. I've one very sensible relation in New York, Thelma Murray, a cousin. She's been closer to us than that, though. She took Gerry in hand once before. Unfortunately, she's away now, in California. She's much more influence over the kid than the rest of us. Well," he sighed again and took out his cigarette case, "enough of this. Why I burden you with all my troubles, heaven only knows. That's not so, I do know. But I shan't tell," he told her with a wicked smile. "Now, what about you? What have you done with yourself while I was away and how's the shop getting on? Did you find someone to take Kate's place?"

Gerry was not mentioned between them again until a little later when Fisher was leaving, early, in order to motor down to Southampton that night. At her door Letty said, "Don't worry too much, it will come out all right."

"If you think so, I can believe it," he answered.

But she didn't think so. Tom. The girl had said he didn't know her name. And Fisher had commented that was most unlikely. Letty thought it unlikely too. Tom, lazy, with a greed for money and with very few principles . . .

She tried to think how that had come about. He hadn't been a bad youngster; a big, awkward, wisecracking kid, he'd been. But too much street corner business, too many evenings given to his gangs, too much wisecracking, too much to drink — and all the rest. The deterioration in his character had been slow but it had come about, from all Carol had told her. Perhaps it hadn't been inevitable. Many boys of his type in just his ordinary circumstances grew up and became good citizens. His circumstances had been fortunate rather than otherwise, parents who loved him, a place to sleep, and food to eat, an average education, a home open to his friends.

His mother, thought Letty painfully, had blamed his leaving home that time on her. She sat on the edge of her bed and faced that. His leaving home had given the final impetus to that deterioration, that much was certain. But *was* it her fault? She did not love him, never had, never could. Had it been intended that she supremely sacrifice herself in order to strengthen Tom Merrick's character? She couldn't believe that; couldn't believe that such a decision on her part would have strengthened it essentially. The weakness must have been inherent.

Late that night she lay awake, trying to decide what to do. Carol came into town the next morning for a treatment. She came in once a week, and she bought enough of Letty's preparations to set up a shop of her own. She had also paid her bill to the book-keeper's grumbling satisfaction.

Letty gave her the treatment; and, in the course of it, told her, low-voiced, what had happened. Carol twisted around under the cool, firm hands.

"Morty's daughter and Tom . . . !" she said. "Well, for godsake!"

It struck her as supremely comic. Then she sobered.

"Better not get mixed up in it, Letty," she warned her, "you'd get in over your head."

"I suppose so. Can't *you* do anything?"

"Not me. I'm having my own troubles." In a lower, more rapid voice she told her that Gordon had come unexpectedly to the doll's house at Long Beach. The other man was there. "For dinner, Letty, perfectly proper, nothing to it, I'd asked some other people, they didn't turn up."

But Gordon had outstayed the young man. There'd been a scene. And he had delivered an ultimatum.

"I've got to take it," said Carol, "on the chin. And like it. There's nothing else to do."

"You don't love this — this other man enough," asked Letty gently. She did not even know his name.

"George? Yes. But what good does that do? He — wants to marry me. We'd be poor and happy, he says," said Carol. "Well, I can't marry him. If he knew he wouldn't marry me. If I hooked him and let him find out after, that would be a rotten trick, wouldn't it? I'd live in fear all my life. And I'm soft, too," said Carol a little wildly, "I couldn't go back to a walk-up and washing dishes, not for any man. Oh, hell, perhaps I could," she muttered, "I don't know."

Letty said nothing. There was nothing to

214

say. Carol stirred again.

"Do you think this Fisher brat would marry Tom?" she asked. "That would certainly fix up the family fortunes."

"Oh, Carol," said Letty, half laughing, "I don't think anything of the kind. I doubt if Mortimer would permit it. He doesn't think the girl knows her own mind for two minutes on end. You — couldn't you do something, really?"

"No. The last thing I want to do is look up my darling brother," said Carol firmly. "He'd prove too troublesome. He has a hundred bucks of mine — or did have it — and that's the last he'll get from me. I'm not going to try and run him out of town again. Your boy friend will have to fix this his own way. He's old enough to handle such a situation," said Carol, "and God knows he's had plenty of experience of one kind or another. Letty, does that astringent tonic of yours do anything to dark circles under the old orbs? I haven't been sleeping —— "

"No," said Letty. "No, it won't help, not actually. You can use a little nourishing cream, the tonic as a pick-up and the herbal eye packs. But what you need is sleep and less gin and cigarettes. Then, if the circles persist, a doctor is indicated."

"You're a helluva saleswoman," said Carol resignedly.

"Are you taking things to make you sleep?" Letty asked her.

"Oh, on and off. They don't give the results they used to," Carol told her.

"I thought so. I saw the bottle on your bedside table. Cut that out, Carol," warned Letty, "a little insomnia is better than a lot of habit."

"Oh, you can talk," said Carol disgruntled, "nothing bothers you. You've your health and your independence and a good business and not a care in the world. But," she said, "it can't go on forever, I'm telling you."

Slangy the note on which she ended but the phrase meant just what it said. She was telling Letty; and she knew, none better.

During the rest of the week Letty thought over the whole situation. There was no help to be found in Carol. And Dan Merrick, provided she went over to Brooklyn and placed the situation before him, would be of no possible assistance. He had absolutely no influence with his son. Perhaps Carol was right; indeed, she must be right, Fisher could handle the matter for himself and in his own way. But Letty was just a little doubtful of that way. Long association with him had shown her that it would be a way arrogant to insolence, roughshod. And Tom had shown himself ugly and undisciplined before. This time it wouldn't be a matter of absurd, borrowed guns brandished in drunken bravado; nor an affair of high and profane words. One revenge for any attack of Fisher's lay nicely in Tom's hand. Gerry Fisher was eighteen. In New York State a girl may marry at eighteen, without her parents' consent. Gerry could do this, in the high, early flush of her rebellion and her romance. If she did, that she would live to repent it, Letty didn't for a moment doubt. Tom, too, for it was entirely on the cards that Mortimer Fisher would cut off his only daughter with less than the proverbial shilling. In fact it was unthinkable, knowing the man and his past relations with his children, that he would do otherwise, unless his pride forced him to dole out a grudging allowance, thought Letty.

Tom was no fool. He would see how readily that weapon lay to service; he would probably use it. There would be a butchered story in the headlines to make a tabloid holiday: *"Heiress Elopes with Life Guard!"*

She could, she thought, spare them all that, with any luck. Her relations with Tom were not friendly, and had not been since their last meeting. But she had generally been able to influence him. Perhaps in this instance she still could.

Her mind was made up. It was now Friday. Mortimer had come to see her on Tuesday.

On Sunday afternoon she would give herself a brief vacation and go to the public beach on whose strewn sands Gerry Fisher had found her new romance and look for Tom and beg him to listen to her. If he would not listen to reason — But he must listen to reason. After all, he must, somewhere, have retained a modicum of common sense.

On Sunday she went in the subway crowded with humanity, strewn with papers, where children cried and dragged at their mothers and where the stale, hot air was stirred by electric fans battling bravely and vainly against a heat wave of early summer and the many odors, all of them unpleasant.

Chapter 12

Arriving at the beach, Letty picked her way across the sand still visible between the strewn papers, the bottles, the mass of humanity. The beach cleaners were busy and efficient but it was impossible for them to keep up with the general, rooted untidiness of thousands of people. There was an incessant noise; laughter, shrieks, the weeping of children. There were luncheon baskets; there were boys running races, playing medicine ball. There were enclosures for games, filled with leaping youngsters. There were obese women and thin women, hundreds of girls in scanty suits, hundreds of men. Everyone was talking, laughing, shouting. Everything was motion, noise, agitation. Bronzed shoulders and backs, arms and necks as red as flame, tossed hair, sand, movement, color, life. And the dirty water creaming in at the edge of the dirty beach bringing with it bits of flotsam, sticks, orange peels, seaweed. In the water thousands of people swam, or hopped noisily up and down, clinging to ropes. It was a still day, very hot. There was not one atom of shade, of relief. There were no breakers, only the water curving to a small, harmless wave at the rim of the beach. Children waded, children leaped back in simulated terror, dug holes to watch them fill with the mysterious fluid, looked for shells, clambered on rocks, sought for the little scuttling crabs; hurt themselves, howled, were comforted; were lost, were found again.

And all this against a background of barkers, carousels, merry-go-round music. And people, more people, coming in by car, by subway, the women in gaudy pajamas, regardless of size or age, or in bathing suits with towels draped around them in order to conform to the law.

Letty looked for Tom. Her eyes hurt and her brain ached with the light and the confusion. She had often come to the beaches, all of them, the noisy ones and those which were a little more quiet, before leaving Brooklyn. Somehow they had seemed to her exciting, amusing, quite normal. Today the beach seemed abnormal, a curious living growth of confusion and crowding. She looked about her at the patient mothers, the impatient mothers. Some of them had brought their children here from the hot tenements, for a breath of fresh air, and would stay with them all day on the sand, cramming their little stomachs with unusual and indigestible food, permitting them to become sunburned to the point of illness, and they would finally drag them home again, weeping, worn out, half sick, and feel that a good day's work had been done. Wouldn't, thought Letty, the city streets, the tenements even, be better? But she supposed not, picking her way across the sand, looking for Tom, cool and slim and lovely in her linen suit and her big shady hat and her sensible small sport shoes.

Then she saw him.

No one was apt to drown today in that still water, unless from too much food or too much heat. Tom was not sitting on the tower dedicated to the life guard. He was standing, in a group of laughing girls, himself laughing. He was very big and very brown, and his teeth were white in his incessant smile and his eyes were brazen and caressing . . .

The girls flocked about him, squealed, wisecracked, pawed at him with their predatory little hands.

Letty came closer and spoke his name. He did not hear her, the still air was filled with shouting. A girl heard her, a small, plump girl in a scarlet sheath. Turning she regarded Letty slowly, insolently. Then she took Tom's arm, clasping it in a little tanned hand with reddened, dirty fingernails.

"Who's the Queen of England, big boy?" she wanted to know.

Tom turned, at that. His expression was ludicrous. His jaw sagged, his eyes expressed unbelief. All the self-confidence, the laughing arrogance dropped from him. He said simply, "Well, I'll be a son-of-a-gun."

"If I could speak to you a minute?" said Letty, smiling at him.

A friendly smile, a little appealing. The girls who giggled and milled about looked at her with distinct hostility. They whispered among themselves. Tom turned back to them, his self-confidence returned. He spoke with a negligent gesture of his big paw, "Scram. Can't you see I've got a date?" he ordered.

The girl in the scarlet suit pouted, sliding her hand over the smooth hardness of his big upper arm. She said, "Boy, are you strong!" And Tom replied, "Baby, you're telling me?"

There was more laughter. Letty waited, standing there. "Scram," said Tom again, a little harshly. The girls scrammed, fluttering into a pseudo-flight, with little flirtings of the hips and wagglings of their rounded rears. "We'll be seeing you," they called back to him.

They were going, not without audible comments. "Mrs. Vanderbilt," said the girl in scarlet, "she's come slumming!"

Now they'd gone. It was a little quieter, here, where they had been. Tom and Letty looked at each other. He asked, "Well, what do you want?" with extreme ungraciousness.

Letty sat down on the sand. She answered:

"To talk to you. Here. Can you sit down a minute?"

He supposed he could. He lowered himself beside her, lay at full length on his lean stomach, his bronzed shoulders gleaming, and looked at her, turning sideways. He said, sneering a little, "It's an honor."

"Please, Tom." She looked at him, the smile erased, a frown creasing her lovely brows. "Let's not quarrel, I came here to —— "

"How did you know I was here?" he asked suddenly. "I haven't told them at home. And Carol — " he looked up at Letty sullenly — "Carol's traveled a long way from a public beach and she not any better than any of the little tarts who come down here to pick up trade, at that."

Letty said, with a sinking heart:

"I knew you were here because — I saw a snapshot of you — and a girl —— "

Tom laughed.

"Want to see more? Oh, I forgot, I haven't my clothes here," he said. "I've an album already. Everyone," said Tom, "wants to have their picture taken with the handsome life guard."

Letty looked down at him, her eyes dark under the wide brim of her hat.

"Tom," she asked quietly, "haven't you made enough trouble?"

"What do you mean, trouble?" he demanded.

"You know. First, that dreadful scene at Sonia's. Tom," Letty asked him, leaning a little closer, "how could you — how could you?"

"Oh, that. I suppose Carol told you." He twisted away from her, propped himself on his elbows, sifted sand through his strong fingers. "Look here, I'm sorry — I didn't mean to — I was pretty well lit, and I was sore at Carol. Yes, and at you, too. So I went there . . . And how did *I* know she had a bum heart?" he demanded querulously. "I didn't do anything, really. All I got was the bum's rush. If I ever see that so-and-so again — " he said, low.

"He may see you first," Letty told him evenly, "and you're liable to find yourself in a station house, with a charge against you."

"What, for instance?"

"Carrying a weapon, for one," she told him.

"You *have* been talking to Carol. It's a sister act. In more ways than one," he said, looking at her slowly, insolently, her smart, simple suit, the handmade blouse, the fine straw of the floppy hat, the sturdy expensive brogues, the stockings, "you don't look exactly on the bread line, Letty."

"Never mind me," she told him. "And never mind about Sonia's now. But there's something you must do for me, unless," she said, feeling her way, "unless you want me to believe that every bit of decency is dead in you, you *will* do it ——"

"Well, what is it?" he asked, astonished.

"Gerry Fisher," she said. "Her father is a friend of mine. He showed me the snapshot of you and of her. He doesn't know I know you. . . . Tom, you must leave the youngster alone. She's a scatterbrained child looking for excitement, thrill, something new. There's nothing in your association that would bring happiness to either of you. Mr. Fisher has forbidden her to see you. If she does so against his will it won't be healthy for either you or for her. And if you have any idea that because she is Mortimer Fisher's daughter things will be made easy for you, you are much mistaken. He is a very determined man. He would turn her out with nothing but the clothes on her back if she disobeyed him in this matter."

She spoke coolly, evenly, her words dropping like little pebbles into the hot clamor all about them. She waited for Tom's answer. To her astonishment he turned away from her and dropped his head on his folded arms and shook with laughter. "Tom!" she said urgently.

Now he looked up, sat up, in one lithe gesture and clasped his hands about his knees.

"So *that's* who she is!" he said. "Mortimer Fisher's daughter! What a swell break!"

Letty's heart shook. So he hadn't known who Gerry was? She had believed that he had. She had done perhaps more harm than good. She said, steadying her voice, so that he would not know the panic that had seized her:

"It's just because she *is* Mortimer Fisher's daughter that I'm warning you."

"Gerry," he said without listening, "she's a cute kid. A hot number, if you ask me. She never told me her name. 'It's more romantic,' she said, 'not knowing names.' She's written me, this week. They kidded the shirt off me . . . Tom, the life guard — it was like a cheap movie. She's nuts about me," he said indifferently.

"That doesn't matter," Letty told him, "she'll get over it. I tell you, Tom, if you try to influence her, if you see her, if she comes here and you don't send her packing, it means trouble, plenty of it."

"What the hell!" he said, suddenly angry, his laughter stilled, his eyes hard on her own. "What difference does it make to you? If you'd stayed decent, Letty, if you hadn't let

226

me down, none of this would have happened. The lousy time I had bumming my way to strange towns — seeing the inside of dirty jails — the business at Sonia's — and this crazy kid chucking herself on my net —— "

Letty looked at him, appalled. He was utterly serious now, oblivious of the crowds, of the people, of the girl in the scarlet suit who kept walking past them, her arm around the slim waist of her closest and most hated girl friend, both of them laughing, making observations. . . .

But there was to be another audience. Mortimer Fisher was driving in from the Island, alone, in an open car. Last night had been excessively unpleasant. Gerry was out of all bounds. Walking up and down, smoking, crushing out one rouge-stained stub, lighting a fresh cigarette, all her rancor against him, her father, her mother, too, her mother who sat white and shaken and utterly helpless in a corner of the big room, poured out in extravagant words. She'd be damned if she'd stop seeing Tom! She'd see him, today, tomorrow, next week. Tell him her name. He was in love with her, she with him. She was sick to death of cake-eaters, sick to nausea of her entire life. She'd be damned if she'd go to Europe, be damned if she'd do anything her father wanted her to do. She hadn't asked to be born! She'd only one life! She'd live it as she saw fit. She'd find some happiness. If they thwarted her, she'd kill herself. No, she wouldn't, she wouldn't give them that much satisfaction. She'd go to Tom, and if he didn't want her she'd go on the *streets*. Anything!

She cast herself on the big couch and burst into hysterical tears, drumming her heels and beating her fists against the pillows, sobbing.

Fisher bribed and threatened. Used to solving problems, rising to all emergencies, accustomed to straightening out all sorts of entanglements seriously affecting many men, he was utterly at sea before this eighteen-year-old child who stormed and wept and uttered insanities and reduced herself and her father and mother to a state of utter exhaustion.

Finally, when she had tired herself out and sat there sullen, her pretty, pert little face ravaged, her eyes swollen, the paint washed from childish lips and cheeks, she listened to a modicum of reason. As usual her mother played no part, save for helpless and unhappy exclamations. But Fisher finally succeeded in wresting a promise from his daughter that she would, as he put it, "behave" herself for, say, a week. If he could prove to her that this Romeo of the beaches was venal and could be bought, would she accept her disillusion? She could do anything her father said — within reason. He offered her a career. She might go on with her singing, study here, study abroad; she would have the way made easy; and he would put no obstacle in her path if, later, she wished to make use of her training.

So the next day, feeling as if he had been physically beaten, he set out to find this impossible young man who had caused all the trouble and who had created so absurd a situation. Yet he felt, driving toward his destination, as if, in a sense, his male sympathies were on the young man's side. After all, what man could resist the sort of attack Gerry would make upon him? Women were fools; but men were damned fools, reflected Fisher gloomily. He had a headache, and he felt like the end of a misspent life. For after Gerry had finally gone to bed, quieted with bromides and promises, he had had a scene with Eva. Irritated beyond all control, he had accused her of being a soft, useless and pitiful creature, unfit for her responsibilities as a mother. She hadn't, of course, answered him back. She never did. If ever, he thought, he could strike one spark from her, of rebellion, defiance, of any emotion, things might be better between them. But she only sat still and permitted his words to fall like hail upon her defenseless head. She only looked at him with wet, unhappy eyes and twisted her hands in her lap and repeated helplessly that the children had outgrown her, that they gave her neither love nor obedience nor even decent respect.

The way was hot and long. The place, when he reached it and parked his car and walked miles, it seemed, from the parking place to reach the beach proper, looked to his hot and tired eyes like a new Inferno which Dante had forgotten to mention. Striding across the strewn sands, his step soft and his heart hard, he became aware of shock. It was simple to find the life guard in that section. A dozen people pointed him out, when he asked. Finding Tom was easy but finding Letty Lawson with him was an amazement.

He thought absurdly — the picture, she saw the snapshot, she's come down here to try and persuade him . . .

But that didn't make sense.

Letty sat in profile to him, her head a little inclined, listening gravely. The young man who, he saw instantly, was a magnificent specimen of youth and vitality, was talking urgently, rapidly. No words were audible at first to Fisher as he approached. And then coming closer, he heard.

"I'll make good. Only give me another chance, Letty. I'd do anything for you, be anything, I swear it, if you loved me —— "

Mortimer Fisher heard. For a single instant he thought he had gone quite insane. Then his mind cleared. He said, "Well, this is rather a surprise," lightly, coolly, and Letty looked up.

She flushed, at once, deeply, darkly. She said, "Tom, it is Mr. Fisher." And Tom, smiling a little, got to his feet.

"No," said Mortimer Fisher. He dropped down beside Letty, and motioned to Tom. "No, go on with your conversation. It was — intensely interesting."

Tom sat down, amazed, looking from one to the other; from Letty's troubled gaze to Mortimer Fisher's hostile, hard eyes. He asked, "Well, what's it all about? A conference?" He looked at Letty accusingly. "You held out on me," he said; she shook her head as Fisher spoke.

"I think you know," said Fisher coolly, "or hasn't Miss Lawson explained?" He hesitated over Tom's name. Letty supplied it at once. He nodded. "I had no idea that you knew each other," he remarked.

Letty said simply, "He's Carol's brother."

"Oh, of course!" Mortimer Fisher regarded them both. Carol's brother. And Letty had lived with Carol's parents for years. That much was explained but not why she had not told him of her knowledge of this boy on the evening he had shown her the snapshots.

"You know why I'm here, Merrick," he said shortly.

Tom knew. He shrugged. He said, "Maybe you take it all too seriously, Mr. Fisher. You and Letty."

Letty's name on the boy's lips was to Fisher an affront. He said, "I hope so"; slowly and carefully as if he talked to a child he began explaining the situation to Tom. His daughter was spoiled, impossibly willful. This infatuation was out of the question. Not that he wasn't sure that Tom was all that was honorable, capable and all the rest. But nothing lasted with Gerry. For Tom's own sake, he thought he should warn him. He wanted, therefore, Tom's promise that he would not try to communicate with her in any way ——

Tom said, and laughed:

"I didn't even know who she was till Letty spilled the beans."

Fisher turned to Letty, trying, as it were, not to see her, her troubled look, her dear and lovely beauty.

"Do you believe that?"

"Yes, yes," she answered. "I'm sorry, Morty."

Tom stirred sharply, and frowned.

Morty, eh?

It was pretty plain to him. Fisher, then, knew Carol. And through Carol, possibly

232

Letty. Letty's prosperity was easily explained, wasn't it? He had been inclined to laugh things off, give Fisher his promise. Now he'd give him a run for his money.

He said, slowly:

"No, I didn't know. Just a cute kid, crazy about me." He lifted his chin defiantly. Fisher looked at him with alien eyes. That was just one of the things you didn't say, no matter what you thought.

"Well," asked Fisher, "what are you going to do about it?"

"She's of age, isn't she?" asked Tom, watching him intently. "She can get married, can't she, if she wants to?"

"So that's your game?" Fisher told him, while Letty drew her breath audibly.

"I don't know," said Tom, enjoying himself, rather.

"Make up your mind," Fisher warned him, "here and now. And if you have any idea of persuading Gerry to an elopement — " He broke off, and continued evenly — "she won't, you know, get a single cent from me, or her mother."

"So that's *your* game?" asked Tom in his turn. He grinned. "It would make a stink in the papers, wouldn't it — with pictures, pretty pictures. *Millionaire's Daughter Loses All for Love?* Flashes of her in a two-room flat, washing dishes at a sink."

Letty said suddenly:

"Tom, don't be a fool. You're just trying to be nasty. You — you don't care for Gerry, you —— "

"You should know," said Mortimer, without thinking. Tom looked at him. He overheard, he thought. He moved his broad, naked shoulders again.

"Whether I do or don't isn't the question."

"Suppose I make it worth your while not to — care?" asked Fisher.

"How?" asked Tom cautiously.

"A job," Fisher replied, "a good one. I've an outfit building a railroad down in South America. Pretty girls, adventure, hard work, good pay. Does that strike you as sensible and worth while?"

"When and how much?" Tom inquired after a moment.

Letty — Letty hadn't softened. Not an inch, not an atom. Every word he'd said had meant nothing to her. Every plea he had made. She didn't love him, she never had, she never would. That was that. He was sick suddenly of the beach and the sun and the stupid, shouting people. South America . . . and pretty girls — and a job — a man's job.

Fisher was answering his question.

"Resign here," he said, "and come to see

me. Tomorrow morning, if possible. In my office. I'll have everything there for you. Your ticket, an advance on salary, a man to tell you what it's all about. A boat sails the end of the week."

Tom hesitated. He looked at Letty. Letty said:

"It's your chance, Tom."

Hell, he might as well. He didn't give a snap of his fingers for any other girl than Letty. Oh, there had been women. He was not without experience, some of it sweet, most of it sordid.

"Otherwise," Fisher was saying, "there are ways and means, you know. I can see to it that you don't hold a job, any job in this town. I have influence."

That was true enough; hounded, jailed, perhaps. The Sonia business coming out. He couldn't look to anyone for help; not his father, not Carol. He rose to his feet and Mortimer rose with him and, turning, held out a hand to help Letty to her feet.

"O.K.," said Tom briefly, "you've got me where the hair's short. I'll be at your office. Tomorrow."

He turned and walked away down the beach.

"Well — " said Letty, inarticulate, wanting to cry, wanting to laugh.

"How did you come?" asked Fisher.

"By subway."

"I've the car here," he said. "We'll drive somewhere and have dinner. I'll telephone home first. I'll see Gerry later this evening and tell her that her young man is purchasable."

They walked across the beach together. People looked after them curiously. Tom once more the center of a crowd of girls was gesticulating, laughing, talking, "Good-by, girls, I'm through," he was saying, "will you miss me?"

They were heartbroken.

"That," bragged Tom, "was Mortimer Fisher. He wants me to take a job with him. Down in South America. I'm a big shot," said Tom, laughing, his heart sore.

The girls were exclaiming. The one in scarlet said:

"But who was the girl friend?"

"Oh, that," said Tom, grinning, "that was an old sweetheart of mine. She wants me back. But I haven't time for women now," said Tom.

Everyone laughed. And a child ran in the water and was caught by a little wave and tumbled. Tom swept the girls aside and effected an easy rescue. The mother ran to him hysterically crying. And the frightened child, choking with water and sand, was restored to her. "I'm a big shot, I am," thought Tom, laughing at himself.

Chapter 13

In silence Letty and Mortimer Fisher walked across the crowded beach and in silence to the parking space. Fisher helped her in and then went through the deft, difficult mechanical maneuvers necessary to extricate the big car from the narrow space. Then when they were clear he spoke, breaking the stillness.

"It's early yet, we can drive out of town, if you like."

Letty stirred restlessly, watching the Sunday crowds, black on the boardwalk, colorful on the streets, the barkers shouting, the souvenir stands, the freak shows, the shooting galleries, alive with people.

"We'd better not go too far," she replied, "if you have to get back early to Southampton."

"That doesn't matter. Shall we go to Arrowhead again?" he asked her.

"Just as you say," Letty murmured.

They picked their way through the traffic, caught the progressive light on Ocean Parkway at just the proper time, and finally threaded their way through downtown Brooklyn, almost deserted at this hour of this special day.

Letty said, after a while:

"I owe you an explanation, Morty."

He did not deny it. However, he said, merely:

"Let it wait. Until we get somewhere where it is comparatively quiet."

She nodded, leaning back, feeling immeasurably tired, feeling as if she had been through an interminable and emotional scene. Yet there had been no scene in the strict sense of the word. There'd been Tom, of course, with his violent talk of love and loss. But she was accustomed to Tom. It was not new ground that had been traversed between them, this afternoon.

She looked at Fisher. His profile was toward her, set, a little stern looking, she thought, rather old and as tired as she felt. A wave of pity for him took her suddenly. Pity was dangerous. She knew that; and so she fought it.

That he himself in many of his reactions toward existence was without pity, she knew. She knew him to be ruthless, in business, in marriage, in even the parental relation. Yet she was excessively sorry for him; and also, more inexplicably, for herself. She felt difficult tears rising in her eyes. Life was such a confusion, it hurried you from one emotion to another, it caught you up in a hundred unexpected ways, set your feet dancing unwillingly to all sorts of unusual and unhappy tunes.

Traffic on the bridge going toward Manhattan was light. There was a constant stream of cars moving in the other direction, moving slowly, with hasty, abrupt grinding of brakes. The skyline swam in a haze of golden light, the tall towers stood out against it, darkly, magnificently.

Once again in Manhattan they entered heavy traffic after they had achieved the uptown portion. Riverside Drive was crowded with cars and so was all the rest of the way to Riverdale and Arrowhead.

It was of necessity a long journey and a slow one, despite Fisher's almost inspired driving. It was six o'clock before they reached Arrowhead. Summer time, daylight saving, preserved the light for them and they went to their table in the open under a daytime sky.

Letty said, a little faintly:

"I'm empty — but I'm not hungry."

She looked away from the menu with a gesture of distaste. "I'll order for you," Fisher said briefly, and did so. She was amazed to find that when the food was set before her, her vague dislike of it passed and she ate with pleasure and appetite. Fisher did not. His plate was scarcely touched, he smoked one cigarette after another, nothing pleased him, he sent back his salad three separate times and finally had the ingredients brought to the table and mixed them himself.

They did not talk much, each too preoccupied with his own secret thoughts. Fisher did, however, speak of Gerry, giving Letty a detailed account of the absurd and unhappy scene he had had with her.

"There'll be another one," he prophesied gloomily, "when I tell her I am shipping her young man to South America to work under railroad engineers."

"Wasn't that the job Burt Barker went out on?" asked Letty, more for the sake of saying something than from any genuine interest. She remembered her meeting with Barker in that office, the fact that he had been out of the country prior to their encounter, and that he was an engineer.

Fisher looked up through the cigarette smoke. He said:

"Burt Barker? Of course. But — I didn't know you knew him."

"Oh, yes. That is, I don't really know him. He is Sonia's son, you know. I saw him when I was working there, once, quite casually. The next time I met him was the day I was coming out of your office and he was coming in. Since then I have run into him a couple of times. Once he came to see me, offered to buy me out, asked me to go back into Sonia's. He is managing it since her death."

Fisher laughed shortly.

"That's rather amazing," he said. "I remember you telling me you'd had an offer."

"*We'd* had an offer," she interrupted, smiling.

"We, then." But his face did not lighten in response. He went on. "I must say it seems rather curious — the beauty business, and Barker. I don't like him," he said evenly; "he's an insolent young cub. He came back from South America primed with the most ridiculous complaints and fantasies. I had the supreme satisfaction of firing him."

He made no other explanations, none were perhaps in order. One was, however, one which had nothing to do with Mr. Barker, except indirectly. Letty pushed back her plate and put out her hand for the cigarette Fisher offered her. She smoked very rarely; but tonight a cigarette was indicated.

She said slowly:

"I told you I owed you an explanation about Tom."

"Yes," replied Fisher uncompromisingly. Then, before she could speak, he amended the affirmative. "That is to say, Letty, you really owe me — exactly nothing. Your life's your own business. But — I couldn't help overhearing something when I came up and found you with him — to, I confess, my immense astonishment. Let us say my curiosity was aroused."

It hadn't been curiosity. It had been an uglier emotion, a dozen emotions, none of them pleasant. Fear, anger, jealousy. Tom Merrick was a young man, ardent, vital. Of course, a good-for-nothing. But women never stopped to think of that. And that he and Letty Lawson had been, or still were, on intimate terms was perfectly apparent. Just as apparent as the fact that Letty had concealed all her knowledge of Tom Merrick from Mortimer Fisher.

Letty said:

"No, whether I owe it or not, I must tell you. You know now that he's Carol's brother; you know I lived with the Merricks. I've known them almost all my life, since childhood, as a matter of fact. I grew up with them. After my father's death I moved into their house, before that I lived next door, their tenant house. You see how it was. Tom and Carol and I played together as youngsters. When we grew up Tom imagined himself in love with me —— "

"Only imagined?" asked Fisher.

"I don't know," she said gravely. "I — I was always his friend but it ceased there. I was never in love with him, not at any time."

She looked away from Fisher's eyes; but she heard his deep drawn breath. He said quietly, "Poor devil," and waited for her to go on.

She did so, with increasing difficulty.

"He never approved of Carol. He — he thought he knew a great deal more about her than their parents did. He was — angry, unreasonably, when I decided to take the course and later the position with Sonia. The first time I ever went out on a party with Carol was with you and — and Mr. Gordon. Tom was waiting for us when we got home. He said certain things," Letty went on hastily, "which made it impossible for me to continue living there. So I left and went to Nelda's. After that, I did see him occasionally, but things grew too unpleasant. Also, his father and mother were angry at me, on, of course, his account. When he left home they blamed me for it. And when Mrs. Merrick died, shortly thereafter, Mr. Merrick thought that — indirectly, I was to blame for that, too. He reasoned it out that if Tom hadn't gone away Mrs. Merrick would not have worried herself into a run-down condition and so — " She broke off with a helpless gesture. "I had to stop going there. And then recently, Tom returned, and because Carol had forbidden her father to tell Tom where she was, he went to Sonia's —— "

She described the scene and what had followed as it had been narrated to her. Fisher listened with increasing interest. Now that he had her assurance that she possessed no emotional interest in the boy, he was once more in a receptive humor. He could forgive young Merrick anything now, even Gerry, provided he removed him from Gerry's scheme of things.

"When you showed me the snapshots," Letty went on, "I recognized him at once. Naturally." She smiled a little. "It was a very good likeness," she added. "I didn't tell you I knew him, I thought I might try to influence him through Carol, or go myself and talk to him, threaten him if need be with the Sonia business, hold Burt Barker's resentment over his head. I didn't want you involved in it, I thought if I could — manage things it would be all over without your even knowing and I'd be spared a lot of painful explanations. I suppose you think that's a pretty lame excuse," she concluded.

"I don't know. I'm so relieved that I'm incapable of judgment. But I do know," he said, smiling at her, "that you did what you thought was best for everybody concerned. So let's forget it. It was just — seeing you there, hearing what the boy said to you that turned things up-side down for me for a time."

She said, low, "I'm sorry, Morty."

"There's nothing to be sorry for. Don't worry. We'll have him away, out of the country, in less than a week's time. Off your hands, off Carol's — although from what you say I fancy she's washed her hands of him already. Perhaps we can do something for the old man too," he went on rapidly, "I know a Bay Ridge contractor who might be useful. I'll ring him up tomorrow. And, of course, Gerry will recover from this momentary blight. She's always recovered before," he said grimly.

"You are a sort of god from the machine," said Letty, smiling at him.

"A machine-made god," he replied, after a moment, "I don't seem able to regulate my own affairs as well as those of others. It's always the way."

There was music now and a gathering of dancers, young couples strolling across the floor in time to the measured beat and a boy crooning through the inevitable megaphone. There were early stars, after a while, above the trees which presided over the dance floor. "Let's go," said Morty impatiently, and beckoned to a waiter.

But they did not drive directly home. There was a side road and he took it, a road which seemed a thousand miles away from the lights of the town, from its confusion. He turned off without warning and stopped the car. He said:

"Letty, I have to say it. I can't wait for you much longer, my dear."

There it was, all of it, in the brief words, the few. She twisted her hands in her lap, wondering, a little helpless. She thought she loved him; she didn't know. What was surety, how did one reach it? Did one come to it by realizing a person was necessary to one, as necessary as air to breathe and water to drink? Was he necessary to her? She thought not, but she didn't know. She knew he was familiar, that she turned to him when things went wrong or right, that he had grown to be a part of her life. But, if that part were torn away by circumstances or by her own decision, would the remainder bleed slowly and perhaps to death? No. She didn't know.

But she was sorry for him, sorry, *sorry*. Because of the essential loneliness she recognized, because of the inadequate wife at home, the thoughtless children, the frigidity where warmth would have meant so much, where warmth should have been, the seeking for warmth elsewhere, for light . . .

He asked:

"I've never asked you — do you care for me, a little? Oh, I know you like me Letty, I know I have your loyal friendship. But love . . . is it too much to ask, too much to expect? I don't expect it, darling. But I do ask it."

She turned now, and put her hands into his own, which sought them so eagerly and held them in so hard and hurting a clasp.

"I don't know, Morty," she said; "I do like you, I more than like you. I — I think I love you. Certainly you mean more to me than any man I've ever known. I'm so grateful to you, too, it's all confused —— "

He said harshly, not drawing her nearer, but keeping her there, her hands in his own, looking at her through the darkness which whispered all about them: "I don't want gratitude, Letty. Erase that from your other emotions. I don't want you to feel that because you believe you owe me something —— "

"No, it isn't that," she said gravely, interrupting him. "Truly, it isn't. It's just that I want to be sure; I *must* be sure. It's for my life, you see. I do understand your situation, our situation. I know that — that you aren't able to be free. I would not ask it of you, Morty. You made your own life long before you met me, you can't unmake it, because of me. You

248

have responsibilities, even," she stumbled on the word so alien to modern usage, "even duties. If — if we love each other, things can't stand still, can't mark time. Everything must be altered for us. I can't believe it a trivial alteration, I can't just take it for granted, go into it — blindly. I —— "

He took her in his arms, closed her lips with his own. He said, when the long, world-shaking kiss had ended:

"You needn't." He released her and sat back. He said:

"I won't hurry you, darling. I won't make it difficult for you. I won't even — do that again. I'll wait, a little longer. Not too long. You're too honest and fine to keep me in torment. But it won't be a torment now. I've your promise that when you're ready, you'll tell me so, haven't I?"

She said, yes, very faintly. He went on:

"We'll be happy, I can swear to that. Terribly happy. Nothing will hurt you, I'll stake my life on it. Perhaps, after all, freedom isn't impossible. If Eva knows that so much depends on it. My entire happiness. Life does owe me something. Success, I've had that. But not happiness. Life owes it to me. Eva's not a hard woman, she'll understand, she must."

"Please," said Letty, "don't talk about that,

don't even think it now."

"I shan't. But — if you love me, Letty, you won't let me down."

"No. Not if I love you," she said.

On the main road the cars went by; their lights would shine out suddenly, blindingly, and then it would be dark again, the stillness broken only by the sound of the tires, the murmur of the engines.

Mortimer set the car in motion. Presently they were on the main road again, driving toward town. Letty said, after a long silence:

"You've a long way before you."

"It doesn't matter. I'll have the companionship of my thoughts," he told her. "And it's between hours; too late for cars going out on the Island for dinner; too early for them to return."

He left her at her house before taking his way to the Fifty-ninth Street Bridge and so out into the Island roads. He said, taking her hands:

"Good night. I'll keep my word; and you, yours."

Then he was gone. She went, suddenly very tired, into the house. In her own quiet apartment alone, she tried to think. What had she said, how far committed herself? She asked herself in a sudden panic of clear reason, if I loved him, would I hesitate, beg for time, hedge and turn? If! Surely I wouldn't, there is no one to consider really but myself, no one to be hurt but myself.

She thought briefly, distastefully, of Eva Fisher. If she could be won to a divorce? She thought further, when I said no one would be hurt but myself, had I forgotten her?

But Eva Fisher didn't, couldn't care for her husband. How then could she be hurt? Her pride perhaps. But that would soon pass, it always did. Only through caring could she be wounded.

Letty regarded herself in the mirror. She was young, she was created for the delicate violence of loving and being loved. She was lonely. This man had been patient, generous, gentle. She thought she understood him, perhaps she did, his loneliness and his desire.

What cowardice within her kept her evasive, held her, balanced between her own desire and her fear? Was it cowardice or warning? She did not know. Meantime she stood atiptoe with expectancy waiting for something, a word, a sign, a symbol. Something that would show her the way, make consent inevitable or refusal the only possible course.

Driving out to Southampton Fisher did not consider the scene which lay before him and which was not to be avoided. His heart was as exultant as a boy's, a very young boy's. He

251

had not rushed his fences, he had waited, in patience, he had been clever. Letty was worth waiting for. He was appalled at the narrow escape he had had in the beginning of their association, heaven alone knew what wisdom had kept him from making an irretrievable mistake, certainly it had not been the wisdom of experience, for she was beyond his experience.

He had been perfectly sincere in saying that it might be possible to persuade Eva to give him his freedom. For the first time in his married life he desired that freedom. Hitherto, Eva had always remained in the background, an immovable obstacle which he could produce on occasion to protect himself, to avoid all danger. He had not been faithful to his wife since the third year of their marriage. But he had never wished her to divorce him, never wanted to leave her. He had not desired to make a second marriage, one which might in its way be as unsatisfactory, eventually, as his first. He had, moreover, a certain harsh tenderness, confused with exasperation, toward Eva. She was so unaccountably futile that she appeared pathetic to him even when he was most angry with her. Perhaps her failure as a woman, as his wife, as a mother, had not been entirely her own fault, possibly it was because her nature was tuned to failure and nothing could change her. He knew, not being a fool, that had they remained in their earlier circumstances, modest, undistinguished people, Eva would have been quite happy and perfectly successful. In a small town, or even a large city, in the most average of circumstances she would have understood her way about, been both occupied and contented. It was simply that the other atmosphere neither became her nor was comprehended by her. She could not adapt herself to it.

No, he had never before wished to free himself from Eva. Now he did. He was quite genuinely in love with Letty Lawson. A year or two before he would not have believed it possible to have so long remained in love with a woman who had granted him no favors other than her companionship, her friendship, a handclasp occasionally and the intimacy of two unconsidered kisses.

He was, as Eva knew, as Letty knew, a ruthless man, with little mercy in him. But he was vulnerable. His heart was vulnerable, and his pride. He had fought his way to success not always by fair means, not always by foul. Many of his enterprises, legitimate in letter, were not as legitimate in spirit. He took advantage of everything, politics, competitors, chance information, information obtained through bribery, through a sort of oblique blackmail, through threats. In business he considered it legitimate to fight with any weapon provided it was what he considered clean. His pursuit of women had had much the same motivation, to satisfy his ambition, his sense of success, and much the same mainspring, an origin in a sense of frustration in one department of his life. He could be generous to a fault, he could be incredibly revengeful. He was neither good nor bad. He was himself, a man, Mortimer Fisher, in love for the second time in his life; and more deeply in love than he had been the first time. And, or so he thought, nearing the ultimate and the infinitely moving victory.

Reaching Southampton he felt braced against any emergency, anything that might happen. He could go to Gerry tonight, almost tenderly, almost with understanding, and tell her that her short and fevered dream was over and that most men are purchasable and that there are boats sailing for South America at the providential end of almost every week.

Driving the car into the garage, walking up to the big still lighted house, he thought of Letty. He had never ceased to think of her. What was she doing? Was she awake, was she thinking of him? Was she asleep, dreamless, or deep in dreams?

She was asleep. On her bedside table the

part-time maid had left a telephone message written in her careful backhand. A Mr. Burt Barker had telephoned, he would telephone her tomorrow, at the office.

The message lay crumpled in the wastebasket. What possible concern of hers was Burt Barker? Letty had thought. An enemy. Her enemy. She had laughed a little at the grandiloquent word. And had thought, fleetingly and with some astonishment, as she fell asleep that, after all, most men were enemies of most women. Even Mortimer. A dear enemy; a dangerous enemy and one who waited, confidently she suspected, for her surrender.

Chapter 14

Gerry's little affair was settled; and settled satisfactorily to everyone but, perhaps, Gerry. However, she had been persuaded; and, certain that man was both cruel and deceptive and women alone loyal and sensitive to heartbreak, she took to demure frocks, a clean-washed face and the writing of very bad poetry. In a week or two that palled and she went off to visit in the Thousand Islands, still subdued; and there she met a famous football player, and so it began all over again, this time harmlessly enough. By the time autumn came, Mortimer Fisher assured Letty, Gerry would be herself again.

He was busy the rest of that summer, out of town a good deal; off with some men on a cruise which had pleasure as its excuse but business as its object; or perhaps it was the other way around. He kept himself fresh in Letty's memory by the ways and means so easy to him, a box of flowers twice a week, books, great piles of new novels, from the bookshops, and even liquor, a bottle of this or that, the modern tribute to one's love.

Letty was glad of the respite. Time seemed to make no change in her uncertainty. He might wait but he certainly would not wait forever, she thought, and he would become impatient, if he was not that already, with her scruples and her questionings and her shilly-shallying. That was only to be expected of him or of any other man. She blew hot, blew cold; she was a straw in the veering wind of her moods. Sometimes she thought despairingly that the best thing to do would be to give him his congé and let him go once and for all, even without knowing the exact state of her own willful heart.

But she couldn't endure to think of his going, in anger and in resentment. She counted on him as a friend, as a vivid personality in her life and as a stimulant, mentally, spiritually. She counted on him, too, although it was not often that she admitted it to herself, as a potential lover.

Then, too, there was the business association. He might talk forever and a day that there was no obligation. There was; there always would be. Aside from that debt of gratitude there remained a money debt. The interest was paid regularly; but the principal remained on her books. She was Letty Lawson, Inc. But not entirely independent.

Tom had sailed for South America, with few farewells, except to his father, to whom he made no explanation beyond "a job, and a swell one." He had made no effort to see Letty again, or Carol. He had gone; removed painlessly from their lives by a man who was accustomed to removing people.

Burt Barker had not rested content with that Sunday evening telephone call. He had called again and again. And finally had become so insistent that Letty made an appointment to see him. When he came to her office she looked at him with an exasperation in which there was some humor. He came in, smiling, but not quite sure of himself, and with the expression of a small boy who has been bad and knows it, but expects that perhaps the fates will treat him kindly this one time and let him off with a light punishment. Regarding him, Letty asked involuntarily:

"Were you careful not to step on any cracks, walking over?"

"Was I *what?*" He stared at her in astonishment. Then he laughed. "So you used to do that, too," he said, "when anything was at stake!" She laughed with him and for a moment, in a mutual understanding, they forgot their rancor against each other.

He said, guiltily:

"No, I suppose I stepped on 'em. I walked

pretty fast. Look here, I imagine you're wondering why I keep pestering you like this?"

"I do, a little," she admitted.

"I owe you an apology and an explanation. Several of them. About that girl, for instance —— "

"Sally?" asked Letty, with slightly elevated eyebrows.

"Sally," agreed Burt Barker. He sighed involuntarily. Sally had caused complications he hadn't really foreseen. Letty watched him, still with amusement. It had reached her, through Nelda, that Sally had more or less made eighteen different kinds of an idiot of herself over Mr. Barker . . .

"What about her?" asked Letty, ceasing to smile. She looked at him directly, her eyes very dark. "You — you sent her here, didn't you?"

"I did," replied Burt. He returned her look. "I know what you think of me for it. It wasn't decent — or ethical."

Letty shrugged.

"The beauty business isn't overburdened with ethics," she said, "but I really can't understand —— "

"No, of course you can't," he interrupted eagerly, "neither can I. But I was sore. That's it. Peeved. You treated my proposition pretty coolly. I'd come in all good faith," he explained. "So I was like a kid showing off. I wanted to make Sonia's the Mecca of all the smart women in New York and points east and west to say nothing of north and south. I deliberately planted her — the operator, in here, in order to see what was going on. I thought forewarned was forearmed, I'd be just one jump ahead of you if I knew what you were up to."

"It sounds like a bad play," she told him slowly. "Did you invite her also to steal my formulas?" she asked lightly.

"Well, no. I did think of it," he confessed with a graceless grin, "but it didn't sound as practical in real life as it appears in the books. No, not that, Miss Lawson. It was a crazy notion on my part, that's all."

"Did you get much information?" she wanted to know, unsmiling.

"Darned little."

"Well," said Letty, "that's that."

"No, I'm not going. Not until I've tried again. Sure, *sure* you won't change your mind?" he asked her.

"Quite sure," she told him.

He rose, but remained standing by her desk, looking down. She thought, Heavens, isn't he tall! Too tall.

She complained, suddenly:

"You give me a crick in my neck!"

"As long as it isn't a pain in your neck," he answered swiftly. He smiled down at her, and when she smiled back,

"In the words of the song, can't we be friends?" he asked.

"I don't see why not," Letty replied, "nor why we haven't been before. Unless — unless you thought I treated your mother badly, leaving the way I did," she added, low.

"No, of course, I didn't," he replied instantly. "And — about the other things I said while I was here last time, forget them, will you, and forgive me? I was pretty muddled . . . her death, you know, and the way it happened."

"I understand," said Letty soberly. She rose and faced him, as well as she was able. Not a short girl, still the great difference in their heights forced her to look up, which exasperated her obscurely.

"About Carol's brother — " she said, thinking swiftly, it is his right to know, "I — I happen to know he's gone away — out of the country," she added, thinking that the destination, in view of all that had gone before, might as well remain obscure to Barker. "It was his last chance to make something of himself. He — he really feels deeply about what — what happened. He was just an unwitting sort of instrument, after all."

261

"That's all right," said Barker embarrassedly, "I understand. The doctor said in any case she had not long to live. Any shock, any excitement — " He drew a deep breath. "I suppose I should be glad she went like that, quickly, without pain," he said soberly. "Of course — at first — I wanted to find him again — I don't know what for. There's no payment possible for such a thing. Let it go," he said, "we won't talk about it again."

She held out the slim, lovely hand.

"I'm glad you came," she said, "and we'll make a truce, won't we?" She laughed up at him, "But if you're going to put spies in every shop in New York —— "

"That would be impractical," he agreed with her. He held her hand longer than was necessary. It stirred gently in his own and he relinquished it. "I'm going to keep on bothering you," he assured her earnestly, "about that other matter. Maybe sometime you'll get tired enough to give in," he said.

When he had gone, with the further assurance that she had not seen the last of him, she sat a moment at her desk and thought. Tired enough to give in . . . ?

Did Mortimer Fisher reason that way too? That one could grow so weary of importunities, spoken or otherwise, that finally one would surrender out of sheer fatigue, sheer distaste of thinking further.

She thought, looking past the roses on her desk, that perhaps she should have spoken to Barker about some of the rumors that had reached her. Yet she did not now believe that he was responsible for them. The girl, of course. And the girl didn't matter. Well, rumors never hurt anyone seriously yet, she thought erroneously, squaring her slender shoulders as if she were replying to a challenge.

But there were rumors of which she knew nothing. They were bred in the exotic atmosphere of beauty salons, they were wafted across bridge tables, across tables in restaurants. They came together, little atoms of gossip, floating, dancing like the tiny motes of dust in sunlight. Separately they meant very little; together they might mean a good deal. Sally helped, or hindered, whichever way you looked at it. A chance indiscreet word of Herbert Gordon's helped too, although he didn't know it and had meant nothing by it. And someone saw Fisher and Letty at Arrowhead, someone who knew Fisher only by sight and Letty not at all. Someone else saw them at the theater once. And so the rumors grew and spread.

How do these things come about? A light word over a cocktail, a whisper during an entr'acte, a chance remark flung out while pondering whether one shall bid no-trumps or spades, or whether one shall order scallops or a vegetable salad.

As usual the last person to hear the rumors was one of the three most closely concerned.

Eva Fisher.

It was summer, but nearing summer's lovely close. Eva was still at Southampton, occupying herself with several of her charitable interests there, the annual fair and after that was over, other things. And she went twice a week to Manhattan to make inspections, sit on committees.

She had few close friends but a vast circle of acquaintances. The woman who knew her best, which was not very well, motored over from Easthampton one day for tea, ostensibly bound only on a friendly social errand but in reality to interest Mrs. Fisher in a protégé of hers, "a young man, my dear, who sings too divinely. Gigli's art and Vallee's sex appeal. If we can get him started . . . a concert or something. I thought a charity concert? If you'd be on the committee, take a box?"

That was disposed of, pretty shortly. Mrs. Fisher would take a box if the charity was worthy. Mrs. Fisher was wise enough to discriminate among her charities. She had no desire to subscribe for a box for a charity which would receive exactly nothing after the expenses were paid; or to subscribe for a box when the funds would go to a home for unmarried mother-cats, or some such vague object.

Her caller was a little annoyed. She had counted on Eva. All her cronies talked depression, used depression as an excellent excuse. Cut their servants salaries, did without a car they didn't need, erased their charitable subscriptions from their books and stopped doing the sort of entertaining they had always hated. Yes, it was a bad time to launch a new protégé, even if he did have a good voice and enchanting eyes and a Southern accent that was "too, too thrill-making" . . .

Eva would pay twenty dollars for the box. But Mrs. Lacey had thought that Eva might do all the hard work on the committee; she herself would lend the decorative effect. Poor Eva, she was far from decorative! Eva had so many nice rich stodgy friends, blue-blooded old ladies with appalling bonnets and enormous bank accounts, whom Eva met on committees, and who liked her for her charitable heart . . .

Eva, sitting in her big living room, her hands gentle and a little self-conscious among the beautiful tea things, irritated Mrs. Lacey. Mrs. Lacey had looks and chic, a famous maiden name and a broker husband who was always one jump ahead of the sheriff. Eva, plain, dowdy, was a thorn in her well-stayed side. If she had had her opportunities! With her appearance and her social background and a husband like Mortimer Fisher, Mrs. Lacey would have set a couple of worlds on fire.

She was not averse to a little dash of platonic preoccupation. She had once used her eyes on Mortimer Fisher but with no effect. They were remarkable eyes. However, one of Mortimer's aversions was entanglements with married women — He had always preferred the frankly unattached, the widowed, the divorced, the ladies who wrote *Mrs.* on the visiting cards for reasons best known to themselves. It was not scruple; it was caution.

So now Mrs. Lacey spoke, out of her irritation.

"I hardly," she said, "know how to begin. But I came over to tell you — " She twisted her fine linen handkerchief. She said, as Eva looked at her with the quiet, faintly frightened eyes around which the lines were so apparent, "It's for your own good, Eva, I'm so fond of you. I thought, Eva has a right to know, a right to protect herself —— "

She was working herself up to the inevitable righteous indignation against husbands in general and Mortimer Fisher in particular. Women, she was proclaiming, must stick together. Only your best friend would tell you. Or words to that effect.

It took a long time, by an involved route. Eventually it was quite simple. Mortimer Fisher had, for months, been seen in the company of Another Woman. Mrs. Lacey made capitals with her agitated voice and exclamation points with her hands and question marks with the remarkable eyes.

Eva took it quietly; but that isn't saying she didn't take it badly. She was sallow, unpainted. She did not easily show a loss of color. But her heart started to bleed, and bleed white. She stammered . . . "Are you *sure?*"

Mrs. Lacey gave her sketchy chapter and unrhymed verse.

"But, who is she?" whispered Eva. A silver spoon tinkled to the floor.

"That," said Mrs. Lacey shrugging, "that, I don't know. She's said to be very young and extraordinarily beautiful." She looked at Eva and was aware of a genuine compassion. After all, this was a defenseless woman. Mrs. Lacey had her moments. She wasn't awfully proud of herself. She said, so sincerely that she shocked herself, "I'm — I'm sorry I told you." That admission wasn't pleasant. She began to hunt for remnants with which to cover her nakedness. "But I thought it was for your own good, my dear," she said. "If I hadn't been fond of you I wouldn't have dreamed — Perhaps it isn't serious at all, perhaps people are just — talking."

A servant came in to clear away the things. Mrs. Lacey chattered lightly of concerts and of this and that. The golf. The swimming. The tennis. Then she rose to go, to drive back to Easthampton in the inexpensive-car-class roadster which was the best poor Lacey could do this year and a lot better than he could really afford. She kissed and clasped Eva in a flutter of merciless pity and Christmas-present perfume. "Do forgive me," she breathed in Eva's ear.

Eva didn't even know she existed.

After a while she went upstairs to her bedroom. It was a great, many-windowed room and "done" by a decorator as a pretty, rich woman's room is usually done. Two-toned, rose and a clear, very pale green. Extraordinarily unbecoming to the woman who slept there, alone. There were too many pillows, too much fine lace. The dressing table was superbly lighted for the art of titivation; the clothes closets, spacious, with matching bags for frocks, built-in places for hats, shoes, gloves, lingerie ——

The bathroom beyond was one created for a modern Venus, who would rise rosy-dripping from the lovely tub, from water tinted and fragrant, and regard herself in many mirrors, smiling secretly. More dressing tables, more gadgets for beauty and bodily care. Great towels, as big as sheets, rose-colored, kittens-ear soft. . . .

Eva, running a tub of plain water, never looked at herself in mirrors.

Fisher's room and bath lay next to hers, a door connected them. The door had not been opened for many years; had never been opened, in fact, since the house was built. Oh, opened, of course, but never in search of companionship, in search of love and laughter.

There had never been a time when that door stood open at any hour, so that Fisher could stand there, knotting his tie, brushing his hair, with stories of a battle won, a battle lost; with petty complaints of husbandly dissatisfaction . . . there had never been a time when that door burst open, when there was no knock, when he came in, unapologetic . . . *Listen to this, Eva. . . .*

Today, after Mrs. Lacey had taken her righteous departure, Eva Fisher sat and stared at herself in the mirror. She heard the older boy come in downstairs, from golf. He was probably begging cocktail material in the butler's pantry. She heard the telephone ring. She heard it answered. It was for Gerry. Gerry was still in the Adirondacks. She thought idly, Mortimer handled that well ——

Mortimer.

Darkness fell. She switched on the cruel lights above the triple mirror, lights which any woman who respected or loved her beauty would have used searchingly and without much misgiving, lights which would warn — in time.

The small, sallow face, the tired eyes which still held an appealing beauty, regarded her. Anxious lines, relaxed skin. And under the plain, hand-knitted sweater frock her breasts drooped.

The brown hair was streaked with gray. It was naturally wavy, drawn back from a too-high forehead in a tight knot that was the despair of milliners.

Eva was slender, fashionably so, perhaps, but far too slender. She wore a child's size in clothes. These were expensive. They came from the right places but they were thrown on her. No one had bothered to show her how to wear them. And the women who sold them to her were vastly uninterested. She was a regular customer, uncomplaining and quick pay. But her own lack of interest communicated itself to them. She bought what she had to have, sensibly, and no more. You couldn't get excited over seeing things on and selling things to a person who couldn't get excited over buying them. And it was no task to sell. They were sure of their sales. So they sold her costly and conservative "numbers" which might have been becoming to her if she had given them a chance. But she didn't.

There on the dressing table was a picture of Mortimer Fisher in a silver frame.

Had she lost him?

She knew she had. Not to this girl, perhaps, whoever she was, but to life.

He had always been very kind to her. There had been the early years of which she could not now think without slow and painful tears. Shy ardor and a braggart spirit — "I'll make good, you'll have everything in the world, some day, darling."

Well, she had everything; except her husband.

Always kind. Even now. Looking in on her, in her room, putting his hand on her shoulder sometimes, saying always, "Anything you want, Eva? Anything I can do for you?"

The estrangement . . . But, no, there had been no estrangement. They did not quarrel, bitterly, were not undignified in their relations. The other night during the trouble over

Gerry, he had said things, flung words at her. She had not attempted to defend herself. He was right. She was an inadequate woman. She had not known how to deal with marriage or with motherhood. Perhaps if Mortimer had not been successful she would have known. She had been born to comfort rather than congratulate. She had been able to cope with her babies when they needed her, when there had been small sorrows to console, hurts to bind. If Mortimer had not become successful, her children might have remained dependent on her. *He* might have remained so.

It was not the passing of that early passion she must deplore. That had always frightened her a little. She was more spirit and heart than flesh and blood. But she had endured it with tenderness and an inarticulate desire to be, to the man she had married, all that he found necessary to his happiness. No, it was not that which wrung her now, sitting before her mirror. Nor did she feel that she lacked his affection. That was there, never put in words, yet she could rely on it.

It was this dreadful sense of inadequacy, of being of no use to any single soul in the world. That was why, she thought vaguely, she had taken to charity as an escape, trying to do something for someone. For strangers, people for the most part whom she never set eyes on.

Charity, in the correct reading of the word, meant love.

Love . . .

She viewed herself now in terror and revulsion. A woman, aging before her time, aging and unattractive, whose children had grown away from her, whose husband had grown away from her.

It had been easy to make excuses at first for their separation, a separation of which the physical side was the least part. He was busy, he was preoccupied, he went where she could not follow, however willing her feet.

Now she faced herself in a mirror, and was immeasurably frightened; and wept, putting her graying head on her thin arms. Mrs. Mortimer Fisher. Wife of Mortimer Fisher. Over in her desk the careful check books with the meticulously written stubs. And the balance. The balance which would buy her anything within reason.

After a while she rose. She went into the bathroom and flooded it with light. She regarded her slim figure with its sagging muscles. She looked at her face, hideous with weeping. She could not cry the way other women cried, lightly, becomingly.

She washed her eyes in cold water and picked up a powder puff to hide the traces of her tears. Someone knocked on the door to her bedroom.

A message. Mr. Fisher would not be home to dinner.

She ate alone in a very large dining room. Through the open windows there was a scent of sand and sea, and of late flowers. She ate very little, was perfectly composed. Her boy had gone out; Gerry was not at home, the other boy at camp.

Mr. Fisher would not be home for dinner.

She thought, I am absolutely alone.

She thought, he is all I have.

But she had the children; fully as much as she had him.

That wasn't so, she thought, further, that was a fallacy. The children could not replace him, ever; and she possessed them in a lesser degree than she did her husband. He was her contemporary. The children of another generation.

I can't lose him, altogether, she thought, in a panic of unreasoning terror.

She bore the girl — "very young and extraordinarily beautiful" — no rancor. She did not give her a thought. Most women would fall in love with Mortimer Fisher, with the man himself, with the success that was as much a part of him as his eyes or his smile or the way he carried himself.

There were other men for very young, extraordinarily beautiful girls. But not for her.

He had always loved youth, beauty, vitality. She couldn't love even as much as she now had of him. She was so unutterably alone.

Chapter 15

It seemed to Eva Fisher that every magazine that came to her hand, every newspaper she picked up, held a special message for her. For all contained articles on beauty; on how to get your man, how to hold him; some were cheap, others had a certain dignity; many contained common sense; and occasionally one was written with an underlying current of authentic sincerity, even beauty. These were the articles read, this the advice taken by thousands of girls and women, naive, sophisticated. Yes, even sophisticated. No matter what the wording, whether appealing directly to the average woman's normal understanding of mere cleanliness and hygiene, whether appealing to her sense of fitness, mental and physical, or merely replying in commonplace, sensible if sometimes endearing words to a girl who signed herself "Blondie," the message was structurally the same. Beauty came from within, true beauty; beauty of spirit and nature; but one could help by externals. One must ally oneself with the thousands in the quest of glamour, of mystery. Eva read, and found herself looking up old magazines, a little bewildered by what she read; by sprightly talk of matching powders and cream rouge; of eyeshadow, blue with metallic lights, violet or brown, of exercises, diets, massage masks . . .

She was not a sophisticate, certainly. She was not even of the Big Town itself, part of its fevered heartbeat. She had given her physical appearance little thought, beyond feeling as dowdy as she looked when she encountered women with a flair for clothes, tended skin and supple bodies. Nor did she really seek a recipe, a spell, for "holding" Mortimer Fisher. She had watched her youth fade, had thought, he doesn't notice. She had seen his eyes light up when a pretty woman spoke to him, flatteringly, gaily, caressingly. Oh, a thousand times. But she was his wife, she belonged to him, they had shared a great deal in those early days. Her position was secure at least, no matter how separated one had become from the other.

Now her position was not as secure.

Young. "Very young and extraordinarily beautiful," Doris Lacey had said of the unknown girl. Mortimer was not young, and he was unaccountable as are most human beings. Eva recalled the novels she had read, novels frank to blatancy about the dangerous age, for women, for men . . .

If he should ask for a divorce? If this were really serious?

She would, she knew, give him the divorce. Anything within her power, which he had asked of her, she had given. Possibly he had asked for a great deal which was not within her jurisdiction to bestow.

If he asked her for a divorce and she gave it to him, what would happen to her? She would, she knew, never lack for money. The children? The children would not be further away from her than they were now, they might even be closer. One couldn't tell. But the children mattered, she realized with terror, so very little, compared with Mortimer.

Living somewhere, possibly alone; alone surely, even if the children were with her, going on with the charities . . . lonely, empty, a failure. . . .

Many women in a like situation went abroad and remained there. If poor, obscurely; if rich, in luxury.

The mere thought was horror. She couldn't. Nor could she live in the same city which held him; nor could she go home. The town had changed, she supposed; and, what was more important, the people she still knew there had their own self-contained lives and in those lives there was no room for her. They wrote her, they came to see her when they reached New York on a visit, the women she had known as girls, a little impressed by all the splendor with which Mortimer Fisher and his name surrounded her. But they would have no place for her, if she came back alone, having failed.

She thought, however, if he does ask for a divorce, in what way would my life differ from my life as his wife?

No, not much outward difference. She saw her husband often — but casually. That was all. He was a man who lived in a house he had built for her, and came to it when it suited his convenience. If he never came, would there be so much alteration?

She knew there would be. She knew now how unchangingly she had leaned on his strength, how the harsh drive of his nature complemented her own. If he wished to ask her to give him up, she must, of course. But — must he wish it?

She had never been able to tell him, not since the long past years, that she loved him and that he constituted her world, the air she breathed. You do not think much about air until your laboring lungs are deprived of it. She had always been inarticulate, and, so he had said, "cold." An easy term. It was not frigidity, it was a curious virginal quality, afraid, timid, which persisted in her. Wifehood, the bearing of children had not altered it. An inarticulate woman, she was also unable through the medium of her body to express that for which she had no words.

For years he had not noticed her save to be abstractedly kind. If she could force herself on his attention? Not in order to rouse a long-perished ardor, that did not occur to her, but to have him look at her as if she were a *person,* someone he did not know very well, with whom he was not familiar. Perhaps if he did so she might acquire courage; courage to ask him frankly, what do you want, is it this other woman, whoever she is?

How did one go about such things? she wondered.

Her attempts were piteous, a little too careless not to be in deadly earnest. Meeting other women . . . "how lovely your skin looks . . . what do you use . . . I've neglected mine dreadfully."

Half a dozen women, half a dozen remedies to confuse her. Soap and water, said one; no soap, and lots of cream, said another. Heavy creams advised the blonde with the dry, delicate skin; light creams which melt on the face, cautioned another. Massage. No massage! Astringents. No astringents!

Eva sent to shops, she bought, lavishly,

with discrimination, and spent hours in her room experimenting, to no avail. The starved, fading skin grew sensitive, blotchy.

She began drinking milk, and eggnogs, taking a nap afternoons in order to gain weight. Mortimer at dinner observed her valiantly struggling through a potato for which she had no genuine appetite.

"You're lucky," he told her idly, "half the women in New York are starving themselves to death."

She smiled at him, looking momentarily pretty, her face a little flushed, her hair loose about her temples in the new coiffure she had copied from a magazine picture.

"I'm trying to put on weight," she said.

He returned to his meal, losing interest, speaking with his usual abstraction.

"You are thin," he said. "Why not see Doctor Carroll? It may be a matter of basic metabolism."

The children were at home. Gerry yawned frankly.

"When are we going back to town?" she demanded. "This place gives me the jitters."

They went back, presently. The boys departed to continue their education under other roofs, Gerry began her music again. The board meetings commenced in earnest.

After one such meeting during that hazy,

golden autumn, mild and lovely, Eva, standing beside a fat and worthy woman who wore a puce-colored dress and priceless stones on hands not overclean, overheard another group of younger women talking, on their way to lunch together at the Waldorf.

"My dear, have you tried Letty Lawson? She's *marvelous!* She makes you over. I'm taking a course there, ten treatments. Oh, of course, I can't afford it but — Yes, Madison Avenue. Be sure to get Miss Lawson herself. She has hands like heaven. I've been as nervous as a June bride used to be, lately. But one facial at Lawson's is like a rest cure."

Later, Eva Fisher opened a telephone book. And in the early morning of the next day she drove to the Madison Avenue business building.

The elevator doors opened and she walked into the reception room. The smart woman at the appointment desk was almost her own age but looked twenty years younger.

"Could I see Miss Lawson?"

"Have you an appointment, madam?"

No, Eva did not have an appointment. She said, "I thought — if she'd see me for a moment . . . ?"

The appointment desk clerk, who doubled in brass as bookkeeper, was no fool. This was a woman over forty, undistinguished, fading, but her frock was custom-made, and there were pearls at her throat.

"If you will come with me — Oh, Miss Rose, will you take Mrs. — Mrs. —— ?"

"Mrs. Mortimer Fisher —— " supplied Eva.

"Mrs. Fisher into a consultation room? If you'll wait there, Mrs. Fisher, I'm sure Miss Lawson will see you immediately," promised the appointment clerk.

Miss Rose, small, brunette, dazzling in her white smock, opened the door of a "consultation" room. She helped Eva off with her coat and laid her hat aside; and said, as Eva hesitated, "If you'd remove your blouse . . . ?"

Presently Eva waited alone in the pretty, quiet room. Her hair was bound back with a soft white towel, she lay full length on the couch, under a soft sheet, a strip of linen binding her breasts, her overthin shoulders bare. Miss Rose had dropped a soft fine blanket over her before she left the room. "You may feel chilly," she said smiling.

Eva closed her eyes. Her every instinct was to escape, to dress herself, to find an excuse, any excuse, and to go . . .

"A new client?" Letty asked the appointment clerk.

"A Mrs. Fisher."

"Fisher?"

"Mrs. Mortimer Fisher."

283

Letty stood quite still. She asked, low, "She wishes to see me, in the office?"

The other woman looked mildly astonished. "No, for a consultation," she said.

"I see." Letty glanced at the appointment book. She was free, at this early hour. She ran her eye down the list of names. "If I am still engaged with Mrs. Fisher," she said evenly, "have Miss Rose take Mrs. Morrow's appointment. I'll come in before it's over. It's her sixth treatment . . ."

She walked toward the room in which Eva waited. She braced herself as she laid her hand on the knob. She had heard of such situations, in books and in plays.

A scene, she supposed, ugly, wounding; recriminations; demands. If she could handle it so that no hint would reach the other people in the shop, if she could control herself —— ?

She went in, walking lightly.

Eva was sitting up, staring into a mirror which did not flatter. Her shoulder blades were sharp. Her neck still firm enough but dreadfully thin. She turned her head as Letty closed the door and smiled, fleetingly, almost apologetically.

"Miss Lawson?"

"Yes," replied Letty. Eva looked at her and stammered, anxiously, color flooding her face and throat, without beauty.

"You were recommended to me — I mean, is there anything you can do for me? I've neglected myself, I'm afraid, and —— "

Her eyes were on Letty's, more eager, more appealing than she could know. Letty saw her thin hands twisting together on the rosy blanket. She said briskly:

"Why, of course, Mrs. Fisher —— "

She didn't know; never had known; had come here by chance, through a casual word, for a consultation. "Is there anything you can do for me?"

Letty's hands were expert and gentle. She turned on the cruel lights, she looked at the texture of Eva's skin through a magnifying glass. She diagnosed and prescribed, conscientiously, automatically.

Dry skin, relaxed. Mrs. Fisher needed a general building up. Rest. Sleep. Attention to her diet. Long brisk walks in the open air. Quantities of water, green vegetables, fats, starches. In the meantime, for the external needs, a course of treatments . . .

Mrs. Fisher listened. She said, "Yes, I understand. If I could begin now?"

Letty's "Of course" was low. Eva Fisher lay back on the lounge and relaxed under the skillful hands, on the cleansed skin the warm rich oils melted; the circulation cream burned for a moment, bringing the blood to the surface, there were cool wet pads over her eyes, she lay in a scented darkness conscious of the firm fingers molding, sculpturing her face into lines of temporary youth; later the mask dried fragrantly and she felt too the cool spray of astringents, and the remarkably pleasant slapping, the brisk tattoo beaten along her shoulder blades and down her back, the tension at the base of her neck gently broken.

Presently it was over. "A little make-up?" asked Letty. Her voice was even, a lovely voice thought Eva Fisher gratefully.

She hesitated briefly.

"I haven't — I don't use —— " she began.

Letty laughed, a small contraband echo of the ironic laughter which was raging in her heart.

"Suppose — just once?" she suggested.

A powder base, patted in, wiped off, cream rouge dotted on in a triangle, and blended, a wisp of cotton soaked in some lotion which contains powder and a healing element, drying, the residue wiped off. Then the fine powder dusted on, and brushed off with a camel's-hair brush. Lip rouge, a very little eyeshadow . . .

Now Letty stood aside. Eva Fisher stared in the mirror. It was a minor miracle, a very minor miracle, but a miracle nevertheless. Her face looked back at her, rested, satiny, the eyes brighter, the lips carefully reddened, the expression subtly changed. She said, and her mouth shook a little, "I *do* look — different, don't I?"

Letty hardened her heart against the pity that invaded it. Her answer was professional merely, but it sufficed. Moreover, it was sincere enough. Eva Fisher did look different.

Before Eva left Letty had prescribed the usual home care for her, had made out a list of things she would need and had arranged for the course of treatments. "Will you take these with you or shall I send them with the rest?"

Eva Fisher went out into the bright sunlight feeling exceedingly self-conscious; feeling as if every passer-by must turn back and look at her with curiosity. She fancied she saw that same curiosity in the eyes of her correctly impassive chauffeur as he opened the car door for her. Returning home, she braced herself against the questions Gerry was certain to ask her and against Mortimer's astonishment or laughter. But Gerry did not come in for dinner and Mortimer, when he did come, was late.

She sat with him while he ate his meal, hurried, a handful of letters and cables beside him, his brows drawn down darkly. "Is anything the matter?" she asked him timidly.

He glanced up at her; but he did not see

her. He did not see the delicately tinted face, the brightened eyes, nor the new hostess gown which she had once been persuaded to buy and which, until tonight, she had never worn, feeling awkward in it, feeling that she did not become its long graceful lines and lovely claret color. He replied briefly:

"Plenty."

The explanation when she heard it was stenographic in its terseness. There was trouble on the South American railroad job. An outgoing government, an incoming government, fighting, revolution. And everything at a standstill with much good money at stake. "I'm off," he said in conclusion, "on the first boat. Someone has to go, someone who can handle things. I've already sent two men from the office. But they've been worse than useless."

Eva touched a bell. "Mr. Fisher's coffee is cold," she told the servant who answered. Fresh coffee was brought. "Take it in the library," ordered Fisher, "I'll be working there this evening."

She followed him in, her gown trailing gracefully about her slippered feet. He sat down at the great desk and she stood there beside it uncertainly. He said with mechanical courtesy:

"I'll work late, perhaps; don't wait up for

me. Gerry at home?"

"No."

"Isn't there something you can do? It's not too late to dress and go to a play . . . "

It was an awkward situation for them both. He was not at home very often; when he was, there were generally guests, of his own choosing, men for poker, or couples for bridge. On the rare occasions when he worked in the library Eva left him alone. Tonight she stood there, hesitant.

His mind so preoccupied that his eyes did not really register what he was seeing, he regarded her. "You're looking very well," he said suddenly and kindly. "Been to see Carroll perhaps?"

She had not been to the doctor's, she told him. His glance left hers and returned to the papers. He reached for the coffee cup on the tray at his elbow. Eva turned and left the room.

He had noticed something, she thought, lying in bed, the reading light on, a pile of books on the bedside table. Something.

But without amazement, without shock, without surprise, without, even, any real interest.

Now, he was going away. The days would be empty of him, and the nights. But would they not be, in actuality, even were he here?

While he was away, she thought, she would take her treatments, her exercise, follow the diet that Miss Lawson had given her, and perhaps when he came back . . .

The hospital committees could do without her occasionally. . . .

When he came back . . . ?

A sudden thought took her and shook her with fear. Fighting, he had said, trouble.

It was late when he came upstairs, very late. She had been lying awake, listening for his step. She remembered when they had looked at this ruinously expensive duplex penthouse apartment. It had seemed enormous to her; and she had asked, "If we could find a little house?"

But he hadn't wanted a little house. He had wanted, however, stairs. He had confessed with the boyishness which endeared him to his friends that he'd always liked to "go downstairs to breakfast."

Now she heard his step and switched on the lights and rose hurriedly and pulled a silken wrap about her. Her face, washed clean, as Letty Lawson had told her it must be, was anxious and even a little childlike, with traces of cream still about her eyelids.

She intercepted him in the hallway, knowing that she would not have the courage to knock on the door of the room adjoining hers. He would think her crazy. But there was a question which could not wait until tomorrow.

"Why, Eva!" he said, mildly astonished.

"I have been thinking . . . This South American trip — is there any danger in it — for you?" she wanted to know, breathlessly.

He laughed and dropped his big hand on her thin shoulder.

"Certainly not. Political shenanigans," he said, forgetting that he quoted one Mr. Burt Barker, "no danger at all. Run back to bed, my dear, you'll take cold."

When he entered his own room he had already forgotten her. He was thinking of Letty. . . . No, no danger, of course, not really. But if Letty thought so? And if he were to say to her, "When I come back, Letty — when I come back . . . ?"

When he was ready for bed he stood by the windows looking down over the Park and the reservoir. A bright, starry night, and the hum of late traffic very distant, muted. He had but to stretch out his hand to the telephone and call a number and her voice, drowsy, awakened from sleep, would respond to his low question. The walls were thick, almost soundproof. Eva would not hear.

He shrugged, and turned away from the window. Letty's telephone did not startle her, that night . . .

But the next night she knew.

Chapter 16

He came to see her that night, shortly after dinner. He said, without any preliminary:

"I'm sailing, tomorrow —— "

"Sailing?"

"For South America. Things are going wrong down there. Everything's mad. Someone with a clear head has to go down and see what's to be done."

"I read," she said anxiously, "that there was fighting. . . . Is that anywhere near where your men are?"

"Too damned near," he admitted.

"Tom — ?" She looked up at him questioningly. She said: "No one's heard from him, Carol told me. Do you suppose he'll get into it? He's just the type," she went on, after a moment, "always looking for trouble."

Fisher looked at her, his brows drawn.

"You do care a lot about that boy," he accused her.

"No. Not in the way you mean. But I care enough to worry about him. After all, we grew up together."

"And me — ?" he wanted to know childishly, "would you care enough to worry if —— ?"

"Morty!" She regarded him with dark, distended eyes. "You don't mean —— ?"

It was enough; her look, her tone. He laughed outright, caught her hands in his.

"No, I *don't* mean," he said, "of course not. Everything is going to be all right."

Now, he was reassuring her, as he had reassured Eva last night, but with considerable difference. He added:

"I don't know how long I'll be away. Not long, certainly. But, Letty, when I come back. When I come back . . . will you be waiting for me?"

She said, low, "I think so, Morty."

She did think so. And yet, now that she had seen Eva Fisher she was obscurely troubled. Not so obscurely at times. It seemed so terribly unfair. She had, she knew, everything; loveliness, tenderness, ardor, with which to hold a man. These things she had and knew she had, without vanity. But Eva had nothing — nothing but Mortimer Fisher's name and his money. Yet in a deeper sense it was she who had everything, and Letty who had nothing. For Eva was, after all, his wife. Useless to argue the title empty; it remained.

She did not tell Mortimer Fisher that Eva had come to her. It was impossible to tell him.

How did one go about such things? "By the way, Morty, your wife came into the shop the other day . . . "

She remembered a girl she had once known slightly, a saleswoman in the dress department of a smart shop. A pretty girl, in love with a married man; happily and dangerously in love. She remembered the girl telling her one day, over a lunch table . . . "He called me one morning, in the store. It was important. He had to go away, to break a date; his train was leaving. I answered, from the floor. His wife was in the department, trying on clothes —— "

Just that, but everything was in the picture, nothing was lacking, a bitter comedy, a touch of drama and of tragedy. The little saleswoman hanging up the receiver on that important outside call and returning, after her noncommittal reply, to the long mirrors where the older woman stood regarding herself with dissatisfied eyes, "Do you think it too young for me? Do you think it becoming?"

No. Letty could not tell Mortimer. If Eva told him — But she thought with a flash of intuition that it was very likely Eva would not tell him.

Still, with her hand close in his own, she made her promise. Half a promise at all events. Then he released her hand and smiled down on her, and looked about the quiet room, his flowers on mantel and table, the few soft lights glowing, the curtains drawn.

"I'll think of this," he told her, "there in South America . . . where I'll probably be sweating and cursing — most of the time. I'll remember."

She knew that he would. She asked, "Morty, you'll write?"

He had never written her. She waited for his lips to answer, conscious of a tightening at her heart. He replied:

"Of course. Not much. I'm a bad hand at letters. Too used to dictation, I suppose. But you'll understand, you'll read between the lines?"

She nodded, forced to be content. She asked, further:

"And if you see Tom, you'll let me know how he is? It would be a kindness to his father. I can tell Carol."

He had forgotten his momentary jealousy. He nodded. "Yes. The boy's all right, or we would have heard. It's his chance down there. Not an easy life, in many ways; and plenty of opportunities to go to hell on a fast express. If there's good stuff in him, he won't; he'll pull through and come back the better for a tough job and a taste of adventure. If he doesn't make good — well, he had his chance, cut loose from everything he's ever known, and all ties."

He left early because, as he said frankly, he was afraid to stay. He spoke, leaving, holding her close, kissing her long and deeply in farewell, "I'll count the days," he said, very low, "Letty, you won't fail me?"

She did not answer. Close in his arms, how could she fail him, how fail love and life and the adventure of loving? Away from him, thinking; thinking of Eva, trying to lay the restless ghosts of her own doubting, how could she be sure?

After Fisher sailed the loneliness began again. The shop was busy, Letty's days were full; that helped a good deal. But the evenings dragged out interminably. She saw a good deal of Carol, who was not going South this fall.

"Depression," said Carol, very well dressed, "and it doesn't matter anyway, I get so bored, traveling, hotels. Here at least you can go to a show. How about a theater one night next week?"

Carol was strange, a little. Nervous, restless. At the theater the following week, viewing a sentimental, rather charming play, she spoke to Letty when the curtain had fallen on the second act. "Look here, do you mind if we clear out? I can't stand it any more, it gets on my nerves."

"What does?" asked Letty.

"Oh, young love and all that sort of boloney," Carol answered. Letty rose and followed her from the theater. Carol had been crying. Her invincible mascara had withstood her tears but there were traces which Letty recognized.

They went to a quiet restaurant and Letty watched Carol drink three cups of black coffee and listened to her light, dissatisfied voice running on, breaking now and then into harshness, or into an appeal for understanding.

"Such a mess," said Carol.

George. She was in love with him, definitely enough. And he'd have to know before long. He wanted her to "give up her job," and marry him. He'd have to know. And Gordon was becoming daily more suspicious; there had been scenes.

"You don't know what it's like, Letty, to be torn in two all the time."

Letty said, low:

"Perhaps I do —— "

"Fisher?" asked Carol, quickening into an interest outside her own ceaseless preoccupation with herself.

"Yes," said Letty on a long breath. Somehow it was better to have admitted it, to have done with secrets.

Carol's face did not change. She nodded once, quickly, like a shrewd child.

"I thought so. But — you love him, don't you?"

"I believe I do," answered Letty after a moment.

"Then, you haven't any problem, really. That is, you care for him, you have no one but yourself to consider —— "

"That's what I keep telling myself — but —— "

"Showdown?" asked Carol briefly.

"I suppose you'd call it that. He's gone away, you know, to South America. But, when he comes back —— "

"I'm a swell one to advise you," said Carol, "and I don't suppose you want advice. It's a damned sight easier to give than take — like medicine. But — Oh, if you love him, that's your own business. But be pretty sure. I know."

After a minute she said:

"I liked Herbert Gordon. I didn't love him, Letty. And without love this hole-in-a-corner business, this left-handed affair, isn't good enough. I don't know whether it would be good enough, even with love."

Letty was silent, considering the dark small

face across from her, now sullen with long thoughts, now sparkling into hard, vivid life.

"If it were George and me," said Carol, "I know I wouldn't stop to think. But it isn't — in that way. He wants me to marry him. Can you beat it?" she said, and laughed. "I can't," she said flatly, "risk his finding out —— "

"If he loves you," said Letty, "and you tell him first —— ?"

Carol looked at her.

"Haven't outgrown high school, have you?" she asked. "Does any man love you enough to risk it — would you be sure enough in his love to risk it for yourself? At first, oh, it might work out — but life's pretty long."

"I don't know," Letty answered after a moment.

"I can't marry him," said Carol, "and I can't tell him; and that's that."

That was that. Letty left her, late that evening, and went home, a little sick with the things that had been spoken between them and the things that had remained unspoken.

The life at the shop continued. Mrs. Fisher came regularly for her treatments. They were helping her; and she was helping herself. She was learning to apply the deft make-up as cleverly as Letty herself; she had put on weight, her body curving into pretty lines, her eyes were bright and rested. She would never be a beauty; she had never been that, even in her youth. But with vigilance and care, and expensive at that, she would achieve something; she would be an attractive woman in a quiet and unsensational way.

Once she said, and Letty's heart pounded so that it hurt her, hammering rebelliously against her side:

"Isn't my skin improved? I do owe you a lot, Miss Lawson. People are saying such kind things lately. Even my daughter notices. She said the other day, 'I don't know what you're doing to yourself but you're getting to be a knock-out.'" Eva laughed, self-consciously. "And she dragged me somewhere and made me buy this frock. It's years too young for me, really." She looked up at Letty. "And I suppose," she said rather engagingly, "you think I'm just another middle-aged idiot."

Letty made the conventional response. Mrs. Fisher said shyly:

"I know I am but — it means more to me than most women. My — my husband is away, in South America. When he comes back I'm going to ask him to take me away for a long holiday, to Europe perhaps. We haven't been away together for years."

The beauty salon atmosphere was under her skin, too, she was pliant in its soft, terribly feminine hands. She was beginning to talk

. . . about herself.

Please, prayed Letty within herself, please don't let her. Make her stop, don't let her tell me any more, don't let her tell me the things which make me so dreadfully sorry for her ——

It was partly to escape from the thought of Eva Fisher that she finally went out to dinner with Burt Barker. He had telephoned her several times, had dropped in to see her occasionally, rather mischievous, his eyes dancing. "Pretend you're glad to see me, Letty Lawson . . . " or "Thought I'd come in and see how my hated rival was coming on. Is that red ink on your desk? Good. Hope so. I like red ink when the other fellow's using it."

He was amusing and irrepressible. She found herself liking him. She had really always liked him even when she thought she didn't; even when she thought herself indifferent, a harder barrier to leap. But she had liked him from that first glimpse of him in Sonia's office.

He was not always merely amusing. The first evening they dined together in a synthetic garden in the East Sixties, which boasted a French chef and an Italian barkeeper, excellent music, food and liquor, he told her something of his life and of Sonia.

"She sacrificed a lot for me," he said, "so

that I might live with my father's people and have most of the things other boys had. I was living there and growing husky and going to a pretty darned good school while she was enduring God knows what. I suppose she could have remarried half a dozen times and been happy if it hadn't been for me. But she thought of me first. I've only really realized that since she — died. Good schools and college and a big allowance and all the rest. I think now she was wrong. Don't misunderstand me. We were good friends, the best of friends, but we couldn't achieve that other relationship, separated as we were. Sometimes I think a hall bedroom and a catch-as-catch-can education would have been a lot better — for us both. You see, you get to thinking you've missed something, something pretty big. Mother and son. Not just — friends. I suppose the kids who have — that other, don't know what it's all about, don't know how lucky they are. But we were both cheated because she wanted me to have everything. Well, she gave it to me, I suppose, just through these sacrifices. But I wish I had her back for about five minutes and could tell her —— "

He broke off and looked at his plate. Then he looked up and smiled.

"I don't know why I'm boring you with all

this," he apologized.

"You're not boring me," said Letty gently, sincerely. She was growing to know and understand Burt Barker; and, through him, Sonia. She felt she could forgive Sonia now for her enmity, an enmity that had borne fruit long after Sonia was beyond the reach of any petty human emotion, ever again.

She had a note from Mortimer Fisher, written soon after his arrival at his first destination, but before he had reached the place where the railroad job was in abeyance. And on top of that note a dispatch came to old Dan Merrick telling him of Tom's death.

Tom, for a few short weeks, had been in his element. Then there had been a scrap of sorts, quite unofficial. Revolutionaries and counter-revolutionaries, with the railroad involved, and Tom, rushing out, glad of the fracas, shouting, very gay now because danger was so close. And so, he had died.

Carol telephoned Letty; and Letty, canceling her appointments, handing her special clients over to the other operators, went at once to the apartment. Strangely, or perhaps not so strangely, Carol was in tears, remembering the brother with whom she had played and laughed and quarreled, the boy of not so very long ago; and forgetting the ugliness and hurt of what had occurred between them

303

since. She held out the dispatch to Letty, signed by the man who had taken Burt Barker's place.

"Poor kid," said Carol, "he had a rotten break."

Letty comforted her as best she could, her own eyes wet. She said, "It was my fault. If I hadn't gone to the beach that day, hadn't meddled — then it wouldn't have happened, Morty would not have sent him out there —— "

"Don't kid yourself," said Carol, "it would have happened, anyway. If you hadn't gone Morty would have seen him anyway, sooner or later, and sent him packing. Probably to this same job. Don't blame yourself. I've been thinking about Tom — and Sonia, that day. I don't blame him any more. When your number's up, it's up. You had no part in Tom's death; nor Tom in Sonia's. It was all meant to be, it all would have happened one way or another," said Carol, "I'm beginning to think nothing we do affects things much in the long run."

Then she said abruptly:

"George knows. About me."

"He — knows?"

"Yes. I didn't tell him. I wish I had. He came here. And Herbert came. That was all. George first; and then Herbert with a latch key. It was as simple as that," said Carol.

Letty was still. Thinking. Visualizing. Then she said:

"What happened?"

"That was simpler still," Carol told her. She rose and went to a little concealed cabinet, opened it, poured herself a stiff, straight drink. She turned, with it in her hand. "George — went. He didn't say much. Herbert stayed. We had one hell of a row. I said, 'All right, I quit.' And he went away, too." She laughed shortly. "Later, he came back. It's all right. I've promised," said Carol, with bitterness, "never to fall in love again."

Letty spoke with some difficulty.

"Carol, why don't you leave him?"

"Herbert? Why? Where'd I go, what would I do?"

"There's work," said Letty shortly.

"Is there? I told you once before, not for me. I'm soft. I never liked working, I was marking time. You know that as well as I do. I'll stick. He's good to me, in his way. He — sort of depends on me. I didn't really know that, until the other night. And I won't — do this again. I'm cured. I hope to God I'm cured," she added under her breath.

Letty said:

"He's — not young, Carol ——— "

"You're thinking, when he dies? You're thinking, there'll be someone else . . . she'll be passed on, from hand to hand?" Carol set down the empty glass she held and sat down again beside Letty on the couch. She laid her arm across the back of the couch and bowed her dark, defeated head. There was silence in the big, pleasant room. She said after a moment: "I'm provided for. That's what he said. As long as I stick. If anything happens to him, there's a trust fund. Mine. He's decent that way, not the sort of a man who takes the trouble to arrange to be a dead dog in the manger. There aren't any strings to it. It's all been worked out on paper, with a lawyer. It doesn't figure in his will, of course. But —— "

Letty loved and despised her. She touched the slack hand. She said sharply, sensibly, "Pull yourself together." Carol was crying, hysterically, without any warning. "You've made your choice, haven't you?"

"I suppose so," said Carol.

"You're drinking too much," said Letty, "and still taking the stuff to make you sleep. Facials won't help, massage won't help. If you've made a bargain, stick to it, as you said you would. You're not keeping your part of it, going to pieces, like this —— "

"I know." Carol ceased to cry. She wiped her eyes and blew her nose, with the forlorn sound of a wounded child. "Only, it hurt, a lot, Letty, the other night. I'm a fool, the least

I can do for Herbert is to — keep my part of the bargain. You told me, all right, I knew it anyway. But — " She sat up and reached out her hand for the cable, crumpled on the table in back of the couch. She stared at it, smoothing it out in her hands. "Tom and I — we both made a mess of it," she said slowly. "He's better off."

When Letty rose to go, Carol went to the door with her. She said:

"I know what you're thinking about me. I never did have any character."

"I'm not thinking — anything," said Letty, moved, "and — you've been decent, Carol. You didn't say — I told you so, to me."

"No, what's the use?" Carol replied. She looked at the other girl for a moment, eyes tilted and narrow and shining in the olive-skinned, small face. There was a pinched look about her full, reddened mouth. "No. And I'm not preaching either. I meant it when I said it was your own life. And it's different with you. If you love somebody perhaps it's sane to take risks. Anyway, it's not just cold-blooded. But — don't be in a hurry, Letty." She said after a moment, "I don't suppose you'd consider me a horrible example?"

Letty kissed her, lightly, gently. The reddened mouth was trying to smile, to laugh it off.

"Don't worry about me, Carol."

"I won't. I've a full-time job worrying about myself." Her tone changed. "Pop's going to give up the house. My sainted aunt is going somewhere else to live. Herbert's found a place in the country for him, someone to look after him, lots of space and air; and a garden in the spring."

"Does he want to go?" Letty frowned. "Morty," she told her, "promised to get in touch with some contractor, in Bay Ridge —— "

"I know. He did. But pop can't work, you see. Heart's gone dickey, or something. He'll like the country," Carol said.

Letty left, walking back to the shop. It was cold now, brisk, the buildings soaring clear and arrogant into the cool blue. Presently it would be dusk.

She thought, I told Carol if she made a bargain she'd better stick to it, however mistaken. That's what I meant. What about me? Did I make a bargain, too?

She thought she had. She cried out within herself — walking along, fast, with that quick sure step, all grace, all vitality, unaware that people paused to watch her, to envy her, perhaps, her youth, her lightness of tread — no, it's not the same. One doesn't bargain with love. One gives, freely.

But she hadn't. Something restrained her,

held her back, whispered and warned. The old cowardice, the old fear, the old uncertainty. She thought, But when he comes back, I'll *know*, and it will be all right, for us both.

Chapter 17

But because of Eva Fisher nothing would ever be right.

She came in for her last treatment of the special course. Hereafter, she said, she supposed she would come in once a week, perhaps less often; and she would use the preparations faithfully. She couldn't thank Miss Lawson enough for all she had done.

In the pocket of Letty's severe little jersey dress, beneath the dazzling white smock, Mortimer's last letter burned like a coal. It was brief. It said that things were very wrong, that they would never be righted, that he supposed he must let the present government take over the uncompleted project and pull out with a loss. It said that Tom's death had shocked him, deeply. "Letty, that poor, crazy youngster . . . you don't blame me, do you?" And it said that he hoped to be home soon — with her.

Eva was regarding herself in the mirror, while Letty's hands moved quietly among the jars and bottles set up on the tray. Someone came into the room and spoke softly. Eva heard Letty's voice asking for a certain egg mask, to be made fresh, in half an hour; heard her ask for an astringent spray, "this one isn't working," and for bowls of ice. But the words had no meaning for her, as she looked in the mirror, the revealing mirror, but, at last, kind.

Mortimer would never really look at her with seeing eyes unless she were different. Different from the woman she'd been all these years. Now, she had altered. Surely, he would see her, surely the blind, kind gaze would quicken into interest, curiosity, anything but that courteous, benevolent indifference. Not, of course with passion. She could not expect that, did not possibly desire it, not even for vanity's sake. It was not vanity that had driven her to Letty Lawson's.

But if he would only *see* her. Then, perhaps, one barrier would be broken, and things would be better between them.

Now Letty was ready for her, the linen was bound about her hair, her breast. The lines of her face were somehow very pure and touching as she lay back, her eyes closed, her nerves quieted. Then, suddenly, as Letty's hands touched her, she began to talk.

Afterward, remembering, she was amazed,

and embarrassed. To talk — to an utter stranger! Why and how had she done it? To lay quite bare so many secret and wounded places in her nature. She did not realize that she spoke without volition; but that, little by little, her surroundings had seduced her into becoming, momentarily, another person, surrendering, in broken sentences, one or a thousand such confidences.

Feminine, soft and scented and relaxing, such was the atmosphere; it was as a drug under which one lies awake yet finds oneself talking, talking, talking, of a hundred hidden things, unable to cease. It was a sort of twilight sleep which acted directly on the brain centers which normally held one in restraint, which cautioned reserve. These cells once lulled, one could forget repressions.

"I had a happy childhood," she was saying suddenly, "we were very poor, I suppose, as people judge things now. My father was an overworked and underpaid doctor. There were three of us children; all dead now but myself. But it was a happy time, somehow. Always enough to eat and drink, country roads, gardens, tumble-down walls, and the smell of baking or preserving. Little towns are good for children, even if they long to leave them when they grow up. Cities are beasts, I think, they take childhood and devour it —— "

"Not always," Letty told her gently, "I grew up in a city. I was very happy as a child."

"You must have been a darling little girl," Eva murmured, without envy.

She said, after a while:

"I married young. A boy I'd always known. There'd never been anyone else. We were pathetic, I suppose. Awfully in love, and quite ignorant — blundering, and sensitive. Happy too, but there was so much struggle. Babies and work and hopes and disappointments . . ."

She was silent. Letty's hands were firm, were cool and mechanical. She thought, as she had thought once before — don't let her go on. But she knew that Eva Fisher would go on, and that she would have to listen. . . .

"Then," said Eva Fisher's voice dreamily, "his chance came. He always knew it would. I knew too. I was sure, and proud but afraid. He — I had a bad head for business. When he'd talk I'd think of other things, something burning on the stove, or a child crying. I always gave him divided attention. Nervous, too, perhaps, worrying about trivial things; colds, thin overcoats, wet feet. I couldn't follow him when he'd come home, eager, excited, to tell me of this opportunity, this risk we must take. He was, you see, an engineer. He had a job in the little town. A fair job, it would be better. People advised against our going away. I was afraid to go; the other seemed so secure. I didn't mind the work. I loved our house. It had a small garden and a place for the children to play."

She was silent, remembering; the arguments, her own timidity. Remembering Mortimer Fisher striding around a living room too small to hold him and his ambitions. "I tell you, Eva, it's our chance. Can't you see it that way?"

She couldn't. She was aware only of risk, for him, for the children. She remembered the day he drew out all their small savings. Without a thought for the future, she'd said. And he'd answered, "Don't you see it is *because* of the future?"

Presently, just when Letty's heart was eased a little of its dreadful tension, she went on. Letty listened as to a twice-told tale. Mortimer Fisher had told it to her — but how differently. This was the other side of the fabric, the pattern was not woven through. On this side — was it the wrong side or the right? — the pattern was different.

The story seemed interminable, told in the brief and mutilated phrases which contained more meaning than their words. Struggle, and terror. Success and more terror. The children growing away from her — "You knew we had three children?" she asked — the man going ahead, taking the roads she could not travel herself, awkward, repressed, timid.

She had what she now termed her work. She told Letty about it. Letty could see very clearly, all this immeasurable love, this devotion, inarticulate, withheld, repudiated, poured out upon the unknown children of the poor.

Sublimating love.

Now she spoke, sighing:

"He's so good to me . . . but there's someone else. Young, lovely. I don't know her. I don't think I know her. A girl, perhaps."

Letty's heart was caged in her breath, struggling for freedom. Eva Fisher said:

"Whatever he wants, of course. But, I don't think anyone could — could care as much as I do. You see, he's always been the same to me, in struggle and poverty, and now. It hasn't changed him, to me. Perhaps this — this girl wants his money . . . perhaps not. He's a very attractive man, it may not be money. If I knew it was money, I wouldn't be so frightened. He's not a stupid man."

Letty murmured something. Anything. Mrs. Fisher said:

"That's why I came to you. . . . I thought, if ever he'd look at me once as if he really saw me. I thought, if he'd laugh at me, perhaps even tease me a little — so we could find ourselves together again, even laughing, just that much. Then perhaps I could ask him, what is it you want, is it something I can give you? I thought, if I could persuade him to go away with me for a little, before he decided . . . otherwise. I'll give up the charity work, everything. It doesn't really matter, it was a makeshift. I'll take an intelligent interest in what he is doing. It seems so strange, to know that he is down there in South America and I don't really know what for or why. He gave up telling me years ago, perhaps because I didn't listen; couldn't understand; wouldn't try to understand."

She added, in amazement, "I don't know why I've said all this. I — Miss Lawson, you do think the treatments have done me good?"

Letty's voice was not steady. She replied: "Of course. I'm not flattering you, Mrs. Fisher. You have the evidence of your own eyes, haven't you?" She achieved the miracle of a little laugh. "And now," she said, "you must be still."

Eva was docilely silent. On the cleansed, cool skin the fragrant soft mask went on evenly, spread by Letty's fingertips. While it dried Eva Fisher must lie quiet, neither speaking nor smiling. Must close her eyes beneath the cooling pads of cotton, must rest, must sleep if she could.

But she had heard Letty's voice shake. She put up her own hands and took the pads from her eyes and stared a moment in incredulity. This girl, kind, gentle, clever, and very lovely to look at — her lashes were quite wet ——

She said, "Why — *Miss Lawson* —— "

Letty took the pads from her and dropped them in a receptacle. "Lie still," she said again, and pressed the fresh eyepacks over the thin, veined lids ——

A moment later the door closed behind her, and she went softly away.

Eva Fisher lay still, feeling the mask drying slowly, slowly. The girl's lashes had been wet. For her. She couldn't understand that. She was ashamed, suddenly, she felt herself flush. Then she was no longer ashamed. Hundreds of women must come here, must talk under the painless anesthesia of this little room. She could no longer remember quite what she had said. But that it had moved this stranger was something she must always recall with gratitude.

She wondered briefly about Letty. Who she was, what she did with her leisure, what man loved her, whom she loved? Someone must love her, she was so very lovely. Nothing hard about her, nothing coarse.

It came to her suddenly how little we know of the lives of people with whom we come into intimate contact, as they serve us; the girl in the beauty shop, the man who dresses our hair, the saleswoman who fits our clothes, the butcher, the baker, the candlestick maker . . .

Letty came in and the dry mask was removed with warm water, the soothing, cleansing cream applied, the astringent sprayed on, the cotton mask soaked with something cool and fragrant applied, the bandage wound across the brow and under the chin.

A little later, rested, refreshed, powdered and lipsticked, Mrs. Mortimer Fisher was ready to take her departure. She halted a moment, before putting on her hat. She held out her hand to Letty.

"You must think me very silly," she said. She smiled fleetingly, a young, shy smile. "But, whatever you think, I want to thank you for all you've done. It's just in the day's work to you, I suppose, but more than you can know, it has helped me. It hasn't just given me an almost brand-new face," she added.

Every nerve in Letty's body rebelled and shrank from taking the small, nervous hand in her own. She took it, and held it a second. She said, with the slight formality that characterized her attitude toward the majority of the women who came to her:

"Thank you for coming. It has been very

pleasant to count you among our clients."

Mrs. Fisher said, putting on her hat at the new angle which now became her and which heretofore had been impossible:

"I'll be back, of course; unless I go away. But in case I go away would you duplicate my last order of preparations so that I may take them with me?"

Letty would.

Later, the long day over, she went home. She thought, how alike, yet how different, the story of the Fisher marriage as told by the two most involved. Two sides of the fabric, two sides of the picture. She found herself briefly a dispassionate, detached onlooker, impatient with Eva Fisher for permitting the opportunity she had had to slip through her hands because they were too nervous to hold it; impatient with her because of her curious inability to break through the frail barriers which had kept her from an understanding with her husband; and amazed, as well as impatient, with Fisher himself because of his blindness. Could he not see how treasurable a devotion had been given to him, silently, mutely, freely, and for all time?

Then her detachment passed. Where do I come in? she asked herself.

She thought, I don't owe her anything. Nothing has been changed.

But she could not force herself to conviction. Everything had been changed. As long as Eva Fisher had remained an abstraction to her she had not mattered; or, had mattered very little. But now she was no longer an abstraction. She was a flesh and blood woman, apparent and real to Letty through Letty's own senses, sight and sound and touch.

And she had told her, badly, unconsciously, of her terror and her despair.

It was lonely at home. Letty looked at the mute mouth of her telephone. Should she call Carol or any of her friends? But the presence of people would not cure her loneliness nor answer her questions.

The house, the apartment was too small to contain her; and too big.

After a dinner which she barely tasted she went out. On the curb she hailed a taxi and drove to the Park and there dismissed it. Impossible to sit still, thinking. She must walk, must feel her blood run free and warm and strong, must through action dispel the unhappy mists of uncertainty.

It was a clear cold night, a night in November. There were very distant stars and the sky was arched dark velvet. The Plaza, the Savoy-Plaza, the Sherry-Netherland were black bulks against the sky, broken by squares of gold. In the Park through the trees, the lights shone,

320

there were the sounds of cars, tires on a frosty pavement, the even murmur of engines. People passed in cars, in evening dress, momentarily she saw them, talking, laughing, in the small moving enclosures. There were some who rode alone; some who sat huddled in the corner, smoking, not talking, alone or companioned.

She must let Mortimer Fisher down.

That much was becoming clear to her. They could not build their happiness on a disaster to another human being. No matter what people said, no matter how they excused themselves, it wasn't possible to do so and live the rest of your life free from torment and self-loathing. Such happiness was never solid. It would crumble in your hands.

All along she had been thinking of her own happiness. It wasn't, after all, a moral scruple that had held her back. It was the question, digging in at her mind and heart like a fine drill, can I be happy, will it last?

She knew now that Eva Fisher would divorce her husband if he asked her to do so; quietly, decently, involving no one, making no scandal. Surely an obstacle was removed by this knowledge. Her own relationship with Fisher would be signed and sealed, it would partake of no hole-in-the-corner element, it would be an association one could publish to the curious, or incurious, world.

But by her own insistence on sacrifice, Eva Fisher had created a greater obstacle than her refusal would have built.

No, thought Letty, I can't do it. Pride somewhere within her stirred. She couldn't let this other woman, the woman with the prior right, be finer than herself, more decent. She couldn't take, at her expense; she couldn't receive, from her hands.

Walking fast, fast, then slow. People stopped and turned and looked. A tall girl, a golden girl, hurrying through the darkness, slim, in a tailored suit, a fur slung about her slender neck.

There were tears on her cheeks. Never to see Mortimer again, after the farewell which faced her, which she contemplated with terror. Never to hear his voice.

Was it Fisher or the loss of love she deplored, over which she wept, walking, alone, in the cold immensity of the night?

That she was followed she did not know. Burt Barker had driven up to the apartment just as her taxi pulled away, with concert tickets in his pocket. It was not the first time he had come. He had come several times after their understanding had been reached. Had called; had dined. He had tried, today, to reach her by telephone, but she had left for home. Then something had come up, he had become involved in a business conference, which had lasted past the dinner hour. He'd sent out for sandwiches and milk, worked with Nelda and an accountant over the books a little longer, and had then jumped in a taxi and driven to Letty's. I'll take a chance, he told himself.

The doorman informed him that Miss Lawson had just gone out, in a cab, by herself. "There," said the doorman, pointing, "I heard her say, 'drive to the Park.'"

So Burt had followed; had seen her get out of the taxi and pay the driver, had seen her strike off alone.

He had had a clear view, very brief, of her face. Desperate it had seemed to him, wounded; yet forlorn as a child's.

And so he had sent his own cab away and followed; and now caught up with her.

"Letty — ?"

That there was still a slight formality between them he had forgotten. She stopped and stared at him, under a street light. Recognition was slow to awaken in her eyes. She had been alone; was no longer alone. But the transition took time. She said slowly:

"How on earth did you get here?"

"I followed you," he answered, "I drove up just as you were leaving. I saw you get out at the Park entrance."

She looked at him, troubled, a little remote. He said, quickly:

"I had concert tickets — "

"Oh, no, not music!"

It was a cry that was wrung from her. He was terrified at its implications. He said, "Of course not," swiftly. He asked, "May I walk with you, or would you rather not?"

She didn't know. She said, merely, "I'm not very good company tonight."

He did not offer the easy, conventional denial. He said only:

"Let's get going."

It was a curious walk. There was silence between them. Yet, to Letty, there was something vaguely comforting about the mere fact that she was not, after all, alone. Barker walked beside her, lightly, quickly, his soft hat pulled down over his eyes, his hands thrust in his pockets. He did not speak. But he was a warm, a breathing human presence, without danger to her; a friendly, breathing silence, there beside her.

Once she said, "You'll think me crazy,"

He replied, "No," shortly enough. He thought, what's wrong, what's happened? Is it business? He thought not. Is it a man? He tried to force his thoughts to stammer into silence but failed. Is it a man?

Something was dreadfully wrong. He looked at her profile, the rounded curve of her cheek, which had not quite lost the heartbreakingly sweet lines of adolescence. Her mouth was tense, and her eyes saw nothing. He touched her arm gently to guide her over a crossing and she started, and trembled.

There were no questions. He did not speak even when walking past the lake she stopped to stare a long moment into the dark waters shattered by starlight . . .

After a long time she complained, as if in astonishment.

"I'm awfully tired."

Barker replied, sensibly, with a question.

"Have you had dinner?"

"I suppose so." She looked up at him, fully, for the first time. "I didn't eat it," she admitted.

"I had sandwiches and milk. I'm starved. I could eat the side of a house," he told her. "Look, let's hop a cab and drive to the Plaza and have something warm. It will do us both good."

She hesitated. The thought of food revolted her. But she was so desperately tired. "All right," she said faintly.

Reaching the hotel, they went into the Oak Room. It was quiet there. Most of the diners had left. They sat in a window and Barker ordered. Hot, good soup, lamb chops, a salad, coffee.

She looked down at her steaming plate, and went white.

"I don't think — " she said vaguely.

"Of course you can," said Barker. "Try. The first six spoonfuls are the hardest."

She lifted the spoon. Her hand shook slightly. Barker's heart contracted. What had happened, why? Why should anything happen to her? He knew what was said, what was thought, what it seemed only logical to believe. It didn't matter, nothing mattered, except that she suffered, that she grieved.

He told himself in astonishment, I do love her. So much that nothing else really counts.

He watched the color come back to her face, slowly, faintly. She regarded an empty plate in astonishment.

"I thought I couldn't but I did," she told him, smiling dimly, "I was hungry, after all."

"Well, naturally."

During the rest of the meal he told her of the business meeting which had kept him from telephoning. "So, I said to myself, I'll take a chance."

"I'm glad you did," she said, and his heart pounded. He said evenly, "So am I."

After coffee and a companionable cigarette, he took her home. She said, in the cab, "If I don't ask you to come in, you'll not think me rude?"

"Of course not," he told her. And later in the hall before her door, he took the key from her hand and inserted it in the lock.

"It's absurd," she said ruefully, "but I'm sleepy."

Emotion, the exercise, the warm food; her eyes were heavy; she lifted the weighted, white lids and looked at him.

"Thank you, Burt," she said, "you've been very good. I — I suppose you think I'm mad. I'm not really. I just had something to think out."

She held out her hand. He took it briefly, firmly. He said, a little embarrassed:

"That's all right. I'll always be around when you want me — I mean," he said hastily, "if I can be of any use."

"You helped," she told him.

They stood a minute in the little foyer of her apartment. Silence, broken only by the sound of a near-by radio playing softly, was all around them. One light burned. He said, loathing himself, yet unable to be silent:

"Letty, forgive me. Is it — Fisher?"

Her eyes were wide now, the drowsiness gone. He stammered:

"I didn't mean . . . but . . . I couldn't help feeling something was wrong . . . I thought — "

She said, evenly:

"I know what you thought. It isn't so. It — it won't ever be. He backed the business, of course. But, as a friend, a good friend. No more."

He knew that he must believe her. Happiness took him, left him shaken; and departed, to be replaced by anger and anxiety. A good friend, nothing more. But she had not assured him that it was not with the thought of Mortimer Fisher in her mind that she walked beside the dark lake and stared into its waters.

He remembered telling her once, when they dined together, of the business in South America, and how she had listened quietly to his denunciation of Fisher and had answered loyally, "I can't believe it. You have it twisted somehow. He's fine, you know, really."

Had she learned that he was not fine?

He left her, walking back to his apartment. Nothing had been explained to him. Yet now the happiness returned and persisted over the unanswered questioning.

Alone, again surrendering to that deadly drowsiness, Letty took off her clothes and opened her windows. She cast herself into sleep as if she would drown in it. She had forgotten Burt Barker and this curious evening. She knew only that she had reached a decision and whether, when full realization came to her, she would die of it or not, she did not care. For the present, she was dead for sleep, and her brain was light and empty.

Chapter 18

Mortimer Fisher returned from South America. He was tired, he was sobered, he had lost a million or so. He had lost more than money. He had seen something more than money involved. He had lost a belief in himself and in his star. He had seen what could come of playing both ends against the middle. He had seen disaster come to men through loyalty.

Well, it was over. There were other ventures. But the heart had gone out of them, somehow. There was, also, at the end of his journey, Letty, waiting. He could talk to her, tell her things, she would understand. She would understand that it wasn't for the sake of money alone that he played at dangerous games, cloaked one enterprise under the guise of another, bribed governments, and sent his men to face unexpected and undreamed-of bullets. She had healing for him. She would give him back his pride and his faith in himself and his faith in the adventure which lay just around the corner. Business, as such, wasn't worth a nickel, a man's thoughts, a man's anxiety. It had to be more than business. He would say to her, "See here, Letty, I didn't mean to start anything . . . you understand, don't you?"

He wondered if Gerry had seen the little notice of Tom Merrick's death in the New York papers; and whether she would blame him. He thought, she won't care, she's over it. Somehow he despised his daughter for this, because he knew she wouldn't care, knew she had forgotten, knew she wouldn't blame him, wouldn't bother to blame him.

Eva was at the boat. He was astonished to find her there. He came down the gangplank to see her, waiting. Her greeting was like Eva, timid, the sort of thing which caused him deep irritation. "You didn't mind my coming?"

Yes, the greeting was the same, but Eva was different. He knew that vaguely through his eyes, and a part of his mind. Perhaps it was her smarter clothes, the angle at which she wore an absurd, expensive hat, the color in her cheeks, the lipstick. He realized that he had never before noticed that Eva used lipstick . . .

In the car he roused himself to reply to her questions briefly, and to say, "You're looking very well, Eva."

"I am well," she told him, "and — and so

glad to have you home again."

That much had been said. He found himself curiously embarrassed. He replied ridiculously, "Why, that's very nice of you, my dear."

He couldn't hurt her by not going home at once. Gerry would be there, and the boys. Tomorrow was Thanksgiving. For once, they'd all be home together.

No chance to see Letty, no opportunity even to telephone her. He wrote a note to a florist and sent it around by the confidential secretary, who had come to the house to see him. There was a card — "Home" was written on it and that was all.

Thanksgiving was dreadful; the boys down from school and college, each with a friend; Gerry, fidgeting through the long, deadly dull meal, wanting to get away, she had a date, she said. And Eva, at the head of the table, smiling at him.

"Doesn't she look swell?" asked Gerry. "I think she's had her face lifted."

Eva, flushing through the delicate rouge, "Gerry, you silly child."

But she did look — oh, not just well, pretty almost. Prettier than he had ever seen her. He stared at her across the table. He was seeing her. Eva knew it and dropped her eyes from his and spoke to the strange boy at her side

. . . murmured something, anything.

Letty spent her holiday with Carol. Herbert Gordon was with his family. "They're always with their families, holidays," said Carol somberly.

In Letty's apartment, Mortimer Fisher's flowers bloomed and lived their short fragrant life. She was glad to be at Carol's. She thought, I can't stand flowers any more. Too sweet, too — funereal.

What she said to Carol that day she did not know; nor did she retain much of what Carol said to her. All she knew was that Mortimer Fisher was back again, and that her respite was over and that she must face him and must tell him; tell him so that there would be no loophole; tell him so that he would go away and she would never see him again.

"What on earth is on your mind?" asked Carol.

"Oh, a little bit of everything. Burt Barker is still anxious for me to sell out, to merge the business with Sonia's. I'd have a share, be on a salary. Sometimes I think it would be practical."

Carol was silent, thinking her own thoughts, something's happened between her and Fisher.

Nothing had happened. But it would happen. Every time the clock struck it was nearer.

On the following evening he was with her. She had sent the maid away. He came, after dinner, looking worn, she thought, on edge. Her heart was sick within her; sick to comfort him, to heal him of whatever ills troubled his mind and body.

If only he would not take her in his arms and kiss her. But he did so and she turned from him and his lips touched the curve of her cheek only.

"What's the matter? Not glad to see me back?" he laughed.

"Of course. Your flowers are lovely, Mortimer."

He brushed that aside. "I would have come, directly I got in — or called you, if you were at the shop. But I had to go home. And yesterday was a holiday and so, of course — "

She thought, they're always with their families on holidays. She said lightly, "That's all right, Morty."

After a moment he started to tell her about the trip. "It isn't the money loss, you understand. I can make it back and more. But the men, some of them, they trusted me, they thought I let them down." He muttered, after a moment, "Maybe he was right — what's his name — Barker . . . ? Perhaps, I didn't see it in that light then. And now it's too late."

She was silent, regarding him. He went on:

"There was only that one fatal casualty, thank God. Young Merrick. You don't blame me, Letty?" She shook her head, without words. He went on after a deep breath, "I knew you wouldn't . . . I couldn't have endured that. The other men, I'll get them jobs, somehow, or carry them until I can."

Then he looked at her, a long moment.

"You've changed," he said. "Letty, I thought it would be different coming home."

She said, no longer dreading the moment now that it had come, passionately concerned that it be over swiftly:

"Yes, I've changed. Or rather, I haven't changed. It's no good, Morty. I've had all this time to think, while you were away. I've made up my mind. I can't. I — I don't love you."

Incredulous, he stared at her, flushing. The color died, he was gray. He said, through a stammer of anger, unhappiness, amazement, "You can't mean that — "

"I do mean it." She steadied her shaking hands one within the other and controlled her voice. "I must mean it. Morty, if I'd loved you really, would I have — made you wait as I did? When you went away, when I stopped seeing you I had a chance to think it all out. I don't love you," she said softly, sorrowfully.

He kept his eyes on her through the growing mist of bewilderment.

"I don't believe you. Why — when I left — "
He said, after a moment, dully, "Letty, I shall
ask Eva to divorce me. I'll be free —— "

"It isn't that," she cried, "not that. If I
loved you would that matter? But I don't. I —
I care for you, tremendously. As a friend. As
something more than a friend. But that's all,
Morty. It isn't enough. If I don't love you
enough to be your mistress," she said with
controlled lips, "I don't love you enough to
be your wife."

She thought, it's like dying; dying must be
like this.

He rose and plunged heavily around the
room; came back to stand over her.

"Letty, you can't mean it . . . the — the one
thing in my life . . . " he said. Then he cried
out at her in exasperation: "I've been patient,
more patient than I ever thought it was in me
to be. I've waited — given you time, I haven't
made demands —— "

"I know," she said. "But it's over, Morty."
"Over?"

"Yes. We can't go on, you see. It wouldn't
be possible, would it? We can't. It's over.
Here and now. I made up my mind . . . "

"But we've so much — " he said bewildered.

An hour of that. Arguments, pleas,
anger, humility. She sat, very erect, her hands

clenched in her lap. Only her hands might have betrayed her. He did not see them. He flung himself down beside her, took her unyielding body in his arms, tried to force her with his lips, his broken words.

"No. Please," she said gently, "please—— "

He let her go and stood up and stared down at her again, this time in defeat. He said, "I *can't* understand."

She answered, and lied, "I can't either. I want you to believe, Morty, that I haven't — haven't been —— "

She couldn't say it, the ugly words. He nodded, shortly.

"I do believe you," he said in amazement, "God knows why."

"You see," she told him, "I thought I did care — enough. But I don't. It was loneliness and growing used to you, turning to you for everything. It was love of love. I must stand on my own feet now," she said, "alone."

He did not see her hands. He looked at her clear eyes, at her quiet mouth. Lost to him, lost.

She was talking, evenly, sanely.

"Burt Barker has made us another offer for the business. It is too good to refuse. Especially now. You've lost a great deal of money. Morty, this, this isn't comparable of course but it will be something off your books. And we can't go on together. When the lease is up, I'll merge with Sonia's. We're solvent now. We might not be later. Times are still bad enough, anything might happen. If you agree, and I think you must, you'll see it's better so. You'll have your money out of it, and a little profit. And I'll still carry on. Mr. Barker has offered me more than a fair salary and a share of the profits."

He heard dimly. He did not wholly understand. There would be time for understanding, later.

He decided slowly, "You've let me down."

"Yes," said Letty, without compromise or excuse.

Presently he went; he went without words, without reproaches or recriminations. It had all been spoken. He said, "Good-by, my dear. I — wish you luck —— "

He didn't. Anger was uppermost now. If it was luck that he wished her, it was bad luck.

The door closed behind him. She sat quite still where he'd left her and thought . . . it's over. She wondered, why can't I cry?

Women, thought Mortimer driving home, were all alike, fundamentally. She'd used him, as long as was necessary.

No, that wasn't fair, really. He believed her. She had told him that she hadn't used him, hadn't kept him dangling between her consent and her refusal.

Eva was waiting up. She called him as he passed her open door, and he went in and looked down at her, too beaten to be astonished.

She was sweet, somehow younger, softer. The room suddenly became her, with its soft lights and elaborate accessories. She sat on the chaise longue, her small feet tucked under her, a book face down on a little table.

She said, "You look so tired."

He sat down on the foot of the couch. He was tired, he admitted.

She spoke then, not too hurriedly.

"If you could get away, Mortimer, and take a real rest? You've never had a long holiday. Suppose — Europe? And if you'd take me with you . . . I'd try not to bore you," she said.

She seemed less taut, less nervous, more sure of herself somehow, friendly, too. Gentle, smiling a little, as he remembered her long ago — when he stopped to remember — which wasn't often.

"Europe?" he asked. "Why, I suppose it could be managed. But you — what about the hospital boards and things?" he asked, trying to smile.

"They can get along without me. There hasn't been a time, really, when they couldn't," she said, with a growing courage, a leaping hope; "after all it was more a matter of writing checks than anything else. I thought I was necessary, but I wasn't. I'm tired, too, Mortimer. I'd like to go away, just the two of us. Somewhere where there's warmth and sun and gaiety. The children don't need us now. The boys are all right. Thelma's back, she'd take them vacations, I'm sure. And Gerry can live with her. She's over that business of last summer, she's seriously interested in her singing or thinks she is. And there's another young man . . . a football player, this time, quite possible. She brought him here while you were away," said Eva, with a soft little triumph, "he's a nice boy."

It was the longest speech he had listened to from her, in years. She added, as he was silent, looking down at her, frowning a little:

"So I thought if it could be arranged? If you could afford it — the time, the money —— ?"

He could afford both. The South American affair was over and done with; the rest of his business ran smoothly. There was no need for new ventures now. No immediate need.

He told her he could afford it. Suddenly, it seemed a solution to him; to get away, to go places, to rest, to loaf, to be gay if one wished to be, to take a boat and sail for weeks, alone with the blue water and blue sky, alone with storm and darkness.

Not alone. Eva would go with him.

He didn't want her. He wanted to escape, by himself. Not to forget, one didn't forget. Oh, he supposed one did, in time; in time, everything passed.

But Eva was waiting, anxiously, her eyes bright, her breath quickened. He said, filled with a bitter compunction:

"I've been pretty rotten to you, Eva —— "

This was her opportunity; she would take it. If it had come six months earlier ——

But it had come tonight. Absurd that courage should be found in a pot of cream, a jar of rouge, a gold-mounted lipstick, a new gown.

"No," she said, "you haven't been rotten. I — I've failed you, pretty much, all along the way, Mortimer. I couldn't help it. I didn't, I suppose, have strong enough roots for transplanting."

He listened, amazed. The soft, hurried voice went on, explaining, asking quite simply for understanding, for pardon.

For the first time he knew something of her loneliness and her bewilderment; for the first time something of her terrified love for her children which could, she said, "do nothing for them." She said, finally:

"It's too late to start over. No one ever starts over. We had our chance and lost it

341

between us somehow. Perhaps it wasn't altogether our fault. But we can go on from here. Together," she said, distinctly, "or alone."

He asked sharply, startled, *"Alone?"*

"Yes. I — Oh, there's been gossip. No need to tell you what, or from whom. If — if you want to be free?"

Twenty-four hours ago it would have been a door opening. Now it was a door which closed. He said slowly, tonelessly:

"No, Eva, I don't want that."

There was a brief silence. She leaned her head against the cushions. She thought, something has happened, something which is hurting him terribly. But it's all over.

He said:

"I don't know what you've heard. I won't ask. It doesn't matter. But — there was nothing in it. I give you my word. You understand."

She moved her head against the bright colors, the smooth silk. He went on. "I haven't always been faithful to you —— "

She said, "I know. I've always known."

"Yes, I suppose so."

He rose and walked around the room; came back to her. He said:

"I'll get passage on the first fast boat. We'll go, without any set plan. You can get clothes, get what you need, over there?"

"I'm all ready," she answered, "now."

"Very well," he told her. He said, "I'm a failure, you know."

He thought he was. He had failed in a mad, gorgeous scheme which would have made him rich, powerful, feared. He had failed with Letty. It came to him that he had failed a good deal of the time. Eva had not failed, in the essential things, in loyalty, in integrity.

He put his hand on her hair a moment, in a brief caress, without passion, without even tenderness. Roughly, almost, a sturdy affection. He said, "We'll muddle through."

A moment later the door closed behind him. Eva Fisher turned her face to the pillows and wept into their bright softness. These were tears of something very nearly approximating happiness. But she did not weep long. She had to remember, now; bright eyes, an unravaged face, patience, gentleness, and as much understanding as love and gratitude would bring her.

A few days later there was an item in the New York *Times:*

"Among the passengers sailing last night on the 'Bremen' were Mr. and Mrs. Mortimer Fisher who have left New York for an indefinite stay abroad."

Chapter 19

The confidential secretary, the invaluable Mr. Watts, telephoned to Letty. After all, it was his name that stood on the incorporation papers. Mr. Fisher had left certain instructions. Could he make an appointment to see her?

Sell and be damned, then. Or, perhaps, be damned if you didn't sell.

Burt Barker, communicated with, was terse and satisfactory. "Good," said Barker, "you won't regret it."

There were conferences, arrangements. And so Letty Lawson, Inc. passed into oblivion. Henceforward, it would be Sonia's. The trade would know; Letty's clientele were informed by word of mouth and correctly engraved cards. Sonia's, by the first of the year, would be expanded into "something bigger and better," said Burt, than New York had yet known. The division of duties was plain enough; Burt in the background; Nelda in her office. Letty given a free hand, managing the clients, doing the diagnosing and advising, in charge of the operators and in charge of the laboratories which would also manufacture her own products.

There would be more salary than she had allowed herself as her drawing account from Letty Lawson, Inc. and a share of the profits that were bound to come. So Mr. Watts, retired from the scene, his brain busy and his tongue silent, with the certified check which represented a good part of the purchase price and all of the Mortimer Fisher interest.

Nothing was left now; not even the independence upon which she had prided herself and which hadn't been independence, really.

Those were very busy days. There was no time for thought except at night; and then she was often too tired to think; moving, settling, the question of leases adjusted, more space engaged in the Fifth Avenue Building which housed the Sonia Salon, wondering if she could hold her clientele with the change; finding that she could; finding that she could persuade them that even if she did not herself give the treatments everything would be as it was before under her direct supervision.

Business as usual; and the heart gone out of it.

Friendship. Friendship with Nelda, glad to have her back again, and no business competition to interfere. "It was a wise move, Letty. Barker's a marvel. So are you. As a team you're unbeatable."

Now she was growing to know Burt Barker, working with him, seeing him often and beginning to talk to him a little, explaining how it had all come about, the business arrangement with Mortimer Fisher; explaining too about the Merricks, and Carol, trusting in his understanding.

A few days before Christmas they were dining together. When the table had been cleared Burt put his hand in his pocket and took out his wallet. From the wallet he took a little clipping from the New York *Times* and laid it down on the table before her.

"So he's gone," he said.

"Yes," said Letty.

"Do you — care very much?" he asked gently. So gently that she forgot to consider it as an impertinence.

She replied, after a moment.

"Terribly. Or so I thought. I still think so — at times."

"Letty, how did it happen?" he wanted to know. "Or, if you'd rather not tell me, don't."

She lifted her slim shoulders. Her eyes were very black under the marvelous fairness of her hair, black in the pallor of her face.

"I don't know, Burt," she said. "I thought I loved him very much. Enough to risk — almost anything. And then I found I didn't.

Call it anything you like — scruples, fear, cowardice. I don't know," she said again.

But she knew. And she would never tell. She would never tell anyone at any time. Sometimes she wondered if Mortimer Fisher, traveling with his wife, stopping as the fancy took him, at the big gay places, at the small quiet ones, would notice . . . the bottles, the jars, gay, beribboned, sealed and marked . . . *Letty Lawson, Inc.?*

When Mrs. Fisher came back there'd be no Letty Lawson, Inc.

No, he wouldn't notice, not if Eva was clever. Perhaps, thought Letty, she would be clever. Perhaps some day he would tell her; and then she would be more clever still. Not with the sharp, quick planning brain of most women but with a sort of animal shrewdness, the domestic animal, threatened, hiding, silent.

No, she would never tell. But suppose he noticed? Suppose he strolled into her room, idly picked up a jar from the dressing table?

There was a laugh in that somewhere, if she could only find it.

She thought, perhaps they'll be happy.

Perhaps they would be, for a little while. Perhaps having failed, and having sensed that he failed, he would alter. Perhaps not. It might be that after a time, after the escape, after the holiday, when he came back to the stimulation of business, rested, his own man again, perhaps there would be another woman ——

Even so, it would never again be quite the same. He could forget the Eva of those early years; but he could not forget this newer, stranger, older Eva who has escaped with him, for a holiday.

Letty was thinking, what will it be like, seeing him again, if ever I do? Then she looked up aware that Burt was talking to her.

"Letty, your attention for a moment. I'm asking you something important. And you're a hundred miles away."

A thousand, three thousand. She smiled at him.

"Forgive me. What is it, Burt?"

"Christmas. Let's have Christmas together. A real one, with a tree and stockings. I'll take you to Lancaster, to my father's people. You'll like them, Letty. Old-fashioned, yes, but solid, the real thing. The only family I ever knew, and for whom I've Sonia to thank. She didn't like them, she didn't understand them, but she knew they'd be good for me."

A home at Christmas time? She had been dreading Christmas. She looked up at him, with soft dark eyes which shone.

"I'll go, Burt," she said, "and I'll love it."

"Good," said Burt Barker. He kept his tone even, matter-of-fact. Almost too matter-of-fact to a woman aware of him, but Letty was not aware.

Christmas brought snow. They were in Lancaster on Christmas Eve. The Barker house was very old and built of brick. There was the big yard in which Burt had played as a child, as a boy. There was the old furniture, some of it priceless, and much of it marred by stumpy boy shoes and desecrating knives. "He was always destructive," said old Mrs. Barker. "I used to go nearly crazy with him. But his grandfather said, once, 'Some day we'll be glad to have these scratches and digs to remind us —— ' "

Old people, the Barkers; a short stocky florid man with white hair and a thin little woman, pink-cheeked, straight as an arrow. Letty had been received with anxiety, very well concealed, and a lovely stately courtesy. She could not know how anxious they were, how they had discussed her, the strange girl, lying side by side in the great old-fashioned bed. A girl. Burt's girl? What would she be like, would she know her luck, did she deserve it?

Then she came, tall and golden and a little shy. They liked her at once. "My business partner," said Burt, grinning. His grandfather asked him, aside, "Just business, Burt?"

"As far as she is concerned," Burt answered.

"But — you?"

"It's too soon yet, you see, gramp."

"Too soon?"

"I — we haven't known each other very long," Burt told him; and the old man nodded, not quite satisfied.

Christmas Eve there were carols and more snow drifting down and candles set in the windows and the spicy smell of the good Pennsylvania Dutch cooking. Christmas Eve there was a tree to trim, a great fragrant tree, very tall, the branches starting at the very bottom, spreading out and up, symmetrical and wide. They trimmed it, the four of them, the new radio Burt had sent out bringing carols and chimes. They trimmed it with strange synthetic fruit, yards of tinsel and tiny bells, with little snowy houses, rotund miniature Santa Clauses and great fragile colored globes and many lights.

On the very top there was a waxen angel. She had been new when Burt was a boy. She still smiled, a pink, sweet smile, and spread her waxen, gilded wings.

Most of the German households celebrate Christmas Eve. Mrs. Barker told Letty, "But Burt likes Christmas Day better. He always said it was more exciting, waiting."

So, after the early supper, came the tree trimming; and then, church. The four of them filing in, going up the old aisles, sitting there hearing the music, smelling the cedar branches and watching the candles flicker.

Letty's heart ached with a burden too great to share alone. She choked a little, feeling the tears in her throat. She reached out her hand blindly. The choir sang and the small Christmas trees sent out their perfume. She touched Burt's hand. It closed over her own strongly. She felt rested, befriended.

Then they were back in the brick house, putting on final touches, hiding from one another in separate rooms, filling the stockings with the packages which the old people had hoarded for weeks, with the things Burt and Letty had brought.

It was almost midnight when Letty went up the wide stairs to her room, and looked down from the landing at the old people and Burt standing below.

She heard the chimes as she lay in bed. The bed was straight and narrow and the worn fine linen sheets were sweet with lavender. The windows stood wide to the frosty air which smelled of snow. It had cleared and there were stars beyond, and somewhere a group of young voices singing.

She tried to think of Mortimer Fisher. Where was he, how was he, what did this time mean to him? But he was elusive, she could not reach him with her thoughts. Just his name in her mind brought nothing, a cardboard figure, lacking life, lacking vitality.

Love did not die in a day or a night; not in many days or nights. The hurt of loss remained, lessening perhaps, but it was there, a sore place, a bruise.

No, love did not perish in a moment, not this love. But it grew dim, it grew remote, as if one had dreamed it. Perhaps some day one would awake to a different world.

She thought of the Christmas seasons of her childhood and of her father. He could come to her always, as if there were not years between, as if he had never gone. There was, after all, no death, she thought, drowsily, nothing really died. Not love, that was altered, transmuted, that reverted, ceased to be something concrete, but became instead a part of you, of your blood and bone, shaping an alteration in you. Nor did people whom you had loved die, they were yours as long as you lived and remembered.

Then suddenly it was Christmas morning and Burt was pounding on her door. . . .

"Merry Christmas, Letty —— "

She came out to him, her fair hair disheveled, her eyes laughing and wide, a heavy robe over her silken pyjamas, her slim feet in slippers. He took her hand and they raced down the stairs together and took the fat stockings from the mantel. A fire leapt on the hearth, he had risen early to light it. They sat down on the floor and opened their packages, the silly gifts from the five-and-ten cent store, and laughed over them together and the old people coming down, smiled to see them. "Merry Christmas, children," they said.

Then, upstairs again, to dress and the smell of breakfast and a ravenous hunger. And church, once more. "You won't mind, will you?" asked Burt. "They always want me to go." And then a long walk before dinner, alone with him.

After dinner the tree. That was an inflexible rule. Little jokes in the morning; church, dinner; and then the giving of gifts.

There was a bracelet on Letty's arm; plain, beaten, handwrought gold. She twisted it and looked at it again and again. "You shouldn't have done it, Burt, I shouldn't have taken it."

"Why not? It's Christmas. We're partners."

They were partners. He touched the pipe she had given him, the striped silk of the tobacco pouch. "This is swell," he said contentedly.

The room was a welter of gay tissue papers,

of ribbons. There was mistletoe beckoning over a door. Letty paused a minute in that door. And there Burt caught her, and kissed her.

She drew away, flushing, trying to laugh.

"If your grandmother saw!"

"She'd understand. And as for gramp — he thinks I'm slow. He all but told me so."

She looked over to the old people, who were sitting together by the fire, absorbed in the entirely absurd puzzle game which Burt had brought them. They were oblivious. Burt said urgently:

"I'm afraid not to be slow — Letty. Shall we go on as we are now, working together, playing together, until the time when, perhaps, you are ready to come home?"

There were tall candles on the mantel. They flickered now. Did he fancy she nodded? Or was it the candlelight dancing, shining on the golden globes pendent from the tree?

She said, suddenly:

"You're dear. I —— "

He said quickly:

"No, you don't. It's just — the Christmas spirit. But some day you will, I think."

She smiled at him, a generous surrender. Not yet. But some day. It was a promise. This time it would be fulfilled. And, as she smiled, the old people looked up, laughing, from their preoccupation. "I don't believe it can be done," said Mr. Barker firmly. "Come here, Burt, your young eyes are better than mine, and you, too, Letty," he added.

They went over together, laughing, and stooped over the little intricate carving of ivory. There wasn't a puzzle you couldn't solve, if you waited and worked and had patience.

THORNDIKE-MAGNA hopes you have enjoyed this Large Print book. All our Large Print titles are designed for easy reading, and all our books are made to last. Other Thorndike Press or Magna Print books are available at your library, through selected bookstores, or directly from the publishers. For more information about current and upcoming titles, please call or mail your name and address to:

THORNDIKE PRESS
P.O. Box 159
Thorndike, Maine 04986
(800) 223-6121
(207) 948-2962 (in Maine and Canada call collect)

or in the United Kingdom:

MAGNA PRINT BOOKS
Long Preston, Near Skipton
North Yorkshire,
England BD23 4ND
(07294) 225

There is no obligation, of course.